NUCLEAR WINTER III

WHITEOUT

BOBBY AKART

THANK YOU

Thank you for reading WHITEOUT, book three in the Nuclear Winter Series by Author Bobby Akart.
Join Bobby Akart's mailing list to learn about upcoming releases, deals, contests, and appearances. Visit:
BobbyAkart.com
Or visit his dedicated feature page on Amazon at
Amazon.com/BobbyAkart

PRAISE FOR BOBBY AKART AND THE NUCLEAR WINTER SERIES

"Bobby's uncanny ability to take a topic of 'what could happen' and write an epic story about it is short of preternatural!"

"Characters with depth coupled with an incredibly well researched topic wasn't enough for the golden man of post apocalyptic fiction. Oh no, he went and threw in a murder mystery just to keep everyone guessing as well as what I believe is one of his best crafted cliff hangers."

"I never would have believed that Mr. Akart could outdo himself! Well, he has! Nuclear Winter First Strike is quite possibly the best book he has ever written!"

"As with any of the best novels, this book really captures your attention and makes it hard to put down at the end of the day."

"Nuclear Winter: First Strike and the Albright family are coming dangerously close to nudging my beloved Armstrong family (Lone Star series) into a tie for first place."

"The suspense, the behind the scenes machinations of governments, the evil unleashed, the world on an uncharted path are all woven into another excellent story."

"I am speechless. By far the most edge of your seat, acrylic nail biting book ever. E V E R.
The characters suck you in on a roller coaster ride of emotions."

OTHER WORKS BY AMAZON CHARTS TOP 25 AUTHOR BOBBY AKART

Nuclear Winter
First Strike
Armageddon
Whiteout
Devil Storm
Desolation

New Madrid (a standalone, disaster thriller)

Odessa (a Gunner Fox trilogy)
Odessa Reborn
Odessa Rising
Odessa Strikes

The Virus Hunters
Virus Hunters I
Virus Hunters II
Virus Hunters III

The Geostorm Series

The Innocents
Level 6
Quietus

The Blackout Series
36 Hours
Zero Hour
Turning Point
Shiloh Ranch
Hornet's Nest
Devil's Homecoming

The Boston Brahmin Series
The Loyal Nine
Cyber Attack
Martial Law
False Flag
The Mechanics
Choose Freedom
Patriot's Farewell (standalone novel)
Black Friday (standalone novel)
Seeds of Liberty (Companion Guide)

The Prepping for Tomorrow Series
Cyber Warfare
EMP: Electromagnetic Pulse
Economic Collapse

NUCLEAR WINTER III
WHITEOUT

by
Bobby Akart

Copyright Information

ACKNOWLEDGMENTS

Creating a novel that is both informative and entertaining requires a tremendous team effort. Writing is the easy part.

For their efforts in making the Nuclear Winter series a reality, I would like to thank Hristo Argirov Kovatliev for his incredible artistic talents in creating my cover art. He and Dani collaborate (and conspire) to create the most incredible cover art in the publishing business. A huge hug of appreciation goes out to Pauline Nolet, the *Professor*, for her editorial prowess and patience in correcting this writer's same tics after fifty-plus novels. Thank you, Drew Avera, a United States Navy veteran and accomplished author, who has brought his talented formatting skills from a writer's perspective to create multiple formats for reading my novels. Welcome back Kevin Pierce, the beloved voice of the apocalypse, who will bring my words to life in audio format.

Now, for the serious stuff. Accurately portraying the aftermath of nuclear war required countless hours of never-ending research and interviews of some of the brightest minds in the world of planetary science.

Once again, as I immersed myself in the science and history, source material and research flooded my inbox from around the globe. Without the assistance of many individuals and organizations, this story could not be told. Please allow me a moment to acknowledge a few of those individuals whom, without their tireless efforts and patience, the *Nuclear Winter* series could not have been written.

Many thanks to the preeminent researchers and engineers at the National Center for Atmospheric Research in Boulder, Colorado. Between responses to my inquiries and the volumes of scientific publications provided, I was able to grasp the catastrophic effect a regional nuclear war would have upon the Earth and its atmosphere. They impressed upon me the danger of inundating our air with the results of these massive nuclear detonations. It would result in a climatic event akin to the eruption of the Yellowstone Supervolcano.

A shout-out must go to Brian Toon, professor of atmospheric and oceanic sciences at the University of Colorado – Boulder. He has been a tireless advocate warning all who'll listen of the consequences of nuclear winter. This quote had a profound effect on me and led to the writing of the Nuclear Winter series—*It could potentially end global civilization as we know it.* In other words, TEOTWAWKI.

At Rutgers University, Distinguished Professor and acclaimed climatologist, Alan Robock, has been studying the potential threat of nuclear winter with a particular focus on the human impact. The incredibly fast cooling of the planet would trigger global famine and mass starvation. His models of fires and firestorms in the aftermath of a nuclear war provided me detailed estimates of the extent of wildfires as well as the timeframes associated with the smoke and soot lofted into the atmosphere.

Now, to the special friends and acquaintances who helped make my characters realistic. Admittedly, my exposure to teenagers is non-existent. Yet, from time-to-time, I have teen characters who speak a different language, sort of. In order to add a sense of realism to their dialogue, I call upon a number of resources to enlighten me on their own unique vocabulary.

Thank you to Pam and Tim Johnson who reached out to their teenage grandson, Simon Andrews. He's credited with a number of phrases in the Nuclear Winter series including—Yeet! Dear reader, this interesting term will be explained within First Strike, book one.

Thank you to Jessica Devenny, referred to me via Pam Johnson and her bestie, Betsy. Jessica's sons, Jacob and Parker, also helped to fill my *teenspeak* dictionary.

Also, Dani's followers on Instagram were up to the task. Instagram is one of the few social media networks where the vast majority of your interactions are positive compared to Facebook and the downright nasty Twitter platform. When called upon, hundreds of terms and phrases were offered. Thanks to you all!

Finally, as always, a special thank you to my team of loyal friends who've always supported my work and provided me valuable insight from a reader's perspective—Denise Keef, Joe Carey, Shirley Nicholson, Bennita Barnett, Karl Hughey, and Brian Alderman.

For the Nuclear Winter series, several avid readers volunteered to make my writing *more better*: Leslie Bryant, Diane Ash, Rusty Ballard, Joe Hoyt, Cecilia Kilgore Sutton, Thelma Applegate, Joyce Maurer, Steven Smith, and Annie Kercher-Bosche.

Thanks, y'all, and Choose Freedom!

ABOUT THE AUTHOR, BOBBY AKART

Author Bobby Akart has been ranked by Amazon as #25 on the Amazon Charts list of most popular, bestselling authors. He has achieved recognition as the #1 bestselling Horror Author, #1 bestselling Science Fiction Author, #5 bestselling Action & Adventure Author, #7 bestselling Historical Fiction Author and #10 on Amazon's bestselling Thriller Author list.

Mr. Akart has delivered up-all-night thrillers to readers in 245 countries and territories worldwide. He has sold over one million books in all formats, which includes over forty international bestsellers, in nearly fifty fiction and nonfiction genres.

His novel *Yellowstone: Hellfire* reached the Top 25 on the Amazon bestsellers list and earned him multiple Kindle All-Star awards for most pages read in a month and most pages read as an author. The Yellowstone series vaulted him to the #25 bestselling author on Amazon Charts, and the #1 bestselling science fiction author.

Since its release in November 2020, his standalone novel, New Madrid Earthquake, has been ranked #1 on Amazon Charts in multiple countries as a natural disaster thriller.

Mr. Akart is a graduate of the University of Tennessee after pursuing a dual major in economics and political science. He went on to obtain his master's degree in business administration and his doctorate degree in law at Tennessee.

Mr. Akart has provided his readers a diverse range of topics that are both informative and entertaining. His attention to detail and impeccable research has allowed him to capture the imagination of his readers through his fictional works and bring them valuable knowledge through his nonfiction books.

SIGN UP for Bobby Akart's mailing list to learn of special offers, view bonus content, and be the first to receive news about new releases.

Visit www.BobbyAkart.com for details.

DEDICATIONS

With the love and support of my wife, Dani, together with the unconditional love of Bullie and Boom, the princesses of the palace, I'm able to tell you these stories. It would be impossible for me to write without them in my heart.

Freedom and security are precious gifts that we, as Americans, should never take for granted. I would like to thank the men and women, past and present, of the United States Armed Forces for willingly making sacrifices each day to provide us that freedom and security. Also, a note of thanks to their families who endure countless sleepless nights as their loved ones are deployed around the world.

They are the sheepdogs who live to protect the flock. They bravely and unselfishly confront the wolves who threaten our country, our freedoms, and their brothers in arms from those who would bring destruction to our door.

Choose Freedom!

AUTHOR'S INTRODUCTION

February, 2021

Since scientific discoveries in the late 1930s made nuclear weapons a possibility, the world began to realize they posed an enormous threat to humanity. In 1942, with the secretive research effort in the U.S. known as the Manhattan Project, a race toward nuclear supremacy began. Since their very first use in World War II, different leaders and organizations have been trying to prevent proliferation to additional countries. Despite their efforts, more nation-states than ever before have obtained nuclear weapons.

Following pioneering research from scientists in the early 1980s, the world was introduced to the concept of nuclear winter. Researchers had known that a large nuclear war could cause severe global environmental effects, including dramatic cooling of surface temperatures, declines in precipitation, and increased ultraviolet radiation.

The term nuclear winter was coined specifically to refer to atmospheric cooling that resulted in winter-like temperatures occurring year-round. Regardless of whether extreme cold temperatures were reached, there would be severe consequences for humanity. But how severe would those consequences be? And what should the world be doing about it?

To the first question, the short answer is nobody knows with absolute certainty. The total human impacts of nuclear winter are both uncertain and under-studied. The aftereffects of the twin atomic bombs dropped on Japan to end World War II were not analyzed in depth. More research on the impacts would be very helpful, but treaties have limited nuclear weapons testing. Therefore research, other than theoretical conclusions, has been limited.

As to the question of what the world should be doing about it, all nations agree non-proliferation is a start. However, there are still more than sufficient nuclear weapons capable of being launched to bring the world to the brink of Armageddon.

Today, nuclear winter is not a hot topic among the world's leaders. When the Cold War ended, so did attention to the catastrophic threat of nuclear winter. That started to change in 2007 with a new line of nuclear winter research that used advanced climate models developed for the study of global warming.

Relative to the 1980s research, the new research found that the smoke from nuclear firestorms would travel higher into the atmosphere causing nuclear winter to last longer than previously thought. This research also found dangerous effects from smaller nuclear exchanges, such as an India-Pakistan nuclear war detonating *only* one hundred total nuclear warheads.

Some new research has also examined the human impacts of nuclear winter. Researchers simulated agricultural crop growth in the aftermath of a hundred-weapon India-Pakistan nuclear war. The results were startling. The scenario could cause agriculture productivity to decline by around twenty to sixty percent for several years after the exchange.

The studies looked at major staple crops in China and the United States, two of the largest food producers. Other countries and other crops would likely face similar declines. Following such crop declines, severe global famine could ensue. One study estimated the total extent of the famine by comparing crop declines to global malnourishment data. When food becomes scarce, the poor and malnourished are typically hit the hardest. This study estimated two billion people would be at risk of starvation. And this is from the hundred-weapon India-Pakistan nuclear war scenario. A larger nuclear exchange involving the U.S., China, or Russia would have more severe impacts because the payloads are much larger.

This is where the recent research stops. To the best of my knowledge there have been no current studies examining the secondary effects of famines, such as disease outbreaks and violent conflicts due to societal collapse.

There is also a need to examine the human impacts of ultraviolet radiation. That would include an increased medical burden due to skin cancer and other diseases. It would also include further losses to the agriculture ecosystems because the ultraviolet radiation harms plants and animals. At this time, we can only make educated guesses about what these impacts would be, informed in part by research surrounding enormous volcanic eruptions.

A note on the impact on humanity, we can look to society's reaction to recent political events. Imagine what U.S. cities would look like if the triggering event for protests and riots was based on lack of food. The social unrest would quickly spread into suburban areas as the have-nots would search for sustenance from those who might have it.

When analyzing the risk of nuclear winter, one question is of paramount importance: Would there be long-term or even permanent harm to human civilization? Research shows nuclear winter would last ten years or more. Would the world ever be able to come back from the devasting loss of billions of lives?

Carl Sagan was one of the first people to recognize this point in a commentary he wrote on nuclear winter for Foreign Affairs magazine. Sagan believed nuclear winter could cause human extinction in which case all members of future generations would be lost. He argued that this made nuclear winter vastly more important than the direct effects of nuclear war which could, in his words, *kill only hundreds of millions of people.*

Sagan was, however, right that human extinction would cause permanent harm to human civilization. It is debatable whether nuclear winter could cause human extinction. Rutgers professor Alan Robock, a respected nuclear winter researcher, believes it is unlikely. He commented, "Especially in Australia and New Zealand, humans would have a better chance to survive."

Why Australia and New Zealand? A nuclear war would presumably occur mainly or entirely in the northern hemisphere. The southern hemisphere would still experience environmental disruption, but it would not be as severe. Australia and New Zealand further benefit from being surrounded by water which further softens the effect.

This is hardly a cheerful thought as it leaves open the chance of human extinction, at least for those of us north of the equator. Given all the uncertainty and the limited available research, it is impossible to rule out the possibility of human extinction. In any event, the possibility should not be dismissed.

Even if people survive, there could still be permanent harm to humanity. Small patches of survivors would be extremely vulnerable to subsequent disasters. They certainly could not keep up the massively complex civilization we enjoy today. In addition to the medical impact, the destruction of the power grid, the heartbeat of most nations, would likely occur due to the electromagnetic pulse generated by the nuclear detonations. It would take many years to rebuild the critical infrastructure ruined by the blasts.

It would be a long and uncertain rebuilding process and survivors might never get civilization back to where it is now. More importantly, they might never get civilization to where we now stand poised to take it in the future. Our potentially bright future could be forever dimmed, permanently.

Nuclear winter is a very large and serious risk. In some ways, it doesn't change nuclear weapons policy all that much. Everyone already knew that nuclear war would be highly catastrophic. The prospect of a prolonged nuclear winter means that nuclear war is even more catastrophic. That only reinforces policies that have long been in place, from deterrence to disarmament. Indeed, military officials have sometimes reacted to nuclear winter by saying that it just makes their nuclear deterrence policies that much more effective. Disarmament advocates similarly cite nuclear winter as justifying their policy goals. But the basic structure of the policy debate remains unchanged.

In other ways, the prospect of nuclear winter changes nuclear weapons policy quite dramatically. Because of nuclear winter, noncombatant states may be severely harmed by nuclear war. Nuclear winter gives every country great incentive to reduce tensions and de-escalate conflicts between nuclear-capable states.

Nation-states that are stockpiling nuclear weapons should also take notice. Indeed, the biggest policy implication of nuclear winter could be that it puts the interests of nuclear-capable nations in greater alignment. Because of nuclear winter, a nuclear war between any two major nuclear weapon states could severely harm each of the others. According to intelligence sources, there are nine total nuclear-armed states with Iran prepared to breakthrough as the tenth. This multiplies the risk of being harmed by nuclear attacks while only marginally increasing the benefits of nuclear deterrence. By shifting the balance of harms versus benefits, nuclear winter can promote nuclear disarmament.

Additional policy implications come from the risk of permanent harm to human civilization. If society takes this risk seriously, then it should go to great lengths to reduce the risk. It could stockpile food to avoid nuclear famine or develop new agricultural paradigms that can function during nuclear winter.

And it could certainly ratchet up its efforts to improve relations between nuclear weapon states. These are things that we can do right now even while we await more detailed research on nuclear winter risk.

Against that backdrop, I hope you'll be entertained and informed by this fictional account of the world thrust into Nuclear Winter. God help us if it ever comes to pass.

REAL-WORLD NEWS EXCERPTS

BRITAIN to BOOST NUCLEAR WEAPONS STOCKPILE

~ Wall Street Journal, March 2021

After its departure from the European Union, the U.K. seeks more sway in the Indo-Pacific region

Following its exit from the European Union last year, Britain is looking to carve its place in a more volatile and fragmented international system while bolstering its economy through greater global trade.

In a radical departure from the past, however, the strategy document outlines an ambitious redirection of London's priorities towards Asia.

"The UK will deepen our engagement in the Indo-Pacific, establishing a greater and more persistent presence than any other European country.

Yet, by far the most surprising development is Britain's announced intention to increase its stockpile of nuclear warheads from 180 to 260, an unprecedented boost of around 40 per cent in the country's total nuclear arsenal. And, just as significantly, the British government has now removed its self-imposed cap on the number of nuclear warheads that are deemed "operational" and can therefore be fired at any given time.

IRAN, RUSSIA DENOUNCE UK PLAN TO BOOST NUCLEAR ARSENAL

~ Channel News Asia, March 2021

Iran and Russia on Wednesday denounced the UK's decision to bolster its nuclear arsenal, with the Islamic republic accusing it of "hypocrisy" and the Kremlin warning the move threatens international stability.

"In utter hypocrisy, the British Prime Minister) is concerned about Iran developing a viable nuclear weapon," Iran's Foreign Minister tweeted. "On the very same day he announces his country will increase its stockpile of nukes. Unlike the UK and allies, Iran believes nukes and all WMDs (weapons of mass destruction) are barbaric & must be eradicated."

"We are very sorry that the UK has chosen this path of increasing nuclear warheads. This decision harms international stability and strategic security," a Kremlin spokesman said. "The presence of nuclear warheads is what threatens peace throughout the world."

IRAN HAS BUILT NEW BALLISTIC MISSILE LAUNCH POSITIONS

~ Fox News, March 2021

Satellite images reveal 4 holes dug into mountainside

The Iranian Khorgo underground ballistic missile site is almost operational after new launching positions were constructed, satellite images obtained by Fox News reveal.

Construction on the ballistic missile site resulted in recent months as the Iranians ramp up work on the launching positions that can rapidly deploy two ballistic missiles each. The Iranian site sits approximately 500 miles from Kuwait, a country that houses more than 13,000 American troops, and less than 200 miles from the United Arab Emirates, a key U.S. partner.

Would Israel Dare Attack Iran's Nuclear Facilities?

~ National Interest, April 2021

There's once again talk that Israel might make a move to attack Iran's nuclear capabilities.

There has been frequent speculation over the last two decades that Israel could launch such an attack on Iran, but while Israel is believed to have undergone various efforts to sabotage Iran's nuclear capability, they have not yet launched a full-on first strike.

The Brookings Institution notes that it would make sense for Israel to strike Iran "sooner rather than later." The question is how Iran would respond to such a strike. Would it order Hezbollah and other proxies to attack Israel? Attack Israel with ballistic missiles? Launch a full-on war in response?

RUSSIA TO BOOST TIES WITH PAKISTAN, SUPPLY MILITARY GEAR

~ ABC News, April 2021

The two nations will boost military ties.

Russia's foreign minister said Moscow and Islamabad will boost ties with Russia providing unspecified military equipment to Pakistan and the two holding joint exercises at sea and in the mountains.

Pakistan wants regional cooperation, though he did not mention Pakistan's uneasy relationship with neighbor India.

The accord underlines the waning influence of the United States in the region, while Russian and Chinese clout grows.

"There's a good reason why this is the first Russian foreign minister visit to Islamabad for nearly a decade: Russia-Pakistan relations are on the ascent," a Russian spokesman said in an interview. He also noted a new 25-year development military agreement between Iran and China.

KIM JONG UN's POWERFUL SISTER SENDS WARNING TO BIDEN

~ CNBC, March 2021

Kim Yo Jong, the powerful sister of North Korean leader Kim Jong Un, sent an eerie message to the United States.

"We take this opportunity to warn the new U.S. administration trying hard to give off [gun] powder smell in our land," Kim Yo Jong said in a statement referencing joint U.S. and South Korean military exercises in the region.

"If it [the U.S.] wants to sleep in peace for the coming four years, it had better refrain from causing a stink at its first step," she added, according to an English translation.

The Trump administration made some initial progress with North Korea, but the negotiations broke down more than a year ago after the U.S. refused to grant sanctions relief in exchange for Pyongyang's dismantling of nuclear weapons and long-range missiles.

The Biden administration has tried unsuccessfully to restart nuke talks with North Korea.

Under third-generation North Korean leader Kim Jong Un, the reclusive state has conducted its most powerful nuclear test recently, launching its first-ever intercontinental ballistic missile and threatening to send missiles into the waters near the U.S. territory of Guam.

EPIGRAPH

"Life on Earth is at the ever-increasing risk of being wiped by a
disaster such as sudden global nuclear war ..."
~ Stephen Hawking, theoretical physicist

There are two problems with our species' survival—nuclear war
and environmental catastrophe, and we're hurtling towards them.
Knowingly.
~ Noam Chomsky, cognitive scientist

The leaders of the world face no greater task than that of avoiding
nuclear war.
~ Robert F. Kennedy, American politician

Nothing conceived by the human mind except Heaven and nuclear
winter is eternal.
~ Jeffrey Zeldman, American entrepreneur

I think I can, I think I can.
~ The Little Engine that Could

PROLOGUE

Wednesday, October 30
Mount Weather Emergency Operations Center
Northern Virginia

Despite the dire circumstances America faced and the unusual conditions under which her government operated, the media from around the world continued to clamor for information. The nuclear detonations had succeeded in collapsing the power grid and associated critical infrastructure across most of America. Nonetheless, information was still being disseminated to her citizens via shortwave radio, satellite television broadcasts, and word of mouth.

President Carter Helton's psychological condition had deteriorated in the initial period following the attacks. Over several days, with the assistance of the White House physician and his close friend Chief of Staff Harrison Chandler, he'd gradually regained control. For the first time since the nuclear warhead struck Washington, DC, he was going to address the nation and then take questions from the media.

His address was going to be like no other in American history. It would rank alongside George Washington's Farewell Address in 1796 and Abraham Lincoln's Gettysburg Address of 1863. Its tone and tenor were completely opposite of other national addresses like John F. Kennedy's inaugural address of 1961 in which he said, "Ask not what your country can do for you, but what you can do for your country." Nor did President Helton call out the enemy like FDR did in his war message to Congress in 1941 following the attack on Pearl Harbor.

No. President Helton focused his efforts on controlling the American people.

In the press room of the Mount Weather Emergency Operations Center in Northern Virginia, the two dozen reporters who'd remained embedded with the Helton administration throughout the entire ordeal shifted uneasily in their seats. They'd been starved for information, receiving only what the president's chief of staff allowed to be leaked to the press pool. This would be their first opportunity to see the president speak and to ask him questions.

The atmosphere was far different from a normal press briefing, where the television media reporters would be standing with their network cameras focused on their pre-address comments. They would be relaying to the viewing audience what they expected the president to say and what it meant. That was not the case on this occasion. There was only one camera that would be focused on the president. Network feeds were unnecessary, as there were no American news outlets capable of receiving them. The broadcast would be sent out via satellite to foreign news networks, who would then share it as circumstances allowed.

The administration's staff tried to convey a sense of normalcy despite their harried looks off-camera. The stage for the address had been set. The *Blue Goose*, the nickname for the large blue podium adorned with the seal of the President of the United States, was an exact replica of the one likely destroyed in the nuclear detonation near the White House. It had remained perched atop a raised stage, awaiting a presidential address, since the moment they'd entered Mount Weather a week ago.

Flanking the podium to the president's right as he spoke was the United States flag, a symbol of America's historic journey from rebellion to exceptionalism. On the other side of the Blue Goose was the flag of the president, the presidential coat of arms on a dark blue background.

Suddenly, with little warning, Chandler announced the president would be coming out within sixty seconds. Any reporters milling about scrambled to take a seat. The muffled conversations of the attendees became an eerie hush as if an invisible hand had hit the mute button. At the start, the media was respectful, as most understood the gravity of this address.

A red light was illuminated on the sole, somewhat antiquated camera that sat in the center of the media seating. Its technology was a decade old but sufficient to broadcast to the U.S. military satellites in low-Earth orbit for further transmission around the globe.

If Peter Albright had been present, he would've been struck by the entourage who accompanied the president onto the stage. To be sure, the director of the nation's Department of Homeland Security was to be expected. Most assumed the secretaries of transportation and energy, who oversaw the nation's critical infrastructure, would be present. Perhaps the secretary of agriculture and her counterpart at the commerce department would be there to address the recovery effort.

But an audible gasp filled the room together with a smattering of whispers when the only people by the president's side were his attorney general and the chairman of the Joint Chiefs of Staff, the highest-ranking and most senior military officer in the armed forces.

Many in the room speculated internally that the president was going to ask for a war declaration from Congress, hence the presence of the CJCS. But what would be the purpose of the nation's top legal advisor being present? They would soon find out, as the president had just settled in behind the podium.

"My fellow Americans, these are unprecedented times. Starting with the unprovoked nuclear attack by Iran on Israel, through the use of nuclear weapons by North Korea on its neighbors and then on the United States, the world has been thrust into a global catastrophe like no other.

"By all counts, millions have perished as a result of the nuclear attacks, and now we face a climatic event that threatens the lives of billions more. It's a catastrophe never faced by modern mankind, and it's one that doesn't discriminate between the rich and poor, or by race, gender, or nationality. The citizens of the world face this calamity together.

"However, my job, as commander-in-chief, is the security of the American people. Other nations are suffering, to be sure, and their leaders are dedicating their efforts to saving lives. As a result, as we've learned, help is not forthcoming from abroad. We have to move forward on our own.

"Through my conversations with the leaders of China, Russia, and European nations, I am assured there will be no further hostilities. Every nation is standing down militarily. This is important as we try to cope with the devastating aftermath and find a path forward toward recovery.

"The first order of business is to regain control of our country. We are facing threats from within. There are those who would undermine our government by taking advantage of our weakened military and law enforcement. These opportunists range from criminals roaming the streets to well-organized militia who seek to subvert the Constitution and establish their own forms of government.

"Therefore, upon the advice of the attorney general and with the strategic planning of our military leaders, I will be taking steps designed to help our fellow Americans during this inexplicable crisis.

"Americans are concerned about their health and safety. Many are starving and without proper shelter. Some are in need of life-saving medical treatment or even life-sustaining medications. We will be outlining a comprehensive plan for helping those in need. It will be a monumental task, one that not only requires the use of all governmental resources but also cooperation from you, the American people.

"The burden of helping one another is universal. It takes a village to achieve a goal of this magnitude, and we will be announcing the mechanism to enlist everyone's participation. Tonight, I am signing a series of executive orders designed to create the largest recovery effort in American history. These orders will grant powers to the Department of Homeland Security, the Federal Emergency Management Agency, and the Joint Chiefs to take the steps necessary to get America back on her feet.

"Now, make no mistake, it will be difficult times for us all. However, I firmly believe by harnessing the resolve of every American who wants to lend cooperation and assistance to this task, we will be able to make our communities safer, stronger, and better prepared to respond to any threats from within or without that hinder our recovery plans.

"Rather than look at this plan as a potential restriction on your rights, look at it in the same vein that the great John F. Kennedy did. It's time for you to help your country through mutual sacrifice and sharing. This is a call to action, and I know the American people will unselfishly respond as we expect them to.

"The actions that I have taken are done with an overriding purpose, which is to ensure the stability of our government while protecting those among us who are most vulnerable. Now, I would like to allow the attorney general to read a statement summarizing the most pertinent provisions of my actions. Mr. Attorney General."

The president stepped back a couple of paces and gestured for the attorney general to approach the podium. The aging lawyer was much shorter than the president but tall in stature when it came to political clout within the administration. Unlike attorneys general of the past, he had the president's ear and was eager to do President Helton's bidding.

"Ladies and gentlemen, I'll get right to it. Following my statement, a copy of the executive order and declaration I am about to read aloud will be distributed to you. It will also be posted by U.S. Marshals inside the glass doors or other conspicuous places at every federal building across the country. It is required by law and the president's executive order that I must read this declaration in its entirety."

Over the next ten minutes, the attorney general read aloud the provisions of President Helton's executive order declaring martial law in America. While trying to contain themselves, the members of the media whispered to one another or unconsciously uttered words of surprise aloud.

During those ten minutes, the declaration gutted the U.S. Constitution. The First Amendment rights of free speech, assembly, and religion were severely restricted under the guise of preventing insurrection and rioting.

The Second Amendment right to bear arms was suspended for the general health, safety and welfare of American citizens. Under martial law, the president declared all privately held weapons, magazines, ammunition, and accessories of any kind to be illegal. Americans were ordered to voluntarily relinquish them to law enforcement or the military. The government would access the database of the Bureau of Alcohol, Tobacco, Firearms and Explosives to identify gun owners. For those who failed to comply, they'd risk having them taken by force.

In order to enforce the provisions of the martial law declaration, the president suspended the Fourth, Fifth, Sixth and Seventh Amendments that protected American citizens from unlawful search and seizure as well as a right to due process or a speedy trial in any legal proceedings.

Further, in addition to specific provisions dealing with penalties such as forfeiture, confiscation, and imprisonment for noncompliance, the declaration of martial law suspended the Tenth Amendment. Designed by the Founding Fathers to limit federal powers, the Tenth Amendment reserved to the states any power not specifically granted to the federal government under the Constitution.

In other words, the president was taking over control of every aspect of America's government at all levels from the state houses to, most importantly, police powers ordinarily falling under the purview of the states.

Even President Helton's many allies in the media shuddered at the broad-reaching, draconian consequences of his actions.

PART I

———

Halloween
Day fourteen, Thursday, October 31

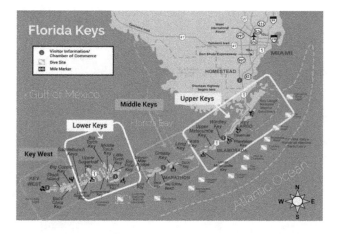

CHAPTER ONE

Thursday, October 31
Munford Residence
Near Amelia Court House, Virginia

Peter Albright was puzzled by what he found in the two-hundred-year-old farmhouse in rural Central Virginia. The home appeared occupied, yet it wasn't. Upstairs, the beds had been slept in. Covers were pulled back, and the sheets were wrinkled. However, all of the pillows were missing. The closets had been rummaged through. Hangers had been emptied, and some had even fallen to the floor as if the residents had been in a hurry.

As he continued to shine his light on the family photos located throughout the home's expansive foyer, he became more certain the family had bugged out when the bombs fell. Most likely, he surmised, they'd gathered the clothes necessary for an extended stay in a bomb shelter nearby. They'd packaged up the food in their cupboards to tide them over until relief supplies came in.

But Peter had an uneasy feeling. Perhaps it was the cold gust of wind that just broadsided the two-story farmhouse. Maybe it was the passing by of a ghost roaming the halls from the home's past.

Nonetheless, he noticeably shivered. He was overcome by a mixture of wide-ranging emotions, exhaustion and the physiological rush of being in someone else's home under eerie circumstances. In the moment, he'd become hyperaware of his surroundings as if life were moving in slow motion, one frame at a time.

The multiple clicks of the rifles' hammers being cocked occurred within milliseconds of one another. Peter's reaction happened equally as fast.

He leapt backwards, recoiling away from the walls depicting the ancestors of the Munford family. As his body flew toward the front door, bullets pierced the wood floor, sending splinters and centuries-old dust into the air. The first two rounds obliterated the dusty footprints Peter had left before his leap to safety.

He crashed into the door hard. His lower back hit the doorknob, causing him to cry out in pain. Stunned, his body slid to the floor in a heap.

The unmistakable blast of the shotgun made his ears ring as the double-aught buckshot blasted a hole in the floor where he stood. This was immediately followed by the shooters loading another round by cocking the lever actions on their Henry rifles.

Peter twisted around onto his knees and tried to turn the door handle. It was locked. In the darkness, he ran his hands all over the mortise lock, an antique door hardware system in which the lock mechanism was combined with a door pull.

"Dammit," Peter mumbled as his fingers found the hole where the bit key was inserted to unlock it.

BOOM!

Another shotgun blast tore through the floor near his feet. Peter abandoned his attempt to flee through the front door and began to scramble on all fours into the parlor. He crossed the threshold separating the two rooms when more bullets flew past his side, striking the ceiling, which resulted in plaster raining down onto his head.

Peter begged his attackers to stop. "Please! Stop shooting! I just need a place to sleep!"

He tried to regain his footing. The rifles fired in unison, blasting through the plank flooring again, ripping into a side table, causing a ceramic table lamp to shatter.

Peter covered his face from the flying bits of shiny porcelain as he stumbled forward toward the wall. He tried to get his bearings. He frantically searched his pockets for his flashlight before he realized he'd dropped it in the foyer.

He had to keep moving. He moved quickly through the parlor toward the large entryway, using the outer walls to guide him. Once in the foyer, he accidentally knocked a painting off the wall and tripped over it. The portrait of a long-deceased Munford landed with a thud on the splinter-covered floor. Peter's body twisted as he fell. He tried to brace himself, but his right arm rammed through the hole the shotgun had made moments earlier.

He was stuck.

He pulled and tugged to free his torn jacket from the shredded flooring. Then, as if he were immersed in a horror movie, someone beneath the floor grabbed his hand.

Peter's mouth opened to scream, but nothing came out. His primal fear prevented him from letting out the blood-curdling shriek his mind wanted to release.

With all his strength, he tore his arm back through the floor and scrambled into the living room, which was combined with the dining area. He clumsily regained his footing and ran several steps in the darkness before stumbling over the rolled arm of the sofa, where he landed facedown on the musty cushions.

BOOM!

Another shotgun blast from below. The buckshot tore a hole in the floor beneath the sofa, rattled off the springs, and ripped through the cushions.

Peter heard the unmistakable sound of the shooter racking another shell into the shotgun. He couldn't react in time.

BOOM!

The pellets from the second shot came through the same opening as the first. This time, there was very little in their way to protect him from the impact. Half a dozen found their way into Peter's midsection and chest. He screamed in agony as he rolled off the sofa onto the rug.

At that point, Peter's anger kicked in to join his adrenaline-fueled fight to survive. He found his way onto his feet and started running toward where he remembered the kitchen entry was located. He pulled his gun from his paddle holster and fired without aiming into the floor in an attempt to frighten off his attackers. The momentary attempt to multitask almost proved fatal.

The loose area rug slid under his feet, and he fell hard to the floor. Two more rifle shots rang out and pierced the floor in front of him. His loss of balance likely saved his life.

He quickly regained his focus and crawled again toward the kitchen before clumsily crashing into a dining chair with the crown of his head. He was immediately rewarded with a goose egg, a hematoma, that began to swell from the trauma. Nonetheless, he was undeterred.

Peter felt the cool air coming through the kitchen and the hallway that led to the back door. It gave him hope and the feeling that he would survive the onslaught. He changed his course and scrambled forward. His hands reached the part of the kitchen where the direction of the floorboards changed.

He picked up the pace, and then he used the kitchen countertop to pull his battered body upright. Recalling how he'd entered the home, Peter stumbled blindly into the back hallway leading to the outside as he tried to find his way out.

In a frantic rush, he pushed himself toward the Dutch door he'd breached earlier. He flung it open and raced into the cold, dewy air. Relieved, he gasped for air, but in his fight to survive, he'd forgotten about the amount of ash and soot that had permeated the atmosphere. He immediately began a coughing fit as he fell onto his knees in the backyard.

The pain. The inability to breathe. His heart pumping out of his chest. None of that mattered to Peter. He was safe.

Or so he thought.

CHAPTER TWO

Thursday, October 31
Munford Residence
Near Amelia Court House, Virginia

Peter stuck his hand into his jacket and felt the warm moisture oozing out of his upper body. The blood from the shotgun wound had soaked all the clothing layers he'd worn to keep warm. He resisted the urge to pull off the wet clothing. He needed to get to his bicycle and get the hell out of Dodge, as they say.

He pulled his shirt over his mouth and nose to avoid inhaling the sooty air. The rusty, metallic smell of blood filled his nostrils, but it was preferable to the smoky air that had circumnavigated the planet. Peter began to walk quickly through the backyard.

BOOM!

The shotgun roared as it sent another round through an opening under the porch. The sound of pellets embedding in the broad side of the barn forced Peter to the ground. Still holding his pistol, he fired twice in the direction of the house. Glass shattered as the rounds entered the kitchen through the windows.

"Stop! I'm leaving!" *What's wrong with these people?*

His attackers never responded, verbally, anyway. Two more gunshots rang out. The bullets whizzed over his head. Close enough to be felt by Peter, which caused the hair to stand up on the back of his neck.

He looked all around him. The ton bales would require him to backtrack, and the barn was too far away to run to. He stuck to the plan. Peter rose to a low crouch and hustled across the yard toward the side of the house. As he did, he held his gun sideways and fired toward the open space under the porch. His first round hit the ground with a thud, so he raised his aim. The second round struck the side of the house.

He became more confident and stood to run toward the driveway where he'd ditched the bicycle. He was rewarded for his efforts by slipping on the moist grass, and he almost fell.

BOOM!

Another shotgun blast with the bellow of a cannon shattered the silence.

Peter screamed over his shoulder, "Leave me alone!" He fired wildly toward the house.

He could hear the muffled voices shouting instructions. The sound of a window rising caught his attention. He fired toward the house again, the bullet embedding in the wood clapboard siding.

His attackers' response was more gunfire, which startled Peter and caused him to fall forward. He regained his balance once again and began running across the yard in a zigzag pattern. The shots followed his path, tearing into the tall grasses all around him.

Then his right leg caught a farm hydrant protruding from the ground. Often used on farms, the hydrant consisted of a steel standpipe attached to an underground water source that utilized a cast-iron lever and plunger handle. Designed to be freezeproof by avoiding plastic, the all-steel device was an immovable object that caused Peter to spin around before landing hard on his back.

The impact knocked the wind out of him, and for a moment, his vision became blurred. His shirt had fallen down from his face, and he once again sucked soot-filled oxygen into his lungs. The incessant coughing began again and gave away his position to his attackers, who immediately unloaded a barrage of gunfire.

Peter had to move. He was on the downslope of the yard now. He winced in pain as he turned his body. Then he forced his prone torso into a roll. Like a kid playing in a sloped backyard, he turned over and over again as he rolled through the tall grass toward the bottom of the hill where the driveway cut through the trees. His body was stabbed with sticks and the sharp edges of rocks protruding from the ground. It seemed like each time, they sadistically found a bruise or an embedded shotgun pellet.

Then, mercifully, the gunfire stopped.

Nonetheless, he kept an eye on the house until it disappeared from sight. In a fluid motion, he made one final roll and bounded to his feet. He rushed through the grass until he found the limestone rock and packed-dirt driveway.

Peter glanced over his shoulder one last time to see if anyone had emerged from the house to pursue him. He pointed his gun up the hill, searching the hazy surroundings that were now slightly illuminated by the rising sun at predawn. His eyes were wild with fear, and his mind raced as he tried to recall how many shots he'd fired.

Then, without any sign of the shooters, he carefully backed down the hill toward the location where he'd stashed his bicycle. With a deep breath of musty air and the odor of his own blood, he swiftly pushed the bike down the hill toward the road, leaving the Munford home behind him.

CHAPTER THREE

Thursday, October 31
Driftwood Key
Florida Keys, USA

Hank Albright wasn't the type to take in every stray dog that came a-knockin'. The Florida Keys was every American's dream of an island paradise. Pristine waters. Island living. Free spirits enjoying life the way they pleased. But, eventually, those who came to the Keys for fun had to pay the bills. Prior to the collapse, there had been a never-ending stream of newcomers seeking a job. They all professed to have extraordinary talents that the Driftwood Key Inn should take advantage of. However, in the end, the resort was a family-run operation with only a handful of longtime employees.

This situation was different. Hank had met Patrick Hollister on occasion. When he first began working for Island State Bank, Patrick had called upon Hank and solicited his business. He didn't expect Hank to completely abandon his existing banking relationship. Maybe a loan to expand his solar array or to upgrade to a newer model boat. Perhaps a small investment account for Patrick to prove his money-management skills.

Hank never switched banks, but he remained cordial with Patrick, seeing him from time to time at business gatherings in the Keys. He certainly knew nothing of Patrick's proclivities and the secret life he led as Patricia, serial killer.

Hank and his right-hand man, Sonny Free, approached Patrick to help him to his feet. The injured daytime banker, nighttime murderer, had risen to his knees, with both hands cupping the sides of his head. Blood was trickling out from between his fingers.

Hank spoke over his shoulder to Jimmy, Sonny's son.

"Let your mom know what's going on. Tell her to get her first aid supplies and meet us at bungalow three. Then get back to the gate and keep an eye out."

Jimmy turned and began running toward the trail, the beam of his flashlight dancing wildly among the palm trees. He stumbled momentarily and then regained his footing as he hustled into the canopy of palm fronds.

Hank and Sonny lifted the battered man off the crushed-shell bridge connecting the inn to Marathon. "Stay with us, Patrick. We're gonna get you some help."

"He needs a hospital, Mr. Hank," insisted Sonny. "He's bleeding everywhere."

"I know, Sonny, but we gotta get him stabilized first. When Jessica returns with Mike, we'll figure out where to take him."

Patrick lifted his head as the mention of Detective Mike Albright's name registered with him in his semi-coherent state of mind. He could feel himself slipping in and out of consciousness as the two men dragged him along the trail. He was fading fast, and his empty stomach began to retch at the taste of blood in his mouth.

Hank and Sonny stopped to allow Patrick to drop to his knees and vomit. Instead, his stomach twisted and flexed because it was empty. All that Patrick managed to do was spit out the blood that had accumulated in his mouth.

"Come on." Hank encouraged Patrick to stand again. Jimmy's flashlight was seen darting toward them along the trail. When he arrived, he was short of breath but relayed a message from Phoebe.

"Mom's getting everything ready. She really needs Jessica's help, though. I don't think she—"

Hank cut the young man off. "She'll do fine. Now, Jimmy, hurry back and lock down the gate. Then I want you to go to the main house and try to raise Mike and Jess on the radio. Tell them to get back here. Hurry!"

Jimmy took off toward the gate, and the guys continued to help Patrick down the trail toward the beachfront guest bungalows. As they got closer, they could hear the low rumble of the portable generator that was dedicated to this particular bungalow.

During mandatory hurricane evacuations, this was one of six freestanding bungalows that could operate on a generator in the event of a power loss. The others drew from the solar array that had been having difficulty charging the batteries necessary for the hydroponic systems and greenhouses. The day prior, Hank and Phoebe had given up on trying to keep the inn's freezers operating.

Phoebe rushed off the small covered porch of the bungalow and met them as they emerged from the trail. The porch lights allowed her to recognize the injured man.

"Patrick? Is that you?"

He didn't respond, as he couldn't remember that he'd met her a few times at his bank branch. The Frees' checking and savings accounts had been with the Island State Bank for years. They never had a need to borrow money, so as depositors, their only contact with the branch manager was a friendly hello now and then.

Phoebe had a small flashlight that she used to walk around Driftwood Key after dark. The inn tried to keep its exterior lighting to a minimum, as it tended to draw turtles toward the main house at night. Sea turtles nest from early May through the end of October in Florida. State and local laws were enacted to ensure all indoor and outdoor lights visible from the beach were shielded so as not to confuse hatchlings. After they were hatched, lights might draw them away from the task at hand—crawling toward the Gulf to start their new lives.

She swept her flashlight across Patrick's face to examine the damage. She then illuminated his body with the beam of light. She shook her head in disbelief. Every part of his clothing was soaked in blood. His face was battered, and his eyes were nearly swollen shut.

While she waited for Hank and Sonny to bring Patrick to the bungalow, she'd prepared the room by spreading an extra coverlet on top of the bed. From Jimmy's description of the beaten man, she suspected they'd be cutting the clothes off him so she could assess his condition, so she had laid out a complimentary bathrobe provided for their guests.

Phoebe didn't have any medical training, but she'd learned enough about basic first aid over the years from Hank and his family. She applied common sense to her decisions as she got to work.

The three of them helped Patrick lie comfortably on the bed. Phoebe turned to Sonny. "There are some blankets stacked in the laundry building. I'm gonna have to undress him, and we need to keep him warm. This robe won't be enough."

"On my way," he said as he exited the bungalow quickly.

Hank had already started removing Patrick's clothing, which consisted of sweatpants and a long-sleeved tee shirt. The dress he'd been wearing when he met his assailants had been torn off in the first brutal attack.

"Sorry, Patrick. Now isn't the time to worry about our dignity." He pulled the sweatpants off and immediately saw his bruised legs. Phoebe hurriedly covered his lower body with a thick blanket that was rarely used in the normally warm climate.

"Help me with his shirt," Phoebe politely instructed her boss. The two worked together to raise Patrick's arms and pull the tee shirt over his head. More bruising was evident as well as cuts and abrasions. Patrick groaned in pain as his arms stretched his rib muscles.

Phoebe wasted no time in cleaning the blood off his body. She used warm water and clean washcloths to wipe him clean but used sterile gauze near any lacerations. She focused on his upper body first, making mental notes of any contusions or open wounds. She then made her way to his lower body, using a hand towel from the bathroom to cover his genitals. As she cleaned him, he began to lose consciousness.

"We've gotta keep him awake, Mr. Hank. We need to keep him hydrated, and I don't know whether Jessica has those IV bags. Will you wipe his forehead with a cool, damp cloth and see if you can get him to sip water out of a straw?"

She pointed to the nightstand, where she'd already set up a shallow bowl full of water and two washcloths. There was also a child's cup that was provided to guests with children who stayed at the inn on rare occasion.

Hank eagerly helped out, following Phoebe's instructions and talking softly to Patrick to calm his nerves. At first, he'd looked confused as his eyes darted around the bungalow, trying to make sense of where he was. He had been more coherent on the bridge when he was discovered than he was now, a direct result of his continued blood loss.

Phoebe set about bandaging his wounds to stop the bleeding. Sonny returned with the blankets and helped her keep pressure on the worst bleeders. Patrick took a couple of sips of water, but he was fading in and out of consciousness, partly from the loss of blood and partly due to exhaustion. He had been allowed very little sleep by his captors, who had abused him mentally and physically until they were finally done with him.

Phoebe checked his pulse and blood pressure. All of Patrick's readings were low but not life-threatening. Satisfied she'd done all she could without Jessica's expertise, Phoebe washed Patrick's blood off her arms and hands.

Drained from the flurry of activity, she sent Sonny to bring her a change of clothes, and then she dutifully took up a chair next to her patient.

CHAPTER FOUR

Thursday, October 31
Near Amelia Court House, Virginia

Peter rode away from the nightmarish encounter as fast as his battered and buckshot-riddled body would take him. He'd lost track of how long he'd been riding, but the pain in his chest and stomach reminded him that he needed to tend to his wounds.

He drove off the two-lane highway onto a country road that led to the banks of the Appomattox River. This stretch of the river was not much more than a creek, but the water was fairly clear and only contained a small amount of silt.

Peter was extremely thirsty, and he needed water to clean his wounds. He stopped at the shoulder of the road and stepped off the bike onto the gravel bordering the asphalt. Each time his feet planted on the rocks, a jolt was sent through his body that seemed to punch every bruise and squeeze every gaping hole oozing blood.

Despite the falling temperatures, Peter didn't hesitate to remove the three layers of clothing he wore above the waist. They were soaked in blood, and ordinarily, he'd just toss them aside. Under the circumstances, however, he considered rinsing them out and hanging them to dry.

He took a moment to glance down at his chest and midsection. Five of the shotgun pellets had punctured his skin. Two were embedded in his chest, and three holes oozed blood out of his belly. Peter gingerly felt the wounds with his fingertips. Three of the five were superficial. The skin had been broken, causing him to bleed, but the pellets apparently had been deflected or slowed enough to prevent them from going deeper.

The other two wounds obviously contained two pellets from the buckshot. He pressed on the puncture holes and could feel something round beneath his skin. The pain took his breath away, and Peter immediately contemplated leaving them there for fear he might pass out if he tried to remove the shot. Then he recalled virtually every television show or movie he'd ever seen that emphasized removing foreign objects to prevent infection. He decided he'd have to play doctor.

First, he needed to hydrate himself. He rummaged through his duffel bags to locate one of the LifeStraws he'd procured at Dick's Sporting Goods the night Washington, DC, was bombed. He also pulled out his military-style canteen and cup combo.

Peter used the LifeStraw to extract water out of the river. To the naked eye, the river water appeared clear and drinkable, but he wasn't sure how the fallout was affecting it. Out of an abundance of caution, he filtered it through the straw and drank until he was satisfied. Then he repeated the process, slowly filling the cup until he had enough to wash his wounds.

He located the first aid supplies he'd taken from Dick's and the CVS drugstore. He dipped the gauze in the water and gently wiped the wounds off to remove the blood. Some was dried already, but all five holes continued to allow blood to seep out.

Satisfied that three of the holes were simply puncture wounds and didn't contain a shotgun pellet, he cleansed them with Betadine antiseptic. After applying Neosporin triple antibiotic ointment, he used large Band-Aids to protect the wounds from dirt and bacteria.

Then he turned his attention to the more complicated process of removing the pellets.

Peter steeled his nerves as he ran his fingers around the pellet holes again. The wounds were circular and somewhat seared. He'd likely been saved by the floor, sofa and layers of clothing that the pellets had had to travel through before reaching his body. He also assumed parts of all of those things had traveled with the pellets as they entered his chest.

The edges of the wounds were raw and flaring out somewhat, different from the other puncture wounds. This had been Peter's first indication that the pellets were embedded. He took a deep breath and went to work on the chest wound first, which seemed to be producing the most blood. He considered taking a finger from both hands and mashing the wound like he was a teenager popping a zit. Then he wondered if he might end up pushing the pellet deeper inside.

He opted instead to use the tweezers that came with the first aid kit he'd found at the sporting goods store. He looked up for strength, and then he gritted his teeth. This was gonna hurt.

Peter slowly pried open the wound, an action that almost caused him to scream in agony. He knew he couldn't because he had to keep his wits about him during the entire process, and he wasn't certain he was completely alone. With the wound slightly agape, he gently pressed on the sides of his skin to urge the pellet to pop out. His eyes grew wide as he fought to keep his hands steady. If his grip on the tweezers slipped, the silver steel ball might be forced farther into his body, and the wound could be expanded.

With a final gentle nudge, the pellet popped out of his chest and rolled down his stomach until it fell to the ground. Peter quickly retrieved the gauze pad and began to clean the wound. Having practiced on the first three, he was able to cleanse and bandage the hole quickly.

Then he turned his attention to the second pellet. The process was similar to his first effort, and having done it once, his confidence grew. Again, in less than a minute, he'd extracted the pellet, which managed to roll into his belly button. Peter spontaneously laughed, causing him more pain than the removal of the bullet.

"I couldn't do that again in a million years," he mumbled to himself with a smile.

He pulled the pellet out of his navel and shoved it into his pocket. This was a story he'd tell his dad and uncle when he got to Driftwood Key.

Peter cleaned himself up, drank some more water, and then dressed in the hunting gear he'd found at the mall. He now wished he'd kept the camping equipment he'd had to leave behind in order to lighten his load. The multiple layers of cold-weather hunting clothes might not be enough to keep him warm out in the open.

For a moment, he thought about looking for a place to sleep. He lay in the grass, surrounded by his belongings and the bloody reminders of what he'd been through the night before. He contemplated what was ahead of him. The length of the trip. The threats he'd face. The challenges of riding a bicycle with his body beat all to hell. His mind wandered, and then it shut down as he fell into a deep sleep.

CHAPTER FIVE

Thursday, October 31
La Junta, Otero County, Colorado

Sheriff Shawn Mobley exited the communications room at the Otero County Sheriff's Office with a disconcerting look on his face. The normally amiable sheriff had shepherded his community through the aftermath of the devastating electromagnetic pulse that had destroyed the power grid for several hundred miles around its point of detonation outside Boulder. The effect was immediate, and all electronics and vehicles that weren't hardened against the powerful pulse of energy ceased to function.

Sheriff Mobley had prepared his department and his community for this eventuality. An Army veteran who was also a proud father of four, as well as a grandfather, he'd studied the threats posed by a massive power outage. He'd researched the consequences of massive solar flares as well as the potential of a nuclear-delivered warhead triggering an EMP.

What he never imagined was being subjected to the devastating climatic impact of nuclear winter. Weather anomalies were beginning to appear, and he'd just received contact via his ham radio network that a flash freeze had engulfed the west part of Otero County toward Pueblo.

He was told a handful of livestock had been frozen even though they were sheltered within barns. However, those fighting the freezing conditions in the fields never had a chance. The reports of a sudden temperature drop to below zero coupled with high winds immediately raised concern for the residents around Fowler located on U.S. Highway 50.

His deputies had really stepped up during the crisis. They'd spent countless hours away from their own families to check on the elderly residents of the county and to assist ranchers in protecting their cattle. The community was close knit, and they came together to soldier through the greatest catastrophe to strike America in her history.

He entered the break room at the sheriff's department without a word. It was five in the morning, and the overnight shift was winding up their workday. His deputies had settled in for a few hands of shotgun poker.

At the sheriff's office, gambling for money was forbidden, so the deputies improvised. The currency of choice was ammunition. Red twelve-gauge shotgun shells were the lowest value. Next came the nine-millimeter rounds used in the Smith & Wessons that had been the department's service weapon for years. Tonight, the guys had raided the ammunition lockers for a couple of boxes of Speer Gold Dot hollow points.

Sheriff Mobley had just received an order of several Glock 17 Gen 5s for his patrol deputies, which were outfitted with Trijicon suppressor night sights. Otero County was generally crime-free, as it enjoyed a low unemployment rate and a stable economy. However, U.S. Highway 50 was often traveled by transients across Colorado, requiring his deputies to be well equipped for every eventuality.

"Can we deal you in, Sheriff?" one of the deputies offered as he reached behind him and slid a chair up to the wood-grained table. Another deputy slid her chair back to the refrigerator and grabbed her boss a V8 Sparkling Energy drink. Sheriff Mobley had been pulling long shifts and enjoyed the boost to keep his wits about him.

"Nah, and I hate to tell you, but I need you to do something for me even though your shift is ending," he replied.

"Sure, Sheriff. Name it."

"Okay. We've had a call from Polly out at the Collins Ranch. There was some kind of weather deal overnight. She said she'd never seen anything like it. The temperature dropped fifty or sixty degrees in just minutes."

"Dang, Sheriff. Did she lose any of their herd?"

"Some, but I'm worried about more than the livestock. A lot of folks don't have the heat sources to withstand that kinda shock to their surroundings. Y'all take the Jeeps and head up fifty. Stop in and check on people. I'll cover the overtime."

The group of four deputies didn't hesitate. They pushed away from their chairs and cleaned up the poker game. After grabbing their gear from their lockers, they retrieved the keys to the department-owned Jeeps from their peg hooks.

Sheriff Mobley was a *Jeeper*, a term used for aficionados of the classic American utility vehicle that dated back to World War II. He personally owned two vintage Jeeps, both CJ5 models. They were made for going off-road, but most importantly, as it turned out, the pre-1972 models' lack of electronics provided him transportation that was immune to the debilitating effects of an EMP.

During his term as sheriff, he'd begun to search the region for similar Jeeps from the sixties and early seventies. Some were wrecks, and others were in need of parts. It became a labor of love to purchase project cars and restore them. The results of his efforts paid off. The department had a fleet of four fully restored Jeep CJ5s that still operated despite the EMP. Coupled with his two personal vehicles, his deputies were able to travel throughout the county, helping their neighbors and providing the safety of law enforcement during a time when looting was rampant around the nation.

He made sure the deputies took fully charged Bao Feng ham

radios with them to communicate with the base unit at the sheriff's department. He'd been diligent about protecting electronics from the pulse of energy as well.

In a vacant lot across the alley from the sheriff's office, six semitrailers had been parked side by side. These were used by the City of La Junta to store supplies, and one of the trailers had been assigned to his department. As part of his preparation for a catastrophic event like this one, Sheriff Mobley had purchased six large and a dozen small galvanized trash cans to create Faraday cages.

A Faraday cage, an invention developed by a nineteenth-century scientist, was an enclosure formed by a conductive material like steel or steel mesh used to block the damaging electrons dispersed when an EMP detonation occurs. When electronic devices are placed within the protective shield, the massive burst of energy that was ordinarily too strong for the delicate wiring of modern electronic devices was spread around the container, and none passed into it.

The sheriff had placed a backup of every electronic device used by his department inside one of the galvanized steel trash cans. He'd wrapped each item in heavy-duty aluminum foil and then cushioned it inside the trash cans with two-inch-thick padding like that used in chair cushions. Finally, he'd sealed the lids in place with aluminum tape used by heating and air-conditioning contractors.

When the EMP hit near Boulder, the electromagnetic pulse didn't penetrate the makeshift Faraday cages. As a result, Sheriff Mobley had the ability to communicate with his deputies when on patrol. He was also able to replace the solar charge controllers and other electronic equipment associated with the department's rooftop solar array.

He'd even secured various types of medical equipment donated by the Arkansas Valley Regional Medical Center in town. As they replaced older, still-operating equipment with newer models, Sheriff Mobley asked to keep the discarded devices. He had also protected this equipment in the larger trash cans. When the EMP destroyed most of the life-saving equipment at the small medical center, he was able to provide them something to work with.

Soon, Sheriff Mobley would learn whether his efforts could help save the lives of a group of strangers who just happened to be passing through his county.

CHAPTER SIX

Thursday, October 31
U.S. Highway 50
Near Fowler, Colorado

Otero County deputies Susan Ochoa and Adam Hostetler followed each other to the westernmost part of the county into the town of Fowler just as the sun was beginning to beg its way through the ash-filled skies. They split up as they drove the residential streets, using the external loudspeakers affixed to their Jeeps to let people know they were in the neighborhood. They asked them to check on their neighbors when the conditions permitted.

The feel of death surrounded them. There were very few birds that inhabited the area, and those were frozen, their carcasses strewn about, lifeless eyes staring toward the sky. Sadly, cats and dogs had fallen victim to the flash freeze as well. Owners, unable to feed their animals, had sent the domesticated creatures out of the house to fend for themselves. Cats were better adapted to the inclement weather, as they squeezed themselves under home foundations or deep into barns. Dogs were another matter. Loyal to their owners, they waited on the porch next to front doors, knowing they'd be let inside eventually. They weren't.

Ochoa and Hostetler made their way west on U.S. Highway 50 toward Pueblo. They slowed at the entrance to the stockyards to see how the cattle had fared. Hostetler pulled in first. However, as he did, Ochoa had another thought and raised him on the radio.

"Adam, I'm gonna make a quick ride out to the Pueblo County line. There are a couple of farms on County Road 1 that I'd like to check on."

"10-4. This won't take long. Let's meet up here when we're finished."

Ochoa continued down the snow-covered highway, which had been partially cleared by the gusty headwinds she faced. A half-mile-long freight train had stalled at the moment of the EMP detonation. Its cars had been filled with cattle heading from Pueblo to the Texas Panhandle. It had been a herculean effort by local ranchers to off-load the railcars and drive the cattle into the Nepesta Valley Stockyards owned by the Lucero family for safekeeping. She wondered if the bone-chilling conditions that had struck the west part of the county killed them all.

Ochoa slowed as she came upon a pickup truck stalled in the middle of the road, heading eastbound. She'd checked it out on a previous patrol to the northwest part of the county, but this time something seemed amiss. Hay was thrown on the asphalt pavement both to the side and rear bumper of the truck. However, there was something else she couldn't quite reconcile.

She eased up to the front bumper and exited her Jeep. Despite her familiarity with the stalled truck, her instincts encouraged her to keep her gloved hand on her service weapon. She made a fist with her left hand and attempted to wipe the ice crystals off the driver's side window. When she was unsuccessful, she removed her cuffs from her utility belt and used the steel double strand to remove enough ice for her to see inside. The interior was empty.

She slowly walked to the side of the pickup, kicking at the frozen hay at her feet. Still wary that an animal might have found its way into the truck bed, she kept her hand on her service weapon. Otero County had battled plague-infested prairie dogs and rodents the summer before. The plague had jumped from animal to animal through flea infestations, infecting the wild dogs that roamed the fields around the county line. These animals were not only infectious, they were considered dangerous.

Ochoa stopped and looked around. Nothing moved, and she began to think her hunch had failed her. She took a few steps toward the west and then turned back toward the pickup. She shrugged and shook her head slightly as she started back to her Jeep.

Then something caught her eye in the back of the truck. Her pulse quickened, and her adrenaline kicked in. She drew her weapon.

"Shit! Are you kidding me? Shit!"

Ochoa rushed to the back of the truck and used one arm to hoist herself onto the bumper. She leaned over the tailgate and rustled through the loose hay to reveal the legs of a man extending from under half a dozen bales piled on top of him. With her weapon trained on the man, she grabbed one of his ankles and shook it.

"Hey, mister! Are you okay?"

No response.

She grabbed both ankles and shook hard. She shouted her question. "Hey! Wake up!"

Again, no response.

Ochoa stood on the bumper, holstered her weapon, and pulled her handheld ham radio from her utility belt. Abandoning all protocol, she called for backup.

"Adam! This is Susan. Need you now! Middle of Highway 50, just east of CR 1. Possible dead body."

CHAPTER SEVEN

Thursday, October 31
Arkansas Valley Regional Medical Center
La Junta, Colorado

Sheriff Mobley was about to leave the department when a member of his communications team rushed to stop him. He was told about Deputy Ochoa's discovery of a body in the back of the pickup truck on Route 50. Amazingly, the man they found was not dead. Both Ochoa and Hostetler confirmed the man was hanging on by a thread. He was suffering from exposure to the extreme temperature drop that had been reported to the sheriff's office.

He took a seat in the chair of the communications deputy and pressed the talk button on the microphone attached to the ham base unit.

"Is he conscious?"

"Negative."

"Both of you need to carry him into a Jeep. Be gentle. Remove his wet outer layers of clothing."

Hostetler responded, "Negative, Sheriff. His clothes are frozen solid. I've never seen anything like it. He looks like that guy on *The Shining.*"

Sheriff Mobley scowled. His voice reflected his sense of urgency. "Come on, Adam. Respect, please. Get him in the Jeep and fire up the heat. As his clothes thaw, remove anything wet and cover him with blankets. Susan, ride in the back seat while Adam brings him to the medical center. Monitor his breathing."

"I have a thermos of hot coffee," she added.

"Good. If he comes to, and if he's coherent enough to drink, let him have some but just a little. I mean, don't let him gulp it down."

"10-4," she replied. There was radio silence for a moment until Ochoa returned to report their progress. "We're coming in. ETA is gonna be half an hour, Sheriff. We're as far away as far away can be."

"Understood. Out." Sheriff Mobley flung himself back in his chair and ran his hands through his thin, sandy blond hair. Throughout the crisis, he'd prided himself and his department on their ability to save the lives of his residents and travelers. Throughout the conversation, as he'd focused on instructing his deputies through the process of bringing the man to the medical center, something nagged at him.

Where did he come from? It was a question he hoped to get answers to because that meant the man would be alive to tell about it. With a sigh, he hustled over to the medical center to alert the emergency room.

Otero County, with its small population of just over ten thousand residents, was fortunate to have its own hospital. Small in comparison to the massive medical centers found in large cities, its history dated back to the early 1900s when it was founded. In the 1920s, its management and operations were turned over to the Mennonite Board with the agreement to expand its facilities. Over the years, it grew before ownership was turned back over to the city of La Junta. Now, the community-owned medical center provided all manner of treatment from birthing babies to treating patients in its intensive care unit.

Sheriff Mobley walked to the hospital to give himself an opportunity to process the weather anomaly that had swept across his county overnight. He'd had several conversations with other ham radio operators in the region about what they'd experienced.

Some explanations were more dramatic than others. Reports of everything freezing instantaneously. Comparisons to space travelers in a cryogenic state. Descriptions of animals instantly frozen, still standing on their legs as if they were an animatronic creation at an amusement park.

There were also the descriptions of the weather event itself. Godly people described it as the Grim Reaper flowing across their fields in the form of a black, shadowy cloud of death. The collector of souls was accompanied by a frigid wind unlike any other they'd ever experienced. During any winter, Otero County was susceptible to icy, subzero temperatures as Canadian air swept down the eastern slopes of the Rocky Mountains, but longtime residents said nothing they'd seen in their lifetimes compared to this.

The sheriff entered the hospital through the emergency room entrance and was not all that surprised to find it bustling with activity. Although most people had been inside during the flash freeze, some had been caught outside checking on their animals or retrieving firewood for their woodstoves.

It was all hands on deck as medical personnel from all parts of the hospital were in the emergency room, treating people for breathing difficulties resulting from taking in the frigid air. Others had suffered frostbite and severe burns to their exposed skin.

One man was suffering a mental breakdown. He'd heard his beloved horse become agitated as his barn was struck with an enormous gust of wind. He ran out to the stable in his nightclothes without a jacket. Within a minute, he realized he was in trouble, and when his horse fell over dead, he did the only thing he could do to survive.

He grabbed a razor-sharp sickle hanging from a support post.

He cut open the belly of his horse and removed her intestines. The small-framed man forced himself into his horse's body cavity and then pulled straw up against himself. He'd lain there for hours, sobbing, but somewhat warm. At least enough not to freeze. He survived physically. Mentally, he'd never be the same.

Sheriff Mobley convinced the emergency room staff to have a treatment room reserved for the incoming patient. They shuffled some of the already-treated patients to other parts of the hospital after he convinced them there might be more exposure victims inbound that morning.

When Hostetler's Jeep roared into the covered entrance to the ER, Sheriff Mobley rushed outside with the nurses pushing the gurney. He wanted to do all he could to keep anyone in his county from dying on his watch.

The medical team quickly moved the man into the ER treatment room. They began their work on the patient but not before they had to encourage remove Sheriff Mobley and his two deputies to leave the room. The three law enforcement officers looked upon the man they knew nothing about with concern and sadness. None of them expected the man to live.

A nurse handed Ochoa two bags containing the man's belongings as she closed the curtain to block their view. The three law enforcement officers walked outside with the bags and laid them on the hood of the idling Jeep.

"We need to go back and fetch Ochoa's Jeep," said Hostetler in a somber tone of voice.

"Let me get the rest of the victim's things," she added as she opened the passenger door and reached into the back seat of the Jeep. She returned with the man's thawed jacket and pants. She was also holding something that puzzled Sheriff Mobley.

"What's with the car parts?" he asked.

"Strange, right?" replied Ochoa. She held them up for Sheriff Mobley and Hostetler to examine. "The vic had the radiator hose stuffed inside his jacket, and his arm was wrapped through the air filter."

"Broken-down car?" asked the sheriff.

"Not that I recall seeing," replied Ochoa. "You know, vis is limited. Plus, once I found the body, I focused on getting him here."

Sheriff Mobley took the parts from her and set them on the still-warm hood of Hostetler's Jeep. He dumped the contents of the man's property bag on the hood and spread everything out.

"Let's look for some sort of identification."

The three of them rustled through the pockets of his clothing until Ochoa found something. "Hey, it's a business card. I don't know if this is the guy or not, but it makes sense." She handed it to Sheriff Mobley, who studied it.

"Owen McDowell. Senior VP with Yahoo in Sunnyvale."

"Should we let the docs know?" asked Hostetler.

Sheriff Mobley handed the card to him and nodded. "Take his things and tell them what you know. Ochoa, you're with me. Let's head up the highway and find this gentleman's car."

CHAPTER EIGHT

Thursday, October 31
U.S. Highway 50
Near Fowler, Colorado

"Sheriff, um, that was County Road 1," said Deputy Ochoa hesitantly. "We're in Pueblo's jurisdiction now." She kept her eyes forward, mostly, with only the occasional side glance at her boss as he continued up Highway 50.

"I'm sure they won't mind. I wanna see where this McDowell fella came from."

Sheriff Mobley relaxed his death grip on the Jeep's steering wheel momentarily and adjusted his stout frame in the seat. He set his jaw and leaned forward, unconsciously causing him to propel the vehicle a little faster on the slick, snow-covered highway.

Despite the darkened daytime conditions, he wore his sunglasses to shield the glare produced by the white cloud cover. What little sunlight found its way to Earth's surface reflected in all directions off the snow and the grayish atmosphere.

"Sheriff, up ahead. Bright blue. Looks like a classic Bronco or Blazer."

"I see it!" he exclaimed as he began to decelerate. He'd already noticed patches of ice under the blanket of snow, and he didn't want to make a bad day worse by plowing into the stranded truck in the middle of the highway. He slowed to a stop, and the two quickly exited the Jeep to approach the stalled Ford Bronco.

Sheriff Mobley noticed the hood wasn't completely closed, and knew he had the right truck. He pulled his tactical flashlight from his utility belt and illuminated it. Despite it being midmorning, the interior of the truck was dark. Ochoa, as she'd done before, tried the door handles first, and then she scraped the ice off the driver's window with her handcuffs.

The sheriff shined the light through the hole in the icy exterior and peered inside. "Looks empty," he muttered.

Ochoa began to scrape away the ice from the rear windows of the two-door classic Bronco. Without saying a word, she began to do so more frantically. She rubbed the window with her gloved hands.

"I see a body! Wait, no. There are two!"

Simultaneously, Sheriff Mobley began pounding on the hood of the truck while Ochoa smacked the window.

"Hey! Are you guys okay?" she shouted.

"Sheriff's department. Open up!" ordered Sheriff Mobley.

"I've got movement, Sheriff! I swear one of them moved."

"Stand aside," he instructed his deputy. He pulled his new service weapon and turned it around to be used like a hammer. He struck the driver's side window with the pistol grip until it cracked. Then he turned sideways and drove his elbow into the breach, causing the glass to break before falling inside. He didn't hesitate to pull up the door lock.

"Are you okay?" Ochoa shouted her question again.

Nobody responded.

Sheriff Mobley struggled to open the driver's side door, which had frozen shut. He placed his boot on the truck's nerf bar, the shiny steel tubular bars that served the purpose of a running board

42

on older trucks. He grunted as he pulled on the door handle. It flew open, causing him to lose his balance temporarily. The sheriff caught himself before falling, and Ochoa quickly moved in to pull the driver's seat forward. She raised the seat back to give her access to the rear passengers.

Despite her hyperactive state of mind, she slowed her approach to the two people curled up together in the back seat. If they were armed, she didn't want to startle them into shooting her. She found a teenage boy on the edge of the seat, bundled up in winter gear. His face was barely visible through the hood of his jacket, which was secured around him with a drawstring.

She leaned in further and placed her ear next to his mouth. She managed a smile as she crawled backwards out of the truck. She made eye contact with Sheriff Mobley.

"He's alive. There's another person crammed in the seat under a pile of clothing and blankets. We gotta pull the boy out first."

"I'll get the Jeep and call it in."

While Sheriff Mobley pulled the Jeep closer, Ochoa tried to revive the young man. For a brief moment he regained consciousness.

"Hey, buddy," she began. "Take it easy, okay? We're gonna get you some help."

The young man tried to speak to her, but his mouth barely moved. Air exited his mouth; however, his words were stifled by his weakened condition.

"That's okay. You don't need to talk. Let me help you out."

"Dad," he said, the word barely audible but discernible by Ochoa.

"Your dad? Is that your father behind you?" She tried to reach under his arms to pull him out, but she couldn't leverage his weight. Sheriff Mobley joined her side to assist.

The young man mouthed the words and spoke whisper soft. "My mom. Dad went for ..." His voice trailed off.

Sheriff Mobley gently nudged Ochoa out of the way and asked, "Is his name Owen?"

Tucker McDowell nodded and then passed out.

The Otero County sheriff's department sprang into action. While Sheriff Mobley and Deputy Ochoa raced back to the medical center with Tucker and Lacey, the other deputies gathered up the parked Jeep. Then they worked together to tow the abandoned McDowells' vintage Ford Bronco to the sheriff's department. Once it had arrived, they were able to confirm the family's identity and provided the information to the medical staff.

As the day progressed, the McDowell family occupied three spots in the small hospital's intensive care unit. Despite being exhausted, Sheriff Mobley remained in the lobby to keep tabs on the California family he and his deputies had rescued. They'd given the young family a chance to live, and he wanted to see their care through to the end.

The attending physician, an acquaintance of the sheriff's, had just completed his rounds and approached to provide an update.

"Shawn, you really oughta go home and get some rest. These folks are in good hands."

"What's the prognosis?" asked the sheriff without addressing the doctor's concerns for his well-being.

The doctor sighed and sat on a chair across from the sheriff. He loosened his tie, one of the few physicians who continued to maintain a higher standard of dress during the apocalypse. His white physician's jacket, however, was soiled from inadequate washing. His shirt was no longer pressed. But he still donned a tie out of respect for those he treated. They deserved professionalism, he'd told his wife the first day after the EMP destroyed the power grid. He'd worked countless hours daily ever since.

"Not good for the father and only slightly better for the other two. Shawn, they're suffering from the worst cases of hypothermia I've ever seen. You know how it is around here; we get cases every winter. You warn people on Facebook and do the PSA radio spots, but they don't listen. They think they can endure what mother nature has to offer."

"This was some kind of freak storm, Doc," interrupted Sheriff Mobley. "The western part of the county got the worst of it. We're lucky your hospital isn't wall-to-wall with these patients."

"It's a good thing, too," said the doctor. "We don't have the necessary equipment to give these people the treatment they deserve. If it weren't for you storing the old stuff in those trailers, we'd have no way to monitor their vitals." He sighed and shook his head before continuing.

"The dad's body temp was just at seventy degrees. I can't stress enough that he's suffering from a profound, potentially life-threatening level of hypothermia. By all rights, he should be dead right now except for the grace of God."

Sheriff Mobley grimaced. "What about the mom and their son? They were pretty bundled up in the back of the truck. Why aren't they waking up?"

"We could wake them, but their bodies need to rest and recover. We're keeping them hydrated and warm. Both of their bodies' temperatures recorded in the low eighties when you brought them in. I suspect they dropped to the mid-seventies overnight."

"And the dad hit seventy?" asked Sheriff McDowell.

The doctor nodded. "You can do the math, Shawn. That means he likely hit the mid-sixties by the time your deputies found him. His vital organs were beginning to shut down, and his brain function suffered. I can't guarantee we can save him, and even if we do, he may have suffered severe brain damage as a result of the exposure."

"Damn," muttered the sheriff as he sat back in his chair and rubbed his temples.

"There's one more thing regarding the dad," began the doctor. "Hostetler relayed to me what Ochoa observed when she found him in the back of the pickup. She said his lower legs had been exposed.

That accounts for the severe frostbite we've diagnosed. I'm afraid it caused permanent damage to his calves, ankles, and feet."

"What does that mean?" asked the sheriff.

"We may have to perform an amputation of both legs below the knees."

CHAPTER NINE

Thursday, October 31
Driftwood Key

By dawn that morning, Jessica and Mike had arrived to help with Patrick. Jessica Albright, Mike's wife, was a trained paramedic and a member of the Monroe County Sheriff's Department Water Emergency Team, aptly known as WET. She was capable of providing advanced emergency medical care for injured patients. Her primary role was to stabilize people with life-threatening injuries so they could be transferred to a higher level of care such as a nearby emergency room.

The closest medical center, Fishermen's Community Hospital, had been closed two days prior after would-be thieves attempted to steal fuel stored for the facility's backup generators.

On any given day, hospitals consume a lot of energy. Their lifesaving devices rely upon electricity to monitor and treat critical care patients. The level one emergency power supply systems dictated by the National Fire Protection Association could be operated using either natural gas or diesel fuel. At Fishermen's, the diesel was stored in elevated tanks to prevent them from being damaged during hurricane conditions.

The thieves had attempted to drain the diesel into fifty-five-gallon drums mounted on the back of a flatbed delivery truck. In their effort to break the locking mechanism on an emergency drain valve, they'd breached the raised tank, and diesel poured onto the ground, emptying the tank within minutes. The sudden loss of fuel caused the diesel generators to seize and shut down. While the tank was able to be repaired, the Keys had no source of diesel fuel to replenish the tank.

This meant the next closest hospital was either in Islamorada or Key West, and they were only treating critical care patients. Patrick's injuries, while brutal, fell just short of life-threatening, so Jessica made the call to keep him there.

She set up intravenous fluids and kept him hydrated. She complimented Phoebe on her excellent first aid skills. However, with her advanced trauma kit, she was able to do some things Phoebe couldn't, including the use of medical staples, an alternative to traditional suturing.

While Patrick was sleeping, Jessica took the time to examine every inch of his body. She was the first to discover that the man had been sodomized. She'd shed a tear as she studied Patrick's badly beaten face. His eyes were very swollen, and both of his lips were cut from repeated punches. There was even an abrasion on his right cheek that resembled the sole of a sneaker.

After a long day, she, Mike and Hank gathered around the fire for a drink. She provided the guys an update on Patrick's condition before their discussion turned to other events of the day.

"Hank, last night's incident with Patrick's sudden arrival at the gate has me concerned," began Mike as he stared off into the darkness.

The three of them were in a solemn, melancholy mood. Patrick's beating reminded them of how depraved their fellow man could be. Depravity was an innate, moral corruption of the soul unique to the human species. No animal on the planet had the cognitive ability, or the penchant, for wickedness.

"Me too," said Hank as he sipped his drink without looking in Mike's direction. It had been a sore subject. He'd made his feelings known to Mike previously that he wished he and Jessica could stick around Driftwood Key. If anything, over the last several days, the opposite had occurred. The sheriff's department had demanded more of their time than ever.

"I know your feelings on this, and trust me, Jess and I have wrestled with what to do," Mike said. "You know, when you're in law enforcement, you have the same sense of duty as those who are in the military. We were hired to do a job, which includes protecting our community."

"And being traffic cops?" asked Hank, allowing his frustrations to pour out. "Seriously, Mike. Is the sheriff asking you to investigate crimes? Are you still pursuing the serial killer? All I hear you guys talk about is evicting nonresidents and leading them off the Keys like the freakin' Pied Piper."

"Listen, Hank," said Mike as he sat up in his chair. "We gotta do what we gotta do. As soon as—"

"As soon as what?" Hank rudely cut him off. "As soon as Lindsey is satisfied that we've rid the Keys of vermin?" Lindsey Free, mayor of Monroe County's government, was also Sonny's former sister-in-law.

"Hank, it's not like that," interjected Jessica. "Mike can't investigate crimes right now because he doesn't have the resources. Also, until we stabilize the Keys by getting people settled in their homes, we'll have crimes like burglaries and beatings."

Hank sighed and gulped down the rest of his drink. He was in a foul mood, partly because he hadn't slept since he'd briefly dozed off on the front porch the night before. The three sat in silence while Hank and Mike stewed about the overall situation.

"Hank, may I finish now?" asked Mike calmly. He respected his older brother and understood he was not used to having criminal activity that routinely took place outside the confines of Driftwood

Key insert itself into his life. After he'd seen Patrick, Mike could only imagine what was going through Hank's head with his son and daughter missing.

"Yeah, sorry," Hank muttered. It was a half-ass apology, but Mike silently accepted it anyway.

"What I was about to say was, for starters, I've got the sheriff's approval to stagger my shifts with Jessica. He's been sending us off in different directions every night anyway, so we weren't able to work with one another. I'm gonna work graveyard, and she'll handle days or early evenings. Here, she'll take the witching-hour patrols. You know, midnight to four or five."

Jessica added, "That'll give me plenty of time to sleep and help watch the key when we're most vulnerable."

"That sounds pretty good," mumbled Hank, hoping that they'd give it all up to stay close to home.

He stretched his glass over to Jessica, who had strategically planted herself between the two brothers. Somehow, she sensed Hank had been waiting all day for an opportunity to bring the subject up. She refilled his glass and passed the bottle of Jack Daniel's over to Mike, who topped off his glass as well. He had to leave for work in an hour but doubted the sheriff would be conducting random breathalyzer tests at the moment.

"Here's the thing, Hank," Mike tried to explain. "First off, we're not getting paid, and everyone from the mayor to the sheriff have acknowledged that. So they do their best to pay us in kind. Sure, it's not the same as money, but under these circumstances, it might be looked at as better than money."

"That's right," added Jessica. "I'm given my choice of medical supplies and gear. Scuba related, too. There's no accountability, and my boss is fully aware we'd use it on our families before a stranger if need be. Today was a wake-up call for me. You can bet during my shift tomorrow I'll be giving myself a raise, if you know what I mean."

The men laughed, so Mike explained how he paid himself. "I will continue to stock Driftwood Key with weapons, ammunition, and accessories. Please understand me, Hank. I know there'll come a time when my contribution to law enforcement will be limited to this place." He waved his arm around his head in a circle as he made reference to Driftwood Key.

"We don't think the county is going to be able to maintain order for very long," added Jessica. "Even with the expulsions and the processing of refugees at the bridges, the locals are becoming increasingly hostile with one another. At first, you had this sense of community. You know. Rah-rah, we're all in this together bullshit. No, we're not. This nuclear winter thing is gonna last a long, long time, and as people become desperate, then watch out."

Mike leaned forward to the edge of his Adirondack chair so he could look his brother in the eyes. The flames of the bonfire grew, casting orangish light coupled with shadows across the brothers.

"Hank, I promise you. We'll circle the wagons here long before it comes to that. But unless we act as your eyes and ears out there, we'll never know what's comin'."

PART II

Day fifteen, Friday, November 1

CHAPTER TEN

Friday, November 1
Near Amelia Court House, Virginia

Daylight was waning when Peter awoke from his long, restful sleep. A light snow had fallen, causing him to shiver. He was also concerned that he'd become infected by the buckshot wounds. His mind raced as his anxiety grew. *Did I miss a pellet? Maybe I should've sterilized the tweezers with alcohol?*

He shot up into a seated position that forced pain throughout his body. He couldn't contain the groan that came from deep inside him. Peter felt like he'd been used as a punching bag on one side and a pincushion on the other.

He'd slept the entire day although the perpetually gray skies made it difficult to determine the position of the sun. He just knew it was getting darker, and he needed to get going, not just to make progress toward home but also to get his body heated up through exercise.

He forced himself to stand and then inwardly complained about his sore legs. Even after the ordeal in Abu Dhabi and the flying episode courtesy of the nuclear blast wave, Peter hadn't felt this kind of pain.

He walked fifteen feet downstream from where he'd unintentionally made camp earlier that day to relieve himself. His urine was dark yellow. As an avid runner, he knew that was a sign of dehydration. He made a mental note to pour his filtered water into the canteen cup and add a Nuun hydration tab to it. The orange-flavored, effervescent tablet the size of an Alka-Seltzer quickly dissolved in water. It was used by athletes to replace lost electrolytes to avoid dehydration.

Peter also took the time to inspect his wounds. The three puncture wounds were already beginning to scab over. The bloody oozing had ceased, and he felt confident after a change of bandages, he'd be good to go. The other two wounds that he'd extracted the pellets from concerned him more.

They were turning red and tender around the edges. Peter chastised himself for forgetting the antibiotics he'd risked his life to take from the CVS pharmacy. He'd had the best of intentions to do so, but he'd fallen asleep. After rebandaging the two still-oozing holes in his upper body, he located a bottle of Keflex 500 milligram capsules. He'd taken this form of antibiotic as a kid when he'd cut himself diving around coral, and therefore, he knew he wasn't allergic to it. He swallowed two capsules for starters with his Nuun-infused water.

Then, in the dimming light, he retrieved his atlas to chart out his course. Originally, he'd planned on riding during the day so he could see the road better. Now, thanks to the residents of the horror house on the hill who had tried to kill him, he'd slept all day, forcing him to travel at night.

Peter traced his finger along the most direct route to the Keys. Ordinarily, he'd follow Interstate 95 along the Atlantic Seaboard. He knew the route, as he'd traveled it several times by car. Along the way, there were long stretches where the only highway was the interstate. The marshlands, especially in the low country of South Carolina and Georgia, would provide him few options besides I-95.

On a bicycle, even under the grid-down circumstances, Peter felt he'd be at risk of encounters far more deadly than the one last evening in which floors and sofas couldn't protect him.

He studied his options through North Carolina. The cities of Charlotte, Greensboro, and Raleigh-Durham stretched from west to east like a trio of giant trolls waiting for an unsuspecting traveler to devour as they passed. He knew the cities had to be avoided, so he considered traveling farther away from the coast, just to the west of Charlotte. This would provide him lots of travel options through mostly rural farmland and away from the cities crowded along the coastal areas.

Peter had told himself when he left that he wouldn't think too far ahead. Originally, he'd told himself that he could walk home if need be. Then, after he'd obtained the bicycle from Jackie's father, he thought he could make it in three weeks if he kept a steady, uneventful pace. Certainly, he couldn't afford any more encounters like he'd had at the farmhouse.

He plotted out his course along U.S. Highway 360 toward Danville, a small town on the North Carolina border. He wasn't sure how far he could travel at night with temperatures approaching freezing, especially after the pummeling his body had endured. But he was determined to push himself so he could get to the North Carolina border by sunrise.

After repacking his gear and reloading his weapon, he hit the road. Peter imagined the four-lane, divided highway was scenic, if he could see it. As he clicked off the miles, he began to question the decision to ride at night. He considered attaching one of his flashlights to the handlebars using duct tape to illuminate the road in front of him. He even held one of them in his hands for a while to see if that helped. If the beam of light happened to catch a reflector off a stalled vehicle, then he could manage to navigate toward it. Otherwise, he decided he'd end up burning through his batteries.

For riding purposes, taking the federal highway was a far better option than pothole-filled county roads, where he could easily puncture a tire or bend a wheel. In this desolate part of Virginia, he hoped to avoid contact with others. But, eventually, major highways run through large cities, and that wasn't a good idea, day or night.

Peter rode for hours and was coming up on Danville, a sizable city of forty-five thousand people. Because it was just after four in the morning, he decided to continue riding until he made it to the North Carolina border. It would mean that he would travel eighty miles that night.

Soon, it became a game to Peter. A competition as to how far he could travel in a given period of time. He'd study the map, calculate the time and distance, and pedal while trying not to think about the difficult task ahead.

It was the thoughts of reuniting with his family that helped him push through the pain.

CHAPTER ELEVEN

Friday, November 1
Driftwood Key

"You know, Hank, I simply can't remember how this happened to me," lied the man who lived the life of a lie. Patrick was feeling better by that afternoon and was now able to prop himself up on the bed. Both Phoebe and Jessica routinely checked on him, as did Jimmy, the young man he seemed to enjoy the company of the most.

"I don't know if you're aware of this, but my brother, Mike, is a detective."

"Yeah. He stopped by earlier when I was just coming out of the bathroom with Phoebe's help." Patrick paused and took a deep breath before he continued. The beatings administered to his ribs and back made the simple task very painful.

"Oh, good. I'm sure he'll do anything he can to catch these guys," said Hank, trying to carry the load of the conversation, as he sensed the pain that talking caused Patrick.

In actuality, Patrick was happy to be breathing again, and the pain was nothing more than a nuisance. He feigned difficulty when it suited him. If the conversation with anyone turned toward what had happened or what he could remember, he fed them a little information and then suddenly experienced difficulty breathing. The ploy worked every time.

Hank apologized for intruding on his recovery and left the bungalow. He made a beeline for the dock as he saw Jimmy returning from a day of fishing. The barely noticeable shadows were growing long as he cut through the palm trees between bungalow three and the beachfront. He remembered that Jimmy had been fishing alone each day, so he jogged down the dock to assist him in tying off the Hatteras.

"Thanks, Mr. Hank!" Jimmy said. The usually good-natured young man enjoyed life regardless of how difficult it had become after the attacks. He quickly tied off the aft line and briskly moved toward the bow to toss Hank a line. Hank, after many years of practice, expertly tied it off to a cleat.

"How'd you do?" he asked Jimmy as he repositioned one of the yacht's bumpers to align with the rubber edge of the dock.

"I have to go farther out each day, Mr. Hank. The water is nothing like it used to be. Pockets, at depth, are cooler like always. In shallow areas, you'd think they'd be cooler, too. Between it being November and all these clouds, I'm surprised how warm it still is."

Hank stepped on board and stood with his hands on his hips as if he could get a better understanding of the water temperatures if he was standing in his boat. Jimmy directed Hank's attention to one of the fish holds on the aft deck. With a grin, Jimmy continued.

"However, you have to remember who you're talking to," he said as he opened the lid. It was full of snapper.

"You are undoubtedly the second-best fisherman on Driftwood Key," said Hank, drawing a laugh from the young man. "Say, did you see many boats out there?"

"No, not really. A Coast Guard cutter passed me, heading north. It was pretty far offshore. I see a few pleasure boats like that one milling about. It was odd 'cause they weren't fishing, which made me wonder why they were burnin' up fuel." Jimmy shrugged and went about preparing the Hatteras to close up for the night.

Hank's mind immediately recalled the night the three men had used the Wellcraft runabout on the other side of the dock in an attempt to steal fuel out of his boat. It hadn't ended well for the three thieves, as Mike and Jessica had turned them into fish chum. It was yet another reminder of why he wished they'd stay closer to home, but he understood their position now.

With the shoot-out over fuel fresh in his mind, Hank had a thought. "Maybe you shouldn't go out alone? With all that's going on, having somebody watching your back might be a good idea."

"I thought about that today when one of the boats got a little too close. I didn't have anything on a hook, so I slowly picked up the Mossberg. When they saw I had a gun, they took off."

Hank decided at that point Jimmy should have someone go with him. The fact of the matter was, he lamented internally, they were short-handed, especially now that Patrick needed more of Phoebe's and Jessica's attention.

He sighed and mumbled, "We'll figure it out."

As they walked up the dock toward the main house with the snapper on a string in each hand, Jimmy brought up Patrick.

"Um, Mr. Hank." He hesitated.

"Yeah."

"How long is Patrick gonna stay here?"

"Why? Do you think he might be a good fishing companion? I'd have to talk with Mike about giving him a gun."

Jimmy's eyes grew wide, and he shook his head rapidly from side to side. "No, nothing like that. Never mind."

"C'mon, Jimmy. What's on your mind?"

"I don't know, Mr. Hank. There's something off about the guy. Mom asked me to check in on him a couple of times today. He just creeps me out, that's all."

Hank was curious as to why. "Did he say something that upset you?"

"No, not really. I'm just saying he was kinda clingy or something. He didn't want me to leave. Wanted to ask questions about the inn and whether I went to college or had a girlfriend. You know. Stuff like that."

Hank slowed his pace, as he wanted to finish the conversation before they encountered Phoebe. "Small talk?"

"I guess."

"And you saw him twice?"

"Yes. First thing this morning and before I went fishing around noon."

"And you said he was talkative?" asked Hank. He stopped to study Jimmy's demeanor.

Jimmy kicked at the sand and turned over a small shell with his toe. He nervously rolled it around as he spoke. "Yeah. I mean, he's probably bored or lonely. Also, um, a little scared, I guess?"

Hank pressed the young man. "Talkative? Both times?"

Jimmy nodded and began walking up the stairs to the porch. Hank lagged behind and glanced in the direction of bungalow three, which was nestled in the palm trees. It was slightly obscured from his view by a wall of tropical plants.

Jimmy's description of Patrick was far different from what Hank had observed just thirty minutes ago. He furrowed his brow and shrugged as he moved deliberately into the house, deep in thought.

CHAPTER TWELVE

Friday, November 1
Mount Weather Emergency Operations Center
Northern Virginia

President Carter Helton was invigorated following the late-night presidential address and press conference two days ago. Outpourings of support from world leaders in Russia and China for his bold initiative bolstered his confidence. While certain members of his cabinet voiced their disapproval at what they deemed to be government overreach, others agreed to do everything within their power to implement his agenda. Plus, as he told his chief of staff, it gave him the opportunity to separate the wheat from the chaff, as they say. He was now able to differentiate his true loyalists from those who might undermine his administration.

He was due to receive several updates with a full analysis on the profound impact nuclear winter had on the climate as well as the devastating effect the EMP had had on the nation's critical infrastructure. Proposals from the DHS, Transportation, and Energy would all be submitted during the morning briefing.

However, in the back of his mind, President Helton was

considering leaving the protection of Mount Weather. He believed that hiding in the protection of the nuclear bunker lent an impression that he was a weak leader. He'd held extensive discussions with military leaders about relocating the government to a military base that had been hardened against the devastating effects of the EMP.

Because Washington, DC, had been destroyed, the president, a native Pennsylvanian, was considering moving America's capital back to Philadelphia, the seat of government during the Revolution. Geographically, a more centralized location like Kansas City made sense, but he was in the unique position to lead the nation into a new era. The choice of Philadelphia would allow him to give something back to the state that had launched his political career.

The amount of government spending required to recreate the equivalent of Washington's massive bureaucracy would be an enormous boost to Pennsylvanians during the recovery effort, as well as the local contractors who'd been longtime donors of the president.

The interim facilities for the new location of government, the Carlisle Barracks, had been an immediate beneficiary of the Helton administration. He'd directed $85 million to build new facilities at the home of the U.S. Army War College after he took office. In addition to upgrading and expanding the second-oldest army installation dating back to 1745, the president had redirected funds from another base in Florida to Carlisle Barracks. The money had been earmarked to harden the base's wiring and electronics from the crippling effects of an EMP.

At the moment, the five-hundred-acre campus of the Army War College would suffice for the basic functions of the federal government. He envisioned Congress relocating to Carlisle temporarily so that the government could once again be together.

Military bases around the country in close proximity to existing FEMA regional offices were used as part of the recovery process. Each cabinet secretary named an undersecretary for assignment to the ten FEMA regions. These undersecretaries coordinated with the military to ensure compliance with the declaration of martial law.

It would take years to rebuild the American government, but at least he had the mechanism to do so. Now it was time to focus on those who would stand in the way of his recovery plan. He would hear first from Erin Bergmann, secretary of Agriculture.

"Good morning, Mr. President," Erin began. She'd been a regular at the president's daily briefings. Behind her back, other cabinet members referred to her as the *doomsayer*, a person who often spoke of foreboding predictions of an impending calamity.

"Good morning, Erin. Got any good news today?"

The president's jovial mood continued, albeit somewhat sarcastically. He, too, was tiring of the gloomy predictions. His overall demeanor was boosted in part from the power he'd gained by the martial law declaration and the antidepressants he was being fed by the White House physician.

His insolent question created stifled chuckles by some members of the cabinet. He glanced at his most loyal advisors, who shared his opinion of Erin. In not so many words, he'd let it be known that Erin, who'd opposed martial law as inconsistent with the intent of the Constitution, would soon be returned to Florida when he relocated the government to Pennsylvania. For now, Erin, and her gloomy updates, were a necessary evil.

Erin bristled at his question. She had no intention of sugarcoating the dire consequences of the nuclear conflict just to curry favor with the president, as most in the room had. If he wanted to replace her and kick her out of Mount Weather, so be it. She was certain she could find a bungalow on a tiny key in Florida, where she could live out her days. She thought about Hank Albright constantly, even asking military officials about how the Florida Keys had been affected by the environmental impact of nuclear war. Until she was no longer included in the briefings or kicked out of Mount Weather, she'd do her job, even if it wasn't what the president wanted to hear.

"Sir, the basic assumption during any nuclear conflict has been that the exploding nuclear warheads would create huge fires, resulting in soot from burning cities and forests. This toxic cloud of smoke is emitted in vast amounts and blends with our clean air.

"Based upon climatology models, it was presumed the troposphere, which starts at the Earth's surface and extends five to nine miles high, would bear the brunt of the pollution, if you will. Those prior models understated the effect.

"The models considered only a limited nuclear conflict under the assumptions the warring nations would stand down before completely annihilating one another. None that I am aware of modeled multiple conflicts across the Northern Hemisphere.

"NOAA has provided us evidence to the effect that the lower levels of the stratosphere have been permeated with the smoke and soot. Similar to the models associated with the eruption of a supervolcano, the Sun's incoming radiation has been blocked from reaching the planet's surface, causing a more rapid cooling of temperatures than ever imagined.

"Due to their high temperatures, this rising smoke and soot have allowed the dirty air to drift at these high altitudes. It's now settling in the mid-latitudes of the Northern Hemisphere as a black particle cloud belt, blocking sunshine for an indeterminate amount of time."

The president raised his hand to stop Erin from continuing. "There has to be a point at which the atmosphere clears. Have you run models to give us some kind of reasonable time frame?"

"Yes, Mr. President. NASA and NOAA scientists have developed a predictive model that points to an eight-to-twelve-year time frame in which we get some relief."

"Not back to normal?" he asked.

Erin nodded. She was expecting this line of questioning. Everyone wanted to know when it would be over. "No, sir. They wouldn't commit to when our skies would resemble what we enjoyed pre-attack."

"Okay, Erin. If we don't know when we can expect blue skies again, can you at least tell me when we'll bottom out? When can we point to a date and tell the American people the worst of it is behind us?"

Erin grimaced and glanced around the room. She was about to add to her reputation as the doomsayer. "Following the rapid series of attacks, the ensuing darkness and cold, combined with nuclear fallout, have begun to kill much of the Earth's vegetation in the Northern Hemisphere. We're receiving reports of wildlife dying out either from starvation or hunters in search of food."

"We have a plan for the latter," interrupted the president. "Soon, the reward in kind for reporting these poachers of our nation's food resources will eliminate the practice of hunting. Please proceed."

"Sir, NOAA advises that the upper troposphere temperatures have risen to the point that a temperature inversion is developing," she said. A temperature inversion was an atmospheric condition in which warm air traps cooler air near the Earth's surface. As a result, pollutants were trapped below with the cooler air. Erin continued. "This keeps the smog and polluted air at surface levels. Coupled with the increased nitrogen oxides produced by the nuclear detonations, our ozone layer has been severely damaged. More ultraviolet radiation is hitting our planet, which will cause skin and eye damage to all animal life."

"Erin, when will we bottom out?"

The president wanted her to give a certain date, which she couldn't. She equivocated, not because she was trying to protect her reputation but because neither she, nor the scientific community, could provide a definitive answer.

"We will experience freezing temperatures across most of the nation above thirty-degrees latitude until late summer of next year, at which time we'll get a bit of a respite. The remainder of the nation, namely south-central Texas, New Orleans, and much of Florida, will be spared temps below freezing.

"In my opinion, we'll bottom out about four years or so after that. How well our planet deals with nuclear winter will depend upon several mitigating factors, including the moderating effects of the world's oceans. The lower latitudes I just described will benefit from the warmer waters coming up from the equatorial regions."

"Are you saying we won't see the worst of this for five years?"

"That's correct."

"What do we do in the meantime?"

"Consider moving large numbers of Americans to points near the equator or into the southern hemisphere," she replied before adding, "and pray."

CHAPTER THIRTEEN

Friday, November 1
Arkansas Valley Regional Medical Center
La Junta, Colorado

Sheriff Mobley had hardly slept the night before. He couldn't put his finger on why the fate of this traveling family weighed on him so much. He made a point to touch base with his own kids and grandchild before turning in for the night. As he tried to fall asleep, he reminded himself how lucky he was to live in a small, close-knit community that most of the world was unfamiliar with.

He thought of the amenities and glamour of living near a big city like San Francisco. The Golden Gate Bridge. Fisherman's Wharf. The cable cars. As a career law enforcement officer, naturally he'd enjoy visiting famed Alcatraz Island. Yet, today, all of those things were either obliterated or damaged. The people who lived in close proximity to San Francisco Bay perished. And those with the foresight to escape before the blast, like the McDowell family, faced unknown perils regardless.

He awoke around five and immediately dressed for work. His first stop was the sheriff's office to coordinate the daily shift change.

After an update from his deputies, he was pleased to learn that there hadn't been any new reports of hypothermia cases as a result of the flash freeze. He attributed it to the time of night it had occurred and the fact most of Otero County's residents were following his admonitions to remain inside to avoid inhaling the nuclear fallout and the soot-filled air.

He arrived at the hospital to check on the McDowell family just as his friend, the attending physician, came in for his fourteen-hour shift. He was standing near the emergency room reception desk, speaking with one of three surgeons the hospital had on staff. He saw Sheriff Mobley arrive and waved him over.

"Shawn, are you here about the McDowells?"

"Yeah. Just wanna see if there's been any change," he replied. He said good morning to the surgeon, Dr. Carl Forrest.

"Not yet," replied his friend. "Listen, I've been speaking with Dr. Forrest, who is concerned about the dad's legs."

The surgeon furrowed his brow as he addressed the situation. "Shawn, this patient is struggling to fight the effects of hypothermia. His body has been weakened by the frostbite to his lower legs, a condition that is impeding his ability to heal."

"I assume you need someone's consent to perform the procedure," said the sheriff. "Are we approaching a point of no return in which a decision must be made?"

"We may actually be past it," Dr. Forrest responded. "Long-term effects like congenital malformation and cancer are not even my concern at the moment. Infection and circulatory disorders are beginning to manifest themselves. After the patient's body was raised to a normal temperature, the threat of traumatic gangrene raised additional concerns."

"How long can we wait?" asked the sheriff.

Before the surgeon could respond, a nurse came running toward them. "Doctors! The boy is waking up!"

All three men hustled down the long corridor and into the intensive care unit at the back of the hospital. It was segregated from the active emergency room so patients could recuperate, yet it was close enough to have access to the trauma team in the event of a medical problem.

Sheriff Mobley gently grabbed the two physicians by the sleeves to slow their pace. "Guys, let's not scare the bejesus out of the kid. This young man has some very adult issues to contend with right now."

The doctors nodded and caught their breath. They casually walked into Tucker's room with apprehension. Two nurses were making Tucker comfortable and stepped away from the hospital bed to make way for the group.

"Doctors," began the head ICU nurse, "his vitals remain stable although his heart rate is slightly elevated. He's been able to drink water on his own although he's complained of a sore throat."

The attending physician reached over the bed rail and held Tucker's hand. "Young man, I'm Dr. Frank Brady. This is Dr. Forrest and Sheriff Mobley. Do you understand where you are?"

As he spoke, he used his penlight to examine Tucker's eyes and throat. Then, with his stethoscope, he listened to his heart and lungs. Satisfied with the results, he put the instruments away.

Tucker pointed toward his throat and swallowed hard. He whispered his response. "Hospital. Colorado."

Dr. Forrest stepped in and looked toward one of the nurses. "Let's get him some ice chips."

Dr. Brady continued. "I'm sorry I asked you to speak, but it was important for us to confirm that you are aware of your surroundings and that you can comprehend the information we are about to give you."

Tucker's eyes darted around the room, and he became slightly agitated. He mouthed the words *Mom, Dad.*

Dr. Brady held his hand up and smiled. "They're alive, son. Let us explain. Don't talk so you can save your strength. Sheriff, would you briefly relay what you and your deputies found."

Sheriff Mobley related the discovery of their bodies yesterday and how they'd brought the three of them to the hospital. He stopped short of discussing Tucker's parents' medical conditions. Dr. Brady took over from there.

"You did an excellent job protecting your mother from the cold. She's still sleeping in the room next door to us. Tucker, hypothermia takes a terrible toll on a body's organs and brain. It's been in your best interest, as well as your parents', that we didn't wake you unless absolutely necessary."

Tucker responded with an imperceptible nod. His eyes began to droop as drowsiness came over him, caused in part by the medications he'd been taking in addition to the trauma his body had endured.

Sheriff Mobley noticed the two doctors exchange a long glance. He knew what they were thinking. The kid was awake. Do they broadside him with his father's true condition and then pressure Tucker for an answer on the proposed amputation while he was awake?

Dr. Forrest spoke up. "Tucker, your father's condition is much worse because he was partially exposed to the frigid air. The sheriff tells us he made an unbelievable effort to shield himself from a sudden flash freeze that swept over your vehicle as well as your dad. For that reason, we have to monitor him very closely for issues that you and your mom were fortunate to avoid."

Tucker comprehended what he was being told, but his eyes studied the faces of the doctors to determine if he was getting the complete story. He pointed toward the white plastic cup of ice chips being held by his nurse. He took a few in his mouth and allowed them to melt. He ate several more over the objection of Dr. Brady, but they seemed to help with the soreness.

"See him." Two simple words conveying a request that was not so simple to fulfill. Then he fell asleep.

CHAPTER FOURTEEN

Friday, November 1
Arkansas Valley Regional Medical Center
La Junta, Colorado

Tucker slowly sipped the warm chicken broth provided him by the nurses. He was slowly regaining his strength with more rest. He was frustrated with himself for falling asleep before gaining approval to see his dad. He wasn't sure how long he'd been out before the nurses and Dr. Brady had awakened him.

Now that he was able to speak with only a minor twinge of pain in his throat, he planned on pressuring his doctor to allow him to see his parents. He was thrilled when Dr. Brady didn't object, although he had no idea there was an ulterior motive for his acquiescence.

Tucker was athletic and young. His body had been able to withstand the extreme cold that had encircled him and his mother that night. It had been a rash decision his mom made that almost killed them. Yet he understood why she did it.

They'd been sitting in the front seat of the Bronco when the first massive wind gust swept over them. Lacey shrieked as the truck shook and then was forced several yards down the highway. Then came another, this time sustained. It inched the truck forward, causing them to wonder if they were on the leading edge of a tornado.

Both of them frantically assessed their options. His mom wanted to search for Owen. Tucker argued that they should stay in the truck for safety. She became distraught and impulsive as she began to put on every item of clothing within her grasp that she could wear in order to search for her husband.

Tucker tried to calm his mother, but the flash freeze did that for him. For several moments, neither of them were able to speak, fear stealing their voices. Ice crystals began to form on the windows until soon, they were unable to see outside. Not that it mattered. The blowing snow and ash created whiteout conditions that reduced visibility to zero.

To Tucker, it appeared that the old truck was contracting. It was if a massive set of icy-cold hands had wrapped their frigid fingers around Black & Blue. It creaked and cracked and allowed the brutal cold inside.

Then, without warning, Lacey pulled the door handle on the passenger door and flung her shoulder against it. It broke the seal of ice and flew completely open with the assistance of the wind.

"I have to find your dad," she said as she swung her body around to exit the truck. She made it three steps before being knocked into the snow-filled ditch adjacent to the highway. Tucker couldn't get his door open, so he scrambled across the seats to help his mother. He was shocked to see how quickly she'd been affected by the subzero temperatures.

She was incoherent as he lifted her under her armpits to drag her back to the truck. The two-door Bronco was difficult to climb into on a good day, much less in epic blizzard conditions.

After a minute of additional exposure to the flash freeze anomaly, Tucker was able to position his mother in the back seat, and then he climbed in next to her. He pulled every available blanket, sleeping bag, and jacket from the cargo compartment and covered them, providing just enough space for the two of them to breathe.

Then he held his mother. He closed his eyes and concentrated in an attempt to will his body heat into hers. He ignored his own skin burns courtesy of the subzero chill. He could only think of keeping his mom alive. And then he joined his mother as a state of unconsciousness overtook them.

Now, two days later, he'd recovered enough to sit up. He was doted over by the nursing staff and constantly checked on by the doctors. However, he had the sneaking suspicion that he wasn't being told the whole story about his parents' conditions. He simply had to see for himself.

With Dr. Brady's approval and supervision, Tucker was allowed to get out of bed and into a wheelchair. He was wrapped in a wool blanket, and his feet were covered with fuzzy, nonslip-grip socks. When he was ready to roll in his wheelchair, Dr. Brady elected to push his patient from room to room himself.

"Thank you, Dr. Brady," said Tucker as they slowly rolled out of his room in the ICU.

"You're welcome, young man. You've made a remarkable recovery considering what you've been through. After we've checked on your family, I plan on moving you to a room in another part of the hospital if you can stand on your own two feet. Our generators aren't capable of operating the elevators in addition to the other loads they're carrying. Our hospital beds upstairs can only be accessed by more mobile patients or by our strongest orderlies carrying you up the emergency stairwell."

"I'd like to stay near my parents," said Tucker as he wiggled his toes and then stretched his calves by moving his feet.

"We'll see," said the doctor noncommittally. He changed the subject to his mother's condition. "Medically, your mom is considered to be in a coma. Most people associate coma with a direct brain injury resulting from some form of physical trauma. A stroke can cause a person to lapse into a coma as well."

Tucker became uneasy. "A stroke?"

"No, not in your mom's case," Dr. Brady replied. "Each of you sustained a different level of trauma from the flash freeze event. That could've been a result of exposure to the elements, age, and physical conditioning. That's why it's not surprising that you've recovered first." He stopped to speak to a nurse before continuing.

"We treat coma patients differently based upon the underlying cause. In your mom's and dad's cases, we've focused on their respiratory and circulatory systems. We have to keep oxygen and blood flowing to the brain."

"Why can't you wake her up?"

"The sudden drop in her body's temperature resulted in her organs being on the verge of shutting down. The consequences of this were reduced blood flow and oxygen supply to the brain. Her brain swelled, and she went into a coma. Leaving her in a comatose state actually aids in her body's recovery because she's not exposed to external stimuli or concern for others. She needs as much rest as she can get, and pulling her out before her body is ready can result in permanent damage to the brain tissue."

Tucker became suddenly quiet as the doctor stated the facts plainly and succinctly. It was a lot for a fifteen-year-old to process, but he appreciated the candor. Once he was rolled into his mother's room, he became full of emotion. He raised his right hand, instructing the doctor to stop short of his mother's bed.

She looked peaceful yet pained. Her face was completely at rest, but her body remained rigid under the layers of blankets designed to keep her warm. A variety of monitoring equipment flashed numbers and lights that Tucker didn't want to understand. However, he did know this. His mom was alive.

After a moment of studying her from a distance, he asked to be wheeled closer. He wanted to hold her hand. He wanted to hug his mother as he had in the back seat that night in an attempt to keep her warm. A flood of emotions coursed through his mind until suddenly, without warning or permission, Tucker stepped up from the wheelchair using the bed's side rails to assist him. Dr. Brady and the nurses implored him to sit back down, but he ignored them.

Tucker leaned over and whispered, "Mom, I love you. It's gonna be all right. I promise." Then he gave her a tear-soaked kiss on the cheek.

CHAPTER FIFTEEN

Friday, November 1
Arkansas Valley Regional Medical Center
La Junta, Colorado

The next visit did not go at all like Tucker had hoped. Convinced to return to his wheelchair, Dr. Brady pushed him farther down the corridor to the ICU room closest to the nurses' station. Owen, he explained, required very close monitoring at this stage of his treatment. The doctor provided Tucker a similar update to the one he'd given on his mother, with one noticeable exception that Tucker instantly picked up on. Dr. Brady never used the word *recovery* in connection with his father's treatment. Phrases like *not out of the woods yet* and *critical condition* were used more than once.

Tucker steadied his nerves as they entered his father's room. At first glance, he saw the same types of monitoring equipment connected to his father's body as he'd observed in his mom's room. Likewise, his dad was wrapped in blankets and seemed to be resting peacefully with his arms by his sides. Then something struck him as out of the ordinary.

"Why are his feet bandaged up like that and not under the blankets?"

Dr. Brady sighed. The moment of truth. Mentally, the doctor determined Tucker was ready. His mettle was about to be tested because a decision had to be made.

The doctor positioned Tucker's wheelchair so he had a full view of his father lying in bed. He nodded toward the door, indicating to the nurses they should leave the room. They eased out and shut the door behind them. Dr. Brady slid a chair over from a corner of the room so that he was sitting by Tucker's side.

Tucker studied the doctor's face and scowled. He choked back the tears and sat a little taller in the wheelchair. After another glance at the monitors and his father's face, he turned slightly and spoke to Dr. Brady. "It's bad, isn't it?"

"Young man, I am not going to sugarcoat any of this. You strike me as very mature, and I applaud your parents for raising you to become the man that you are. We have a situation with your dad that requires an adult decision. Today, in this moment, you have to be that adult."

Tucker swallowed hard and nodded at Dr. Brady without breaking eye contact. Apprehension supplanted sorrow as he prepared himself for what he was about to hear.

"Based upon what we learned from the sheriff's office, your dad was caught completely off guard by this weather anomaly. The flash freeze hit the west end of the county the hardest. From what they could tell, he did his level best to avoid the frigid air by trying to bury himself in hay in the back of a pickup.

"His efforts kept him alive, but unfortunately, he wasn't totally covered. The deputy discovered his body because his legs were protruding out from the hay just below the knees. Both extremities suffered fourth-degree severe frostbite."

"What does that mean?" asked Tucker.

"Well, first degree is skin irritation and pain, the level of frostbite you and your mom suffered. Although, there was evidence of second-degree blisters on your mom's hands but no major damage. Fourth degree, the level suffered by your dad, is indicated when the frostbite is so severe it causes bones and tendons to freeze."

Tucker's eyes grew wide as he immediately looked at his father's feet. He ran his fingers through his hair and then wiped away the tears that began to seep from his eyes.

He took a deep breath and asked, inwardly knowing what was coming next, "What are you saying?"

Dr. Brady furrowed his brow. He'd learned throughout his medical career that one of the most difficult tasks he faced in addition to saving lives was informing the family of a loved one's death. Explaining to a son that his father was about to lose half his legs ranked right up there.

"The best treatment for fourth-degree frostbite is hyperbaric oxygen therapy, a process involving breathing pure oxygen in a pressurized room. We don't have that kind of facility here, and it's doubtful any of the major hospitals in Denver or Colorado Springs have one that is functioning due to the EMP. Even if they did, there aren't any helicopters that survived the EMP either."

"Isn't there something else you can do?" asked Tucker.

"Tucker, I'm gonna have to shoot straight with you, okay? We've waited as long as we can to make a decision."

For the next several minutes, Dr. Brady explained the options to Tucker. He soaked in the information and then asked to have some time alone with his father. He sat there, crying, asking God why this had to happen to his family. Then he asked for guidance to help him make the most difficult decision of his life.

CHAPTER SIXTEEN

Friday, November 1
Arkansas Valley Regional Medical Center
La Junta, Colorado

"How are our patients doing?" Sheriff Mobley asked the ICU nurses as he took another sip of coffee. He'd spent the day defusing a domestic dispute between a local couple who were considered by the community as head over heels in love. He chalked up the heated argument to temporary insanity from being locked down during the adverse conditions.

Dr. Brady appeared from another patient's room and responded to the sheriff. "Mom is stable but still out. Dad's slipping. We can't make any progress because of his lower limbs. A decision has to be made, Shawn."

"What about Tucker?"

"He's doing as well as can be expected, physically. Mentally, I took him to visit his mother, and although he seemed distraught at the shock of seeing her that way, he handled it like the strong young man that he is."

"I can feel a *but* coming," said the sheriff. He finished his coffee and handed the Styrofoam cup to the desk nurse, who graciously threw it away for him.

"Shawn, I had to lay out his father's condition and treatment options for him. We're out of time, I'm afraid."

Sheriff Mobley looked up and down the corridor, which was empty. "Is he in his room? May I talk to him?"

Dr. Brady pointed towards Owen's closed door. "He asked to be left alone. That was half an hour ago."

Sheriff Mobley gently rapped his knuckles on the counter and winked at his old friend. "Give me a little time. Maybe he needs a sounding board."

He walked to Owen's room and stared through the small glass window in the door. Tucker was sitting in the wheelchair, staring at his father's face. Sheriff Mobley slowly turned the knob and cracked the door enough for his head to fit through.

"Hey, Tucker. Can I come in?"

Tucker sat up in the wheelchair and took a deep breath before exhaling. "Yeah, sure."

First, Sheriff Mobley asked Tucker how he was feeling. He complimented him on how much better he looked since they'd met when Tucker woke up for the first time. Then he walked around to the opposite side of the hospital bed and studied Owen's face. He grimaced and then allowed a slight smile.

"Your dad's a helluva fighter. What he did to protect himself saved his life."

"Yeah," mumbled Tucker, whose attention turned to Owen's feet. "My mom's still out, and the doctor said it's too dangerous to wake her up right now."

Sheriff Mobley came around the bed and sat in the chair vacated by Dr. Brady earlier. "That's what I hear. She's gonna pull through, Tucker, if her body is allowed to heal itself."

Tucker sighed and rolled his head around his shoulders to relieve some tension. "This really sucks, you know."

The sheriff nodded. He gently patted Tucker on the back. "Ya wanna talk about it?"

Tucker shrugged. "I guess. Might as well. I mean ..." His voice trailed off as he pushed himself up and grasped his father's bed rails.

"Shouldn't you be sitting—?"

Tucker ignored the question and allowed his thoughts to pour out of him. "I've got some really crappy options," he began. He rubbed his hands along the rail, gripping it for comfort and strength as he spoke.

"Tell me what you're thinkin'," interrupted Sheriff Mobley, giving Tucker a moment to gather his thoughts.

"Okay, well. My mom's in this sort of long sleep, coma thing that I'm told isn't serious. However, it's necessary for her recovery, so they aren't comfortable waking her because of brain damage.

"Dad's legs were left exposed to the flash freeze. Dr. Brady said he has the worst kind of frostbite from his calves to his toes. Basically, everything from the bottom of the knees down is dead.

"The problem is his legs need to be amputated because his body is spending too much effort to save the legs and not enough to heal the rest of his organs. Their solution is to amputate and focus on saving his life."

"That's what I've been told," added the sheriff, allowing Tucker to catch his breath.

"Well, Mom can't make the decision, and they want me to." He turned to Sheriff Mobley. "Do you hear what I'm saying? They want me to approve cutting off my father's legs."

Tucker closed his eyes and began shaking his head side to side. Tears flowed out of his eyes as he imagined being responsible for his father's inability to walk.

Sheriff Mobley looked away briefly as he tried to avoid crying along with Tucker. He felt a deep sadness for the teen, who was faced with such an important decision alone. He gathered himself and joined Tucker's side. The father of four placed his arm around Tucker and spoke in a softer tone. "Sometimes, life throws us a curveball. It's not fair, and we're left to deal with it regardless of how old we are."

Tucker nodded. "Dr. Brady says that if we amputate, Dad has a better chance to live. If they don't, we could lose him soon. Maybe even today."

Sheriff Mobley let out an audible gasp. He hadn't heard that from Dr. Brady. But then again, this decision had been looming over the medical team for more than a day.

Tucker continued. "He says that even if we don't amputate, the potential gangrene or infection could take his entire leg, basically confining him to a wheelchair forever. At least with the lower legs only being removed, they can fit him with prosthetics that will allow him to walk. Maybe even hike and stuff."

The two of them continued to stare at Owen. "And a better chance of recovery, right?"

Tucker chuckled and nodded. Finally, somebody had associated the word *recovery* with his dad's condition.

"No guarantees, of course. He was pretty definite about what would happen if Dr. Forrest doesn't amputate."

Sheriff Mobley stepped away from Tucker slightly so he could gauge his reaction. "What would your father do if the roles were reversed?"

Tucker laughed. "He'd Google it. Well, I mean, he'd Yahoo it since that's where he works. Somehow, Yahooing something never caught on like Googling did. Anyway, he'd weigh the options and then make a decision."

"And what do you think it would be?"

Tucker jutted out his chin and smiled at his father. "He'd rather have three-quarters of me than none at all."

CHAPTER SEVENTEEN

Friday, November 1
Driftwood Key

Jessica and Mike were like two ships passing in the night. She returned from her shift driving one of the county's surplus Ford F-250 pickups. The vehicle wasn't recognized by Jimmy as it eased across the bridge toward the front gate, so Jessica stopped well short of the entry and turned off the headlights. She shouted at Jimmy to stand down. Mike, who was preparing to exit the key for work, immediately recognized her voice.

She pulled through the gate onto the key, and the married couple spent a few moments together before Mike left. He already expected a long night, as he'd volunteered to work the blockades at the toll bridge. He wanted to see for himself whether they were secure and what kind of crowds had amassed on the Homestead side of the bridge.

"The sheriff and the mayor spent most of the afternoon and evening huddled up in the Islamorada office," said Jessica after the two broke their embrace. "It was a hot topic among any governmental personnel she encountered, and the coconut

85

telegraph was all abuzz." The phrase was an oft-used term paying homage to a song performed by Jimmy Buffett, "Coconut Telegraph," referring to a rumor mill in the islands.

"I can only imagine," said Mike as he shook his head. He held his wife's hand as they leaned against the truck and enjoyed the silence of the evening except for the random ticking sound coming from the Ford's hot engine. "Any idea what they're up to?"

Jessica sighed. "Supposedly the mayor wants more cops on the street. Residents are complaining about the huge uptick in home invasions each day. The sheriff says his manpower is stretched thin because of the checkpoints at the bridges."

"I feel a demand for working longer hours coming."

Jessica nodded. "That's part of the solution. The other suggestion by the mayor was to deputize a bunch of people. She wants warm bodies."

"Armed, too?" asked Mike.

"I assume. You and I both know that the investigation of these types of crimes will never happen. Heck, you can't even spend time tracking down the only serial killer in Florida Keys history."

"No shit. Listen, I understand we all have competing interests here. The mayor wants people to feel safe in their homes, and the sheriff is trying to minimize the number of potential criminals on our streets by eliminating the nonresidents. The *unknowns*, as he calls them."

Jessica walked away from the truck and shrugged. "Well, I hope he deputizes the *knowns* because, otherwise, we could find ourselves working alongside someone with a gun who doesn't know how the damn thing works."

Mike rolled his eyes and laughed. "Anything else exciting?"

Jessica smiled and walked back into his arms. "Yeah. Your partner wanted me to let you know he might have a lead on the killing that took place near Islamorada. He said it came as the result of a random conversation he had with a bartender up there."

"Hey, there's some good news," said Mike cheerily. If he had his way, he'd be chasing every lead to find the serial killer regardless of the apocalypse.

"The other good news is the fact that there haven't been any more bodies turn up since they found the one in the dumpster several days ago," added Jessica before asking, "Do you think he's moved on?"

Mike stuck his chin out and stared in the direction of Marathon. "I want to believe so. Maybe. Somehow his MO may have been thrown off by the power outage. It's possible he remained in Key West after the last murder and saw how quickly we descended upon the crime scene. It's all speculation, but I do know he's taken a breather."

"Stopped the bleeding, right?" asked Jessica with a chuckle.

"Yeah," agreed Mike, with the insensitive choice of words. He glanced at his watch, but he wanted to give Jessica a heads-up on their patient. "Speaking of stopping the bleeding, apparently Patrick is recuperating nicely. He's sitting up in bed on his own and making it to the bathroom without assistance."

"Good for him."

"You know, Jess, I've dealt with victims of crimes my entire career. Including the families of murder victims. In every case, both victims and families are determined to find the perp. I mean, you know, I've shared this with you. They're uber-helpful. Any little detail is sent my way. They watch a damn episode of *Blue Bloods* and call with some theory or another. I have to humor them sometimes, and I always respect them because I can't imagine what they're going through."

"Where are you goin' with this, Mike?"

He hesitated before responding, "I just don't get that same feeling with Patrick."

Jessica rubbed her husband's shoulder. "Do you think it's PTSD?" It was common for the victim of a brutal sexual assault and beating to want to block out the event as a coping mechanism.

"I don't know," he responded as he stared off into the distance.

Jessica had a suggestion. "Try spending some more time with

him on a personal level. You know, not as Mike the detective but as a concerned member of the Albright family. Maybe he'll open up?"

Mike glanced at his watch. He would be late, not that anyone would notice. He was most interested in catching up with his partner in Islamorada to see what he'd learned about the body they'd found in the hammocks.

"Yeah. We'll see. Love you." He gave her a kiss on the cheek and climbed into his truck. Jimmy quickly opened the gate to let Mike out. He drove off into the darkness with his mind focused on the serial killer who'd eluded him.

CHAPTER EIGHTEEN

Friday, November 1
North of Winston-Salem, North Carolina

Before dawn that morning, Peter found a looted gas station near the Virginia-North Carolina border. It allowed him an opportunity to sleep for several hours, which was sufficient rest to ride well into North Carolina before stopping for the evening. He'd traveled an extraordinary number of miles early that Friday, and he'd be pleased to make it another sixty miles or so to the outskirts of Winston-Salem by nightfall. A good night's sleep there would put him back on a daytime travel cycle.

Peter had been diligent about staying hydrated and checking on his wounds. Between the mall and his foray into CVS, he'd obtained a duffel bag full of first aid supplies and considered them to be more important than toting his sleeping gear.

Despite the long rides, his body was responding better than expected. His various pains were subsiding, and his excellent conditioning as a runner aided his stamina, which helped him avoid taking breaks. After crossing into North Carolina, the terrain became less forgiving. He started to experience more hills, which both challenged his energy levels but provided him a respite as he coasted downhill.

He stopped to drink from a roadside stream. He had a temporary lapse of judgment during which he cupped the water in his hands to slurp it down. He thought he was sufficiently far enough away from DC to avoid the radioactive fallout, but then he reminded himself that the nukes might have struck nearby. Charlotte was a major banking center. Raleigh-Durham was a high-tech corridor. There were also numerous strategic military bases in the region, including Fort Bragg and Seymour-Johnson Air Force Base.

He pulled out his LifeStraw and filled the stainless-steel cup that came with the canteen. He added his electrolyte supplement and drank it down. Peter had to remind himself that he could take nothing for granted when it came to the harmful effects of nuclear winter. The radiation was only one aspect. The soot and ash flowing through the atmosphere could also be harmful to his airways and digestive system.

He studied the map and identified a town close to Winston-Salem called Stokesdale. It appeared to be about ten miles north of the city and a logical place to head west for fifteen or twenty miles before finding a desolate road that would lead him due south.

Peter approached the town as the sun was setting and temperatures were dropping. It seemed to be getting slightly colder and darker each day, which was not unexpected. He was, however, surprised by how low the temperatures had dropped below what he considered to be normal for early November. Once again, he reminded himself he was in uncharted territory, and therefore, he should expect the unexpected.

Which was exactly what he got.

He navigated through a wooded area during his approach to the town. One winding turn after another minimized his visibility of the road ahead. He took a deep breath and pedaled harder as he rose up a steady incline on the tree-lined road that obscured what little light remained that day.

His body was screaming now, the hill seemingly being the last straw his muscles could take as he pedaled to the top of the rise. He kept going, determined to make it to the point he'd identified on the map before turning west. His breathing was labored, but he kept pressing on.

Almost there. Peter encouraged himself to continue up the hill. He stood on the pedals and pushed downward to keep a steady pace. He was not going to quit, but, in his mind, he hoped the intersection would provide another vacant gas station or business to shelter him for the night.

Peter looked ahead and saw that the top of the hill was approaching. Like reaching the apex of a roller coaster, he arrived at the top and began to sail down the hill, building up speed to get to his destination sooner. Peter leaned back on the seat and arched his back to relieve some tension. He took a deep breath of the musty air inside the gaiter he'd been wearing from time to time.

He was coasting at a high rate of speed as he crossed through the intersection with several abandoned businesses in sight. As had been his practice, when the stop sign appeared, he ignored it. He hadn't encountered any operating vehicles since his Mustang stopped running.

This time was different.

As he entered the intersection, a car appeared out of nowhere from the west. Peter struggled to slow the bicycle to stop. When he couldn't, he chose to pedal faster to beat the approaching vehicle, which he did. Barely.

He abruptly applied the brakes and skidded to a clumsy halt, almost toppling his bike over as he lost control for a moment. He stepped off the pedals to straddle the frame. Peter furrowed his brow and physically wiped his eyes with the back of his hands. He looked in wonderment as the passing vehicle slowed at a curve and applied the brakes before speeding eastward.

"Wow! Didn't expect that," Peter said aloud.

HONK!

Peter jerked his head around. Another car was approaching, and they were laying on the horn to force him out of the road. Peter pushed off and shuffled to the shoulder to avoid getting hit by the second car. This time, he got a better look at it. It was a late-model Mercedes.

Once again, he rubbed his eyes as if he were dreaming. Then he rubbed both hands on his thighs as if to confirm he was really standing by his bicycle. In the growing darkness, he studied the buildings around him. None of them showed signs of life, much less electricity. Yet two late-model cars had just sailed past him.

Peter took a deep breath and held it. He focused all of his senses on his surroundings, straining as he listened for any signs of machinery operating, whether it be another car or a small appliance. He cupped his hands to his ears in an effort to block out any ambient noise caused by the wind rustling through the trees. He concentrated.

Then he heard it. It was the low rumble of a truck approaching from behind him. He pushed his bicycle off the shoulder of the road behind a dumpster standing between a gas station and a barbeque restaurant.

Peter pulled his weapon and crouched next to it. Peering around the edge of the dumpster, Peter saw headlights appear on the road he'd just traveled along. The truck had lumbered up the hill and was coasting down the other side toward the stop sign. Only, he stopped, whereas Peter hadn't.

After a second, the driver of the diesel farm truck began to drive past him, shifting gears as he picked up speed. Peter wanted to call out and ask him a simple question.

How?

CHAPTER NINETEEN

Friday, November 1
Stokesdale, North Carolina

Peter eased up out of his crouch and assessed his surroundings. There were several older homes at the intersection together with an auto repair business on the back side of the gas station. The barbecue restaurant was attached to a hair salon. Despite the vehicles that had unexpectedly passed him, the rural crossroads was devoid of life except for a dog nosing around the back of the building.

Peter breathed a sigh of relief. He watched the dog sniffing around in search of food and wondered if the older pup might help him find something to eat as he suddenly realized how hungry he was.

The pup noticed him and immediately made a beeline to Peter's side. Tail wagging and the tags on his collar jingling, the family pet turned scavenger used his friendly nature to introduce himself to Peter.

He crouched down and held his right hand out for the dog to

sniff him. Peter spoke in a calm, reassuring tone. "Hey, buddy. Are you looking for some yummies?"

The dog responded by wagging his tail even faster. He sniffed at Peter's arm and then sat down, eagerly allowing Peter to scrub on his neck. His panting and smiling face confirmed to Peter that he wasn't likely to bite him.

"I wish I could help ya. I'm pretty sure the MRE bars I have would suck for you as much as they suck for me."

Peter stood and rummaged through his bag in search of the Clif protein bars. Most of them had chocolate, but he found one that substituted carob, a powdered form of the dark brown pea produced by the carob tree that tasted like chocolate. He broke off a small piece and allowed the Heinz 57 pup to try it.

"Um, did you even taste that?" asked Peter with a chuckle. The dog panted, and his eyes seemed to ask for more. "All right, a couple more bites. Let's not overload that stomach."

Peter fed his new friend half and ate the other half for himself. It was hardly enough but satisfied him until he could find shelter. The dog raised his nose in the air and caught a scent of something. He darted off between the buildings and glanced back at Peter before disappearing.

He suddenly felt exposed. Thus far, he'd been riding along with very little human contact, thank goodness. Either the people he'd encountered had tried to kill him or they had already been dead. Peter had developed a survival mindset in which everyone was a threat and the world would be lacking any form of operating electronic device. Yet, here he was, roughly three hundred miles from Washington, and he'd just witnessed three vehicles that had survived the electromagnetic pulse generated by the nuclear warhead destroying the city.

Peter needed to process this as well as rest for the next day's ride. He considered his options. Unlike the small communities he'd ridden through previously, these businesses didn't appear to be looted. There was no electricity, at least as far as his eyes could see.

This was puzzling to him as well. If the EMP didn't impact the cars, why would it take down the electric grid here?

He paced back and forth behind the dumpster, contemplating all of this. Finally, he pushed his bicycle between the buildings. At the rear of the simple block building, which contained the restaurant and hair salon, there was another business that built storage sheds. They were the kind you found at most home improvement stores. Shaped like small cabins and Dutch barns, the simple structures could be loaded on the back of a flatbed delivery truck and installed on blocks just about anywhere the owner desired. They'd become popular for some as tiny houses, a way of living inexpensively and, in some cases, off the grid.

Now that he'd seen signs of activity in the form of moving vehicles, Peter assumed law enforcement was active as well. He was not comfortable breaking into the businesses to look for food and shelter. He looked to the inventory of storage barns as an option that might not draw the owner's ire if he was discovered.

He checked the door handles of the first few floor models lining the front of the business. They were all unlocked. After a look around, he decided on a small, near-windowless storage building in the middle of the business's inventory. The lack of windows would insulate him from the cold, and the centralized location within the property might give him a heads-up in the event somebody else had the same idea.

Operating vehicles meant people were more mobile. The lack of electricity meant they were still going to be desperate.

Peter wheeled his bicycle inside and unloaded the gear. Then he laid the bike crossways across the barn door and used his bungee cords to secure it to the interior door handles. This barricade would give him peace of mind as he slept.

After rebandaging his wounds, he laid out the various pills that had become part of his daily regimen. The Keflex followed by the potassium iodide. He also took a multivitamin, vitamin C, D, and E supplements as well as a zinc tablet, most of which helped build his body's immunities to disease. He had a sufficient supply to last him six months although he was certain he'd be back at Driftwood Key by then. Meanwhile, as he traveled, he'd be more likely to encounter diseased animals or people. And, as he'd proven, the prospect of being injured was high as well. The vitamins and supplements would help protect him while his nutrition was lacking.

After settling in, Peter took a sip of the Chivas Regal scotch he'd packed at the golf course. It caused him to wince as it went down, but he allowed himself another swig. He chuckled to himself as he imagined a doctor assessing his mental state. On the one hand, he was taking extra precautions to keep his body safe with various supplements. On the other, he was swigging a premium scotch without regard to the countereffect on his medication.

"Sometimes, you gotta just say *screw it*. Right, Pete?"

He took another sip. Within minutes, the lack of food in his stomach immediately resulted in a buzz. Peter, who'd never been a heavy drinker, had become a survivalist much like his sister. He recognized the importance of keeping a clear head. He capped the bottle of Chivas and stored it away before he took one swig too many.

Peter inhaled deeply, leaned against the wall of the shed, and laid the AR-15 across his lap. He closed his eyes and ran all the scenarios through his head. He tried to recall everything he'd ever learned about EMPs.

After all the calculations and possibilities were run through his mind, he came to the conclusion that the effect of the ground detonation in Washington had been limited to a certain radius. He became convinced that the power grid had been taken down due to the cascading failure similar to what had happened in India years ago.

Most likely, he decided, appliances and electronics like computers could function the farther he traveled away from DC. And, as he'd witnessed, vehicles were moving, although not in large numbers.

This meant his options for getting home just widened. As Peter drifted off to sleep, his entire focus changed. He needed to find a ride, one with at least four wheels.

PART III

Day sixteen, Saturday, November 2

CHAPTER TWENTY

Saturday, November 2
Mount Weather Emergency Operations Center
Northern Virginia

President Helton was about to learn not all EMPs were alike. The electromagnetic pulse generated by the nuclear warheads had a differing effect on the U.S. depending upon whether it was an impact explosion or if the warhead detonated above the Earth's surface.

Homeland Security and its experts were called in to brief the president on the impact the EMPs had on critical infrastructure and anything dependent on the use of electricity. While trying to help those in need, he was constantly looking forward to the rebuilding effort.

"Mr. President," began the DHS director, "since the nineties, an argument raged in Washington as to whether the EMP threat was overhyped or a grievously overlooked existential threat to the nation. Generally, the debate centered around the funding of the various means to insulate our critical infrastructure from the effects of an electromagnetic pulse.

"These EMPs, whether naturally created by the sun in the form of a coronal mass ejection of solar matter or manmade as delivered by a high-yield nuclear warhead, impact us in similar ways. When a nuclear device explodes at high altitude, say between twenty-five and two hundred fifty miles above the Earth, it produces powerful gamma rays that radiate outward.

"As the gamma rays collide with molecules in the Earth's atmosphere, they are directed toward the planet surface in the form of a powerful electromagnetic energy field. The EMP does not directly cause human injuries, but it does destroy most electrical equipment and computerized devices as a surge of high-voltage current seeks out wiring or cables that act like antennas."

The president raised his hand slightly to stop the director's presentation. "Before you continue with what has been affected, let's talk about the range these detonations had. They're all different, correct?"

"Yes, Mr. President. For one, we're dealing with several different types of detonations. This may seem illogical, but the higher the altitude of the burst, the farther the pulse of energy travels. The gamma rays spread outward from the detonation site. At twenty-five miles above the surface, they enter the atmosphere where ionization occurs and produce an electromagnetic wave. This wave travels unimpeded, and it radiates everything below it.

"The only example of this type of high-altitude EMP detonation occurred near Denver at an altitude of around twenty miles. Our analysis leads us to believe that this warhead was destined for Cheyenne Mountain, but our ballistic missile interceptors took it down near Boulder. The gamma rays radiated outward in a radius several hundred miles across the U.S.

"Now, contrast this with the ground burst in Washington, which radiated out a much shorter distance. The line of sight from ground zero was much shorter than the Colorado air detonation."

"Okay, I understand," said the president. "Now, is it possible for you to identify, either by your modeling or actual in-the-field research, what parts of the country were directly affected by the EMP effect?"

"We've begun that process through modeling, Mr. President. Next, with your permission, we'd like to utilize the military to assess the range of each nuclear detonation. Those parts of the nation that are outside the reach of the gamma rays will be able to achieve some sort of normalcy first. Assuming, of course, that the power grid can be restored."

"Normalcy?" asked the president.

"Sir, I suppose that was a poor choice of words. Nothing will be normal for years to come, as Secretary Bergmann indicated in yesterday's briefing. By normal, I mean vehicles and computers could still operate. Audio-visual equipment, for example, would work, enabling Americans to both receive and transmit information to satellites for further dissemination."

"Hospitals, too, I presume."

"Yes, sir. Most hospitals outside the EMP blast radius would have operating medical devices once electricity is restored. For a while, as we've discussed, they can operate using their generators, many of which are hardened against electromagnetic pulse energy already. However, they need fuel to function. Without the power grid, they have to rely upon propane, natural gas, or gasoline. All of which require their own power sources to be extracted and then delivered."

The president sighed. The nation's ability to function wasn't totally destroyed. It simply meant he'd have to marshal the unaffected assets wisely. However, he thought to himself, without a functioning power grid, the task of recovery was near impossible.

"Our managed blackouts didn't work to prevent the complete collapse of the grid, did they?"

The director grimaced and shook his head. "Sir, it was the only option we had, but you're correct, the rolling blackouts simply prolonged the agony. It didn't give us time to prevent the cascading failure."

"What steps do we need to take to restore the grid? At least in the areas where the EMP blast didn't have an effect."

"Sir, prior studies have pointed to as many as fourteen bulk-power transformers that are especially vulnerable to the thermal damage resulting from an EMP event. These massive transformers, all made in China, I might add, convert high-voltage electricity from one transmission location to another, enabling it to move from the source of generation to the end user.

"Their proximity to the EMP blast determines whether it is ruined or simply rendered inoperable. Further analysis is needed to understand the extent of damage using site-specific data, including the overall condition of the transformer. That said, the cascading failure will necessarily result in the removal and replacement of the computer systems for each transformer. These are unique to the transformer and must be rebuilt to those exact specifications."

"How long would it take to replace a transformer and its computer system?" asked the president.

The director shook his head side to side as he contemplated his answer. "Years, under normal circumstances. Because Japan was hit by the DPRK's nukes, China is our only source for replacement components. We're totally reliant upon them at this point."

The president slumped in his chair, allowing the director's final words to hang in the air.

CHAPTER TWENTY-ONE

Saturday, November 2
Central North Carolina

A dog barking incessantly in the distance awoke Peter that morning. He'd passed out sitting up, and eventually during his sleep, he'd slid over on his side, sleeping in a fetal position to ward off the cold. The barking dog might have been his new friend, but when several others joined in, a cacophony of breeds awoke the rural neighborhood just like a rooster might on a farm.

Peter gripped his rifle and forced his sore body to stand. He rolled his eyes as he questioned if it would ever recover. He unstrapped the bungee cords from his bicycle and eased the door open. It was daylight. Well, as much as daylight was allowed to appear during nuclear winter.

The sounds of the dogs barking in the distance were louder now but sufficiently far enough away not to concern him. After he relieved his bladder, he slipped back into the storage building and plotted out his day.

He was beginning to establish a routine after only a few days on the road. He checked his wounds and took his medications. He repacked his duffels and backpacks, reassessing his ammunition supply as he did. Thus far, he'd only expended nine-millimeter rounds from his handgun. He was certain it wouldn't be the last time.

He also decided to keep extra magazines in his cargo pants pockets for his handgun and the AR-15 rifle he'd taken from the men on the bridge. He would be traveling near a major metropolitan area as he swung to the west of Winston-Salem. The historic city of a quarter million, built during the infancy of America's tobacco industry, would present challenges if someone approached him.

He'd have to tread lightly and be pleasant to everyone he encountered. He'd also have to be prepared to shoot them just like he'd shot the men on the bridge. His mind was prepared to travel through a kill-or-be-killed environment. It was wholly out of character for him but a necessary consequence of the changing world.

The circuitous route he would have to take to avoid the city would take him to the town of Wilkesboro, sixty-five miles northwest of Charlotte. From that point, Peter believed, after studying the map, he could travel due south through the Carolinas, into Georgia, before entering North Florida. All of the major cities along the way could be avoided.

Peter was a beast that day. Perhaps it was the fact he'd rested his weary body. Maybe it was the fact he began to see more signs of life. Several times along the route, he was passed by vehicles traveling in both directions as he approached Wilkesboro. Only one car slowed down as they approached Peter, and it appeared to be out of courtesy, as they didn't want to startle him on a sharp curve.

The combination of all the positive things he'd experienced as he rode gave him a second wind. By his prior calculations, he was able to easily ride eighty-plus miles in seven hours. He approached Wilkesboro with several hours of daylight remaining, so he continued on his southerly track.

As he rode closer toward I-40, the number of homes with people appearing outside increased. There was one property near the road frontage that caught his eye. A man and a woman sat in white rocking chairs, slowly easing back and forth with surgical masks over their faces. The older man had an oxygen tank with a breathing mask dangling from the valve by his side. The portable oxygen device must've been used by him for a respiratory ailment. Now, despite the horrendous air quality conditions, he was sitting outside.

Peter decided to take a chance. He was starving for information, probably more than he was hungry for food. He turned his bike toward the house and dismounted near their mailbox. He slowly walked it up the sidewalk, which had a dusting of ashy snow.

He stopped short of the porch when he saw an old double-barrel shotgun lying across the lap of the woman, who continued to rock back and forth while maintaining a watchful eye on Peter. He held up his hands to show he hadn't planned on drawing his weapons on them.

"Hi! I'm Peter Albright. I don't want to bother you, but I just wondered if you could help me with some information."

The older man cupped his hand to his ear and looked over at his wife. "What did he say?"

"He has questions." She shouted her answer to him.

"About what?" he asked.

"I don't know, Charles. He ain't asked 'em yet." She raised her voice so he could hear.

If Peter wasn't apprehensive, he would've found the scene comical. He inched his bike forward until he was just a few feet away from the covered stoop. Neither of the rockers seemed to be concerned with his approach.

"Whatcha wanna know?" she asked, pulling down her mask as she spoke.

Peter kept his face covered. "Hi. Well, ma'am, I was—"

The old man interrupted him, waggling his finger at Peter as he spoke. "You gotta pull that thing down, or I can't hear ya. Go ahead now. Pull it down."

Peter glanced around and then pulled down his gaiter. "I was wondering if you could tell me if the power is out around here."

"Yup, just a couple of days ago," the old woman replied. "It was on and off for a bit after the bombs dropped. Then it just never came back on."

Peter decided to tell his story to gain their trust. He hit the high points of where he had been located at the moment of the blast and how he'd managed to survive since. He left out the parts about the gunfights, naturally.

She told him what they'd heard on the radio following the nuclear attacks. Tears poured out of his eyes when he heard about San Francisco. They both noticed that he'd become emotional and exchanged looks. Without saying a word, the old man nodded, and his wife stood up.

"Young man, why don't you come inside and take a load off your feet. I'm gonna fix up some beans and cornbread. I've got some pepper relish to put on top if you like it."

Peter's eyes grew wide, and his stomach immediately began to growl. "How? Um, how are you cooking it?"

The woman laughed as she helped her husband out of his rocking chair. "We're country folk," she said with a chuckle and then waved her arm around. "This ain't nothin' for us."

CHAPTER TWENTY-TWO

Saturday, November 2
Bethlehem, North Carolina

Their names were Charles and Anna Spencer. Both were in their early eighties, having resided in the small community just north of Hickory all their lives. Anna had taught school at nearby Bethlehem Elementary, and Charles had been a trucker working for Freight Concepts just down the road from their home. The company specialized in hauling furniture manufactured by companies in Hickory to warehouse destinations across America. He'd developed respiratory issues from years of smoking cigarettes while on the road.

"Ma'am, I can't tell you how much this means to me," said Peter as he wiped his mouth with the paper napkins she provided. Anna had encouraged him to eat all he wanted. There was plenty, she assured him, although he couldn't imagine where she stored it. The house was full of furniture, but it appeared they only had a limited amount of food. Perhaps that was by design, Peter thought to himself as he offered to clear the dishes.

"Not on your life, young man," admonished Anna as she raised her hands. "You're a guest in our home." She pushed her chair back and immediately grabbed his bowl.

"Young man, have you heard about the farmers' market tomorrow?" asked Charles.

Peter politely raised his voice so his host could hear him. "Farmers' market? As in selling their harvest?"

Charles laughed. "Well, it's something like that. People have been gathering each morning to trade with one another. One man's bushel of apples is worth another man's bottle of bleach."

"Barter?" asked Peter.

"That's right," Anna replied as she set a small plate in front of him, full of sliced apples. Peter wiped a tear from his eyes. In his lifetime, no one had shown him this much kindness in a time of need other than his family.

Charles reached over and squeezed his wife's hand. He smiled as he spoke. "It's more than that. You are determined to get to your family, and there is a way that might become easier for you."

Peter slowly munched on an apple, savoring the flavor. "I have my credit cards. Do you think I could buy a car?"

The trio laughed, and after several jokes about how the banking system had probably collapsed just like the Spencers' grandparents had warned them it would someday, Anna explained, "My husband is referring to the truckers. You see, like Charles, most of the drivers who work for Freight Concepts live nearby. This is their only terminal, and all deliveries start right here. When they're done with their trip, they come back to Bethlehem empty."

Charles took over from there. "Most of them, like us, had small farms. They also had trucks big enough to take livestock to the stockyards over in Catawba, or if they had chickens, Tyson up the road would take all they had."

Peter finished the apples and gave Anna a thumbs-up. She offered him more, but he declined. His stomach was truly full. He was concerned how the sudden influx of beans and apples might wage war on his digestive system. The excessive gas might cause the Spencers to throw him out in the cold.

Charles continued. "We all have farm diesel stored. Me and the missus topped off our tanks the day after the bombs hit. The day after that, the supplier ran dry. Others like us did the same. Now they're finding a way to profit from it."

"How's that?" asked Peter.

Anna laughed. "Well, it ain't no Uber, but it serves the same purpose. They're takin' folks west and south away from where the bombs dropped in DC and New York. Folks who weren't ready for something like this are searching for seclusion or, like you, family."

Peter's eyes lit up. Greyhound bus or chicken truck, he didn't care. *How do I get south?*

"Do you know how much? I mean, they must charge something."

"We don't know 'cause we don't go down there," replied Anna. "It's getting more crowded every day as people have started walking along I-40 from Charlotte into the Smokies." The Great Smoky Mountains were located at the southern end of the Appalachian Mountains along the North Carolina-Tennessee border.

Peter's elation suddenly turned dour as he thought about the reality of paying someone to drive him to Florida. He didn't have any money or bushels of apples to trade. He grimaced and sat back in his chair.

There had to be something, or some way, to make this work.

CHAPTER TWENTY-THREE

Saturday, November 2
Driftwood Key

Since Patrick's arrival several nights ago, there hadn't been any activity at the gate separating Driftwood Key from Marathon. Hank had begun to feel foolish for his constant nagging at his brother about keeping one of the family's law enforcement officers at the inn at all times. Despite Hank's vivid imagination that conjured up marauders at the gate, the only person attempting to enter Driftwood Key had been a harmless banker who'd been beaten to within an inch of his life.

It had just turned dark when Hank arrived at the gated entry to the inn, with an AR-15 slung over his shoulder. The rifle was equipped with a suppressor confiscated by the sheriff's office during a drug bust. Mike had taken a few liberties with the evidence locker after the collapse sent everything into disarray.

Armed like a soldier, he hardly looked like one. His uniform consisted of Sperry Top-Sider deck shoes, khakis, and a Tommy Bahama half-zip sweatshirt. His appearance on patrol that night looked more like that guy Dale who drove the motor home in the early episodes of *The Walking Dead* than an armed sentry who should be reckoned with.

Mike had had to leave early to deal with a looting situation in Key West and wasn't due back until midnight. Because it was just after dusk, Hank sent Sonny and Jimmy to join Jessica at the main house for dinner. He told them to get some rest, assuring them he could handle any wayward soul who ventured across the bridge connecting their key to Marathon.

A chill came over him as the slight breeze off the Gulf brought with it dropping temperatures. He cursed himself for not sending Jimmy or Sonny to Walmart to purchase cold-weather clothing, if it was even available. He'd tried to prepare based upon the warnings he'd received from Erin Bergmann and Peter. In the back of his mind, he'd doubted their cautionary advice to expect nuclear winter to live up to its name.

As he mindlessly wandered along the shoreline, he thought of Erin. He'd become smitten with her in a way he hadn't felt since his wife was alive. Erin was attractive and intelligent. Their conversations ranged from serious, such as geopolitical affairs, to silly, as was the case on their last day together when they went fishing. She had been whisked away that day because of the impending doom that was about to be unleashed on America. They'd barely had time to say goodbye much less discuss whether they'd ever see one another again. He thought about her every day, and the fact that she was still on his mind was an indication of how deep his feelings were for her.

Hank glanced upward in search of the moon and the stars. As a lifelong resident of the Keys and an accomplished boater, he knew what day of the month the moon was supposed to be full just like landlubbers knew what day the mortgage was due. Prior to the attacks, on a night like this, he'd look up to an impeccable midnight blue sky with a bright white orb peeking between a few clouds passing by. The stars would appear to be dancing around it, a nighttime sailor's delight, who relied upon them for navigation. Now the constant blanket of gray, sooty cloud cover blocked out everything the heavens had to offer and radiated nothing but misery inward.

"We need a hurricane," he said aloud. Then he laughed. He'd heard a friend of his make that statement when Hank had had to travel to Georgia once. It had been the middle of August, and the sweltering summer heat coupled with near one hundred percent humidity was oppressive. His friend complained about the weather and was certain a hurricane brewing off the coast would suck all the moisture and heat out of Georgia to fuel its wrath.

Hank wasn't one to get offended, as he prided himself on living his life without a chip on his shoulder. However, having lived through those devastating subtropical cyclones, he'd gladly live with the inconvenience of heat and humidity.

He continued to walk back and forth along the bank of the brackish water separating Driftwood Key and Marathon. His mind wandered from topic to topic, having conversations with himself. Most were lighthearted; others were analytical. He'd become lost in himself when he noticed headlights on the other side of the mangroves.

Vehicles were operating only sporadically through the Keys as gasoline became in short supply. Government vehicles seemed to be the most prevalent, and there were a few residents who elected to leave their homes to join relatives up north. Nobody was joyriding, and there certainly was no place to shop or eat out.

Hank held his position and studied the location of the vehicle, which was roughly a thousand yards across the water. There were several older homes nestled among the trees on the other side. Hank knew the families. Like him, they'd grown up on the Keys. One owned a charter boat operation, and another owned Barnacle Barney's Tiki Bar, which was adjacent to his residence. Early on, he'd touched base with his distant neighbors, who indicated they'd be fine if the power outage didn't last too long. He'd suspected that most longtime residents of the Florida Keys felt the same way.

Suddenly, another set of headlights flickered through the trees, barely noticeable unless Hank focused on one particular spot. There were now two vehicles parked across from the inn but not directly on Palm Island Avenue, which led to Driftwood Key's private access bridge.

With a wary eye on the two vehicles, Hank moved quickly back toward the bridge. He was certain he'd locked it after Mike had left earlier, but he felt compelled to double-check. He felt his pants pocket for the air horn. When he remembered he'd left it on the granite block that held one of the gate's posts, he walked even faster.

Then he began to run as he heard the vehicles' tires spinning, throwing crushed shell and sand against their rear quarter panels in the otherwise deathly silent evening.

"They're coming!" he shouted spontaneously.

Hank couldn't see their headlights, but he sensed the vehicles maneuvering across the way to make a run at the gate. He pulled the rifle off his shoulder and pulled the charging handle as Mike had taught him. In the darkness, he struggled to see the safety so he could flick it off.

Sweat poured off Hank's brow as apprehension and fear swept over him. He'd been caught unprepared for what was coming. He reached the gate and crouched behind the granite block. He felt exposed. And alone.

He nervously searched the granite block with his left hand to find the air horn so he could issue a warning to the others. His awkwardness, fueled by anxiety, caused him to hit the canister with his knuckles, sending it flying off the granite block and tumbling down a slope until it wedged in the riprap.

"Dammit!"

He tried to gather his wits about him by holding his breath. He heard the slight crunching of tires on the crushed shell. Hank squinted, trying to block out any movement or distraction as he tried in vain to see the other side of the water in the pitch-dark night.

He steadied his rifle on the block and trained his sights on the center of the road. He listened for a few moments, hearing a snap in the distance, followed by the slow-moving tires crushing the shells beneath them.

Hank lifted his head from behind his rifle and peered around the gate post. At first glance, the bridge entering Driftwood Key looked like it always did since nuclear winter set in—a shadowy, multihued fog of grays and whites with the occasional mangrove tree making an appearance on the other end.

A few more seconds of hyperawareness and laser focus enabled Hank to see what he was facing. A truck, flanked by darkened figures, slowly approached along the bridge. They were being invaded.

CHAPTER TWENTY-FOUR

Saturday, November 2
Driftwood Key

As quickly as this threat arose and Hank began to sweat, he now seemed to get a grip on himself. He was alone and unable to issue a warning to the others without giving away his position to the people who approached. Hank closed his left eye and looked through the gun's sights. He studied the column slowly making its way across the concrete surface of the bridge. The pickup was flanked by two men, who each carried a hunting rifle. When the driver gently tapped the brakes for a brief second, Hank was able to make out a second truck with two more men flanking its front fenders.

They couldn't be more than a hundred feet away from the gate and in the center of the bridge when Hank slid his finger onto the trigger. The group was disciplined, resisting the temptation to storm the gates and crash through them with the front bumper of the pickup.

He steadied his aim but stopped short of pulling the trigger. Did it make sense to fire on the guys on foot when the truck was likely to accelerate toward the gate and breach their security? The suppressor might keep his position concealed long enough to take additional shots at the truck as it passed. Eliminating the men with guns was a tempting thought, but the greater risk to the rest of the compound was the speeding pickup barreling past him toward the main house.

He glanced over his shoulder, expecting to see his backup emerge from the trail. When they didn't, he realized he was on his own. He'd only get one or two shots before he'd come under return fire. If the sound of the air horn couldn't bring the cavalry, gunfire certainly would.

Hank adjusted his aim toward the driver and steadied his nerves. The magazine had thirty rounds, and he'd need them all. He quickly squeezed off two shots; the spitting sound emitted by the suppressor allowed the bullets to reach the windshield at supersonic speed. They both found their mark, obliterating the windshield and embedding in the upper body of the driver.

The truck swung wildly to the right and crashed into the concrete guardrail before stopping. The man on the truck's left flank was pinned against the concrete and screamed in agony as he attempted to free his leg from the bumper, which continued to push forward as it idled.

Then the night exploded in a hail of gunfire. One round after another careened off the steel gates and the concrete underneath them. One round sailed well over Hank's head, but it was a reminder that there was a lot of work to be done.

"Move the truck!" a voice ordered from behind the bed.

"I'm on it!" a man responded.

Hank fired again, sending two more rounds toward the back of the pickup in an attempt to shut down the men who were firing upon him. They'd all scrambled for cover after Hank took away their battering ram. For now, at least.

"Hank! Hank!" shouted Jessica.

"Are you all right?" asked Sonny as they could be heard rushing along the trail leading to the main house.

Their questions were answered with gunfire from the attackers. The bullets ripped through the palm fronds and embedded in the trunks.

"Stay low and take cover!" Hank yelled instructions to them.

The tires of the pickup truck began to squeal as the driver forced it into reverse. The man it pinned groaned over the racket as he was released from the front fender's grip. The smell of burnt rubber filled the air and reached Hank's nostrils, giving him an idea.

"Shoot out the tires. Now!"

Jessica and Sonny joined him in immersing the pickup in a variety of bullets ranging from Sonny's shotgun pellets to Jessica's .45-caliber hollow points from her Kimber 1911. The truck was being pelted by the shotgun blasts, but it was the expert shooting of Jessica that took out the front two tires. Each time a bullet penetrated the outer wall, the tires exploded from the sudden release of air pressure. Now it sat in the middle of the bridge, a disabled hunk of steel unable to breach the gate but providing excellent cover for the attackers.

A gun battle ensued that could be heard for miles, as the unusually quiet conditions coupled with the low cloud ceiling kept the sound confined near the ground.

Hank and Sonny took up positions behind the granite blocks holding the gate in place. Jessica crouched to keep a low profile and rushed to Hank's side. She patted him on the back.

"Trade guns with me," she whispered with an urgent tone in her voice. Hank didn't hesitate as he took her handgun, a weapon he was far more familiar with. "How many rounds have you fired?"

"Ten or twelve, I think."

She reached into the back pocket of her jeans and handed him a full magazine. "Don't waste these. I need you to give me some cover. Try to skip the bullets under the bed of the pickup truck. This will distract them and maybe even find a leg or two. With a little luck, you'll breach the gas tank."

Hank muttered, "Okay." He raised the weapon and rested it on the granite block to keep his aim steady. "Ready."

Jessica tapped him on the back and whispered, "Now."

Hank fired. She raced off to his left as the .45-caliber rounds careened off the pavement, creating sparks underneath the truck. A man screamed in agony as one of the bullets found his shinbone, shattering it as the hollow-point bullet expanded.

Jessica moved away from the gate to get a different angle at their attackers. As Hank's bullet hit the man's leg, she was able to get her bearings. Then she got some help.

There was a reason criminal conspiracy laws had become so effective in taking down any form of crooked enterprise. Most criminals will roll over and snitch on the others to reduce their own punishment. Or, as they say, there's no honor among thieves.

On the bridge, the attackers in the second pickup truck decided to cut their losses and flee. Jessica heard the truck's doors slam. A second later, the driver threw the truck in reverse and turned on his headlights so he could have a better view as he drove off the bridge. As a result, he left his partners in crime lit up and dumbfounded.

Jessica didn't hesitate; she took aim and unleashed a salvo toward two men who'd broken their cover. She didn't miss. The men were riddled with bullets and thrown to the pavement. She gritted her teeth in anger and stood. With the barrel of her rifle seeking any movement from the men still alive, she patiently waited.

Then she got her chance. The man Hank shot in the leg tried to run-hobble away. He turned his body sideways and continued to fire wildly toward the gate, missing his targets. Jessica, however, did not. Her first shot struck him in the good leg, and the second ripped through his neck, killing him instantly.

She ran toward the gate, where both Sonny and Hank were standing. Her eyes grew wide as she darted between the two men toward the disabled pickup.

"Get back down," she growled at them. "This may not be over."

Both men rushed back to their protective cover. Switching the rifle to her left hand, Jessica jumped on top of Hank's granite block, swung her right arm through the post, and hurled her body around until she landed at the front side of the gate just feet from the water's edge.

Using the concrete railing for cover, she caught her breath and readied her rifle. She crouched as low as she could and began to ease around the barrier, focusing her eyes on the concrete surface of the bridge.

Although she'd arrived late to the party, she believed there was still one attacker unaccounted for. If the driver of the truck was dead, then the only attacker left was the man pinned against the guardrail, who might still be alive. A wounded animal was a dangerous animal with nothing to lose, she thought as she walked heel to toe, studying the undercarriage of the pickup for movement.

She took several steps closer until the large rear tires provided some clearance to see the other side. She could discern the shape of a man's legs spread apart as if he was leaning against the guardrail. She squinted her eyes to search for any movement. She had to be sure he was dead, and there was only one way to do it without exposing herself.

Jessica lowered her body to a prone position on the bridge. She aimed at the man's foot and gently squeezed the trigger. The powerful NATO 5.56 round entered the sole of the man's shoe and tore a hole through his foot.

No scream. Not even a twitch of his already dead body.

She jumped to her feet and raced for the back of the pickup, swinging her rifle's barrel from side to side as she swept the bridge in search of targets. There were only two, and they'd already been eliminated.

After a long moment during which she stared at the darkness on the other end of the bridge, serenity had returned to Driftwood Key as Jessica gave the all clear.

CHAPTER TWENTY-FIVE

Saturday, November 2
Arkansas Valley Regional Medical Center
La Junta, Colorado

Lacey's mind had taken a respite, an unconscious sleepy slumber, during which time she had minimal brain activity and showed no signs of awareness of her surroundings. Her eyes had been closed, but not clenched shut. No sound, no pain, no external stimulus triggered any form of response from her. Even basic reflexes such as coughing and swallowing were greatly reduced.

A coma was the body's way of healing itself following a traumatic injury. It had been two days, and it was time to wake up. Slowly, at first. Lacey began to hear things around her. Shuffling of feet. Whispered conversations. The occasional words of encouragement from what she thought was an angel, but it was actually one of the ICU nurses.

Then she heard Tucker's voice. Oddly, he was retelling her stories of family outings. Backpacking through the Redwood National Forest. Camping at Wild Willy Hot Springs. Hiking to Burney Falls. Standing atop the Cone Peak at Big Sur.

His voice was comforting. Familiar. Yet something was wrong. Owen was missing from the storytelling sessions. Tucker mentioned his dad as he spoke, but Owen wasn't present. His smell. His touch. His loving voice whispering in her ear.

Inside, Lacey was becoming agitated and apprehensive. Where was her husband? Why couldn't she hear him joining in the conversation reminiscent of their evenings around the dinner table at night? It was all so confusing.

Then, in an instant, as if a thousand roosters had crowed at once, Lacey awoke with a start. Her body lurched as if it had been shocked with an overcharged defibrillator. She took in a deep exhale, filling her lungs through her mouth, but seemingly unable to expel it. Lacey McDowell was awake, and she choked out a scream to let the world know it.

Tucker rushed out of the room to the nurse's station to let them know his mom was waking up.

"Find Dr. Brady! Stat!" a nurse shouted from just outside her room. She turned to Tucker who was headed back into the room. She firmly grasped his arm. "Young man. Please wait here until the doctor examines your mom."

Within seconds, three nurses had rushed to Lacey's side, checking the machinery around her and feeling her neck and wrist. Her eyes were forced wide open and wild with perplexity as she tried to process her surroundings.

"Mrs. McDowell, my name is Donna Ruiz. Everything's okay. Please calm down while we check you over."

"Where?" Lacey tried to ask, but it came out as a whispered breath of air. Her intubation tube had stolen her ability to speak.

Nurse Ruiz seemed to sense what she was saying. The long-term ICU and emergency room nurse had seen people come back from the brink of death before.

"Honey, you're fine. You're at the hospital. The doctor will be here in a—"

As if on cue, Dr. Brady rushed into the room, penlight in hand. "Did she just come out?"

"Yes, Doctor," replied Ruiz. "Her vitals went through the roof, but she's calming quickly. Only her pulse is elevated."

"Good, very good," said Dr. Brady, who leaned over Lacey and performed his own examination. He tested her eye, motor and verbal response. He studied her arms and legs for evidence of unusual spasms.

He flashed his penlight across the front of her face. "Follow my light with your eyes." She did.

Then he removed her covers and grasped her hand. "Squeeze my hand, please." She gave him a firm grip.

As he checked her heart and lungs, he spoke to her in a casual tone. He took a personal approach to keep her calm. "Lacey, welcome back. As you can see, we have you in the hospital. There's a lot to discuss, but I need you to remain calm. Your heart rate is slightly elevated, and we're gonna give you some medicine to slow it down. You're breathing remarkably well. I'm gonna have Nurse Ruiz remove your breathing tube so you can speak with us. How does that sound?"

Lacey stared at Dr. Brady's face and nodded. She had a thousand questions she wanted to ask, the first of which was simple—where's my family?

Ruiz leaned over Lacey and gently removed the tube. "Lacey, you're gonna feel a little discomfort." She expertly slid it out, which immediately opened Lacey's throat.

She began coughing violently, so Ruiz lovingly touched her face to comfort her. Seconds later, the nurses adjusted Lacey in her bed, propping her up slightly so she could get a better view of her surroundings.

Lacey conducted her own self-assessment, carefully testing her limbs to see if they functioned. She wiggled her toes and fingers. She tensed her muscles in her legs and arms. She slowly turned her head side to side. Other than the normal stiffness associated with lying perfectly still for days, she felt fine.

"Doctor," Nurse Ruiz whispered into his ear. "Her son is very anxious to see his mom. Can we let him in?"

Dr. Brady furrowed his brow. "Give me a moment to test her mental acuity."

He turned to Lacey. "Do you feel like you can talk? I know your throat is sore. We'll fix that in a moment."

She nodded and whispered yes. This resulted in another coughing fit, from which she quickly recovered. Nurse Ruiz allowed her a brief sip of water.

"Okay. Do you know what state you're in?"

"Colorado," she whispered.

"Good. And what year is it?"

Lacey scowled, which caused Dr. Brady some concern. He thought she was struggling to find an answer.

"Lacey?"

"It depends. How long have I been out?"

Dr. Brady stepped back from her bed and stuffed the penlight into his pocket with a smile. "I'd have to research where sense of humor falls on the Glasgow Coma Scale, but I think that means you're fine."

The Glasgow Coma Scale was a clinical tool used to measure a patient's level of consciousness after a brain injury. Physicians focus on eye opening response, verbal interaction, and motor skills.

Nonetheless, he wanted to go through the rest of the procedures.

Lacey forced a smile and looked toward the door. "Owen? Tucker?"

Dr. Brady raised his index finger in the air. "Just a moment." He left her room and spoke briefly with Tucker before letting him in.

"Can I see her now?" Tucker asked before Dr. Brady was able to close the door behind him.

"She is doing very well, young man, but it's important that we not allow her to become agitated. Her brain is still recovering from a very traumatic event, just like yours did. She needs some time to process what is happening before she takes in any unsettling news."

Tucker sighed and looked up at the ceiling. "How do I hide Dad's surgery from her?"

Overnight, Dr. Forrest had performed the transtibial amputation on Owen's lower legs. It was one of the most frequent forms of amputation due to the rate of diabetes in America. Dr. Forrest was successful in leaving Owen with two well-padded residual limbs that could easily tolerate prosthetic replacements. He was still in recovery and remained in a coma of his own.

"I'll be with you the entire time," Dr. Brady responded. "Let's just stay positive and tell her that your dad is still fighting the good fight. Okay?"

Tucker forced a smile and nodded. He was fully dressed now. Sheriff Mobley had retrieved the family's Bronco and pulled it into the local auto repair garage across the street from the sheriff's office. He'd secured the McDowells' belongings at the station and delivered clothing for Tucker early that morning. His appearance would never suggest to his mother that he had been in the same medical condition she was just a day ago.

He eased into the room first, and his face beamed with the broadest smile of his life. "Hi, Mom."

Tucker tried to remain calm as the doctor had suggested, but he couldn't control his emotions. Tears flowed out of his eyes, and he rushed to her side. Lacey gingerly raised her arms to accept his embrace, allowing his warm salty tears to pour off his cheeks and join hers. For a minute, the two held one another without speaking, not that words were necessary.

When they finally let go of one another, Lacey's piercing eyes looked into Tucker's soul as only a mother could. Tucker felt it immediately and tried to look away, seeking Dr. Brady for moral support. His mom suddenly found her strength and squeezed her son's hand before he could bolt out of the room. He'd never been able to lie to his mom, and now was no different.

CHAPTER TWENTY-SIX

Saturday, November 2
Arkansas Valley Regional Medical Center
La Junta, Colorado

Lacey and Tucker spent the next hour talking with Dr. Brady. The family's attending physician was also no match for the strong-willed Lacey McDowell. Her reaction to the news was expected, but her sadness extended to both her husband and Tucker. She felt guilty for not being there to help her teenage son make such a difficult decision. She assured him that she would've supported his choice, and she meant it. After the shock of what had been required to provide Owen a chance at living was over, she swelled with pride as she realized her son had become a man.

She'd first become impressed with Tucker's survival instincts when they sought shelter as the threat of the nuclear attacks materialized. Under the high-pressure conditions inside the fallout shelter, Tucker had kept a cool head and did everything to help his parents stay safe. Then, after they began their trek east, he had been so nonchalant with dealing with the dead bodies on the highway overpass that she became concerned. His acceptance of death, especially at the hands of two gunmen, had shocked her at first.

It was during those few minutes alone in the Bronco before the flash freeze overtook him that Tucker had assuaged her fears. He'd explained to her that he was never one to stir up drama, much less fabricate it, as many of his teenage friends did. In a very adult way, he'd stated there were enough challenges growing up without making up any.

He'd talked about drug use by his friends. Teenage pregnancies that parents were unaware of. Cheating on exams and term papers that went undiscovered. He'd been completely honest with her in those few minutes before they nearly froze to death.

As they talked in the hospital room alone, she realized Tucker had handled the freeze anomaly better than she had. It was her concern for Owen and the impulsive decision to charge out into the frigid air that had put them in peril. Tucker saved her, and now, with his ability to make a very heart-wrenching decision, he'd given Owen a better chance of survival as well.

On Dr. Brady's orders, without objection from Lacey, she took some time to sleep. She was feeling much stronger and even took in some solid food, if you could call lime Jell-O and a cup of applesauce solid.

While she napped, Tucker donned his jacket and took a fifteen minute walk down the street to speak with Sheriff Mobley. He hadn't stopped by the hospital that morning, and Tucker wasn't sure if he was aware of his mom waking up.

To his surprise, Tucker learned that Sheriff Mobley had spent the entire morning making arrangements on behalf of the McDowell family. He was aware of Lacey's condition, but he chose to give Tucker time alone with his mom before he stopped by to introduce himself. In the meantime, he'd done several things to benefit their anticipated travels.

First, he encouraged Tucker to keep his family in La Junta for as long as they wanted. One of the locals offered up a fully furnished rental property down the street from the hospital to be used for as long as the McDowells wanted it. Families prepared foods for them. The city manager gathered up packaged MREs to feed them on their journey once they chose to leave. Sheriff Mobley filled their gas containers and topped off the tank to their truck. And, with the help of several townspeople, they found a radiator hose to repair Black & Blue.

Except, Sheriff Mobley had a conversation with Tucker about the pristine condition of the vintage Ford. As they traveled southeast toward Florida and out of the Rocky Mountain region, they'd eventually come into only slightly more hospitable weather conditions. Also, based on reports, the EMP effect dissipated near Texas. Nonetheless, an operating vehicle like the classic Bronco would be a prize possession of anyone with criminal intent.

His solution? Make it ugly. It needed to be painted to appear run-down. A primer-gray fender here and some poorly spray-painted camouflage there. Even the gas cans should be painted to blend in with the truck. Then, to top it off, a nondescript tarp was recommended to hide one of the most valuable assets in America, gasoline.

Tucker asked Sheriff Mobley to hold off on the extreme makeover for Black & Blue until he spoke with his dad. He hoped that the amputation surgery would enable him to come out of his coma.

As they were having this conversation, Owen did just that.

A young male orderly had rushed into the sheriff's office after running the mile from the medical center. He had been told by Dr. Brady to find Tucker and the sheriff. They piled into Sheriff Mobley's Jeep and rushed back to the ER. Before coming to a stop, Tucker had flung the door open and raced through the entry doors toward the ICU. He was met in the hallway by Donna Ruiz, the ever-present nurse.

With Tucker barreling down on her, Ruiz stood in the middle of the hallway with both hands raised like a third base coach giving a signal to a base runner to stop.

"Tucker, Tucker, slow down. The doctors are still with your dad."

"Is he awake? Is he okay?" Tucker nervously looked past her toward his dad's room. He then looked toward his mom's. He wondered if she knew, or maybe she was with him already.

"They're still examining him," Ruiz replied. "Both doctors said your father's situation is a little more complicated than your mom's. They need you to give them a little time, and then they'll explain."

"Does Mom know?"

She nodded. "Yes. In fact, I'd like you to join her so the doctors can speak with you both as soon as they come out."

Tucker nodded his head rapidly, and she gently took him by the arm. As she led him down the corridor, he craned his neck to look in the small glass window in the center of his father's door. The doctors in their white coats and several nurses obstructed his view, resulting in a sigh of disappointment. It was all he could do to restrain himself from pulling away from the nurse and bursting in there.

He entered his mom's room and was amazed to see her sitting in a wheelchair, dressed in pajamas provided by the hospital staff. Clothing had been donated by several families who were aware of the McDowells' predicament. Lacey was wearing red and white striped flannel pj's from Victoria's Secret.

"Hi, honey," she greeted him with a smile. She stretched her arm up to grasp Tucker's hand. "Where've you been?"

"I walked down to the sheriff's office," he replied and then briefly explained what he'd learned, especially the part about the town rallying to help them.

"Have they told you anything about your dad?" she asked.

"Nothing, except I saw both of his doctors and a few nurses in there just now. Nurse Ruiz said they'd come see us here, and reminded me that dad's condition was more complicated."

Tucker looked down at his feet. He was unsure whether the term complicated was in reference to the amputation or his exposure to the bitter cold. He pulled a chair next to his mom and sat down; then he told her more about what Sheriff Mobley had done for them. They made small talk in an effort to pass the time until the doctors arrived.

The door opened slightly, and Dr. Brady was giving instructions to Ruiz about another patient in the ICU before finally entering the room. Tucker immediately stood to greet him, and Lacey tried before plopping back into the wheelchair. She'd need more rest and some nutrition before she could stand on her own.

Dr. Brady held the door open, and shortly thereafter, Dr. Forrest joined him. He allowed Dr. Brady, as Owen's attending physician, to speak first. He addressed Lacey.

"Okay, as you know, your husband is awake and somewhat alert. There are a couple of things you need to know, so I'm gonna get right to it so you can see him before he nods off.

"We performed a series of tests on Owen just as we did for the both of you when you woke up. There are some positive signs. His eye response is fairly good. He responds to our verbal commands. When we asked him to perform certain physical functions on command, he was unable to do so. His inability to do this could be related to his drowsy state or general disjointedness. Time will tell. But the larger concern is related to his verbal responses."

"Are you saying he can't talk?" asked Tucker.

Dr. Brady scowled as he tried to find the words to explain Owen's condition that could be understood by a layman.

"The brain is a very complicated part of the body, Tucker. The Glasgow analysis is designed to assess brain function without conducting more invasive tests. The verbal response test is designed to determine his higher cortical function. In other words, how does his brain allow him to communicate coherently, react, remember, and even react to pain.

"Unfortunately, Owen is having difficulty responding to us. He uttered incomprehensible sounds, and when he did manage to speak, the words were used inappropriately to the questions."

"My god," said Lacey, who began to cry.

"Now, let's be clear," said Dr. Forrest. "We are in the early stages of your husband's recovery process. Traumatic brain injuries like his may take weeks or months to fully recover from. He'll need to be seen by a neurosurgeon, probably at one of the hospitals in Colorado Springs, when he's able to travel. After that, the normal course is physiotherapy and reoccurring psychological assessments."

Dr. Brady stepped in. "The good news is that he's alive."

"Does he know about his legs?" asked Tucker.

"There's no indication that he does," replied Dr. Forrest. "In fact, it's not that unusual during a post-op recovery. Many amputees believe the limbs are still there until they observe the results of the surgery for themselves."

"Can we see him?" asked Lacey.

Dr. Brady answered her. "Absolutely. In fact, we hope that your presence might help him become more alert and responsive to verbal stimuli. The key is to remain calm and speak words of encouragement. Owen needs to know he has your love and support."

Tucker quickly moved behind his mother and grabbed the handles of the wheelchair. "Let's go."

"All right, but remember, let's not overload him with information. Keeping him relaxed will be the best medicine right now."

Dr. Brady led the way as Lacey and Tucker followed close behind. Tucker had already seen his dad after the surgery, so he wasn't shocked by the sight of him without his lower legs. When Lacey saw him for the first time, she covered her mouth, and tears flowed down her cheeks. Her family's life often revolved around outside activities. Owen would be crushed when he learned of the amputation.

For now, however, she rejoiced in his being alive and awake. Tucker pushed her wheelchair until she was at Owen's side. Then, like her son had done before her, she disregarded her doctor's orders and pushed herself out of her chair to grasp the bed rails. She needed to be as close to Owen as possible. Tucker wrapped his arm around her waist and supported her so she could lean closer.

She wiped away the first flood of tears and regained her composure after a few sniffles. She lovingly touched his face and said, "Honey, I'm here for you. I love you so much."

Owen's eyelids fluttered and opened slightly, staring directly upward. Both Dr. Brady and Dr. Forrest stepped a little closer to the bed.

"Recognition," whispered Dr. Brady. "A great sign."

Lacey continued. "Tucker's here with me. Our son is a very brave young man. You'll be so proud of him."

Owen's eyes shifted from left to right. Then up and down. Tucker picked up on his eye movements and presumed his dad was searching for him. He continued to hold his mother and leaned over the bed.

"I'm right here, Dad. We're all together again."

Then Owen did something that sent elation through the minds of everyone in the room. He blinked rapidly, and a slight smile came over his face. Lacey began to cry again.

"That's right, Owen. We're all here. All three of us are together again, and we're gonna make it through this. You'll see. We love you so much. Just hang in and get—"

Lacey stopped mid-sentence as Owen's body convulsed, and then his chest heaved, lifting him off the bed. Alarms started going off, and lights flashed on the monitoring equipment on both sides of the bed.

Nurse Ruiz rushed around the back of Lacey and Tucker. She shouted to the doctors, "He's in V-fib!"

Ventricular fibrillation was a dangerous level of arrhythmia, or irregular heartbeat. Owen's heart rate elevated rapidly, and the cardiac monitor indicated rapid, erratic electrical impulses.

"What's happening?" asked Lacey in a loud voice.

"What's wrong with my dad?"

Dr. Brady approached Owen from the other side of the bed. Just as he arrived, Owen went into cardiac arrest and flatlined. A solid, horizontal line appeared on the electrocardiogram monitor affixed to Owen. It meant all electrical activity had ceased in the brain.

"Please move back," ordered Dr. Forrest. Ruiz assisted Lacey back into her wheelchair and brusquely pulled her against the wall. Another nurse was forceful with Tucker as well. They needed to save Owen's life, and now was not the time for politeness.

"No pulse!" shouted Dr. Forrest, who pressed two fingers to Owen's carotid artery.

Dr. Brady was pumping on Owen's chest in an effort to restart his heart. He shouted instructions as he did.

"Bag him!" A reference to the use of a large, balloon-like manual resuscitator that forces air into a patient's lungs.

"Push epi!" he ordered next, looking directly at the monitor and Ruiz. She immediately injected epinephrine into Owen's saline drip. Epinephrine increased the arterial blood pressure in an effort to reverse cardiac arrest.

"It's not working!" shouted Dr. Brady, who ferociously pumped his hands on Owen as he attempted CPR.

"Charge the paddles!" shouted Dr. Forrest. Dr. Brady stopped pumping Owen's chest and quickly peeled back his blankets to open up his hospital gown. His chest had been shaved, and strategically placed electrodes affixed to the electrocardiogram device were visible.

Ruiz handed the paddles to Dr. Forrest and then yelled, "Charged, two hundred!"

"Clear!" said Dr. Forrest, and the medical team immediately reacted by standing away from Owen. He placed the paddles and deployed the device.

Owen's body lurched upward as the strong electrical current passed through his heart's muscle cells, momentarily stopping the abnormal electrical energy and encouraging the normal heart beat to resume.

Everyone held their breath and studied the heart rate monitor. The horizontal line remained unchanged following the first attempt.

Dr. Forrest was not giving up. "Charge again!"

"Charged!"

"Clear!"

He tried again. Once again, the jolt of electric current forced Owen upwards, but as before, the monitor told the story. There was no response.

Dr. Brady frantically resumed chest compressions while Ruiz continued to manually force air into Owen's lungs. It had been almost six minutes. Generally, at least fifty to sixty percent of sudden cardiac arrest patients survive if defibrillation procedures take place within five minutes. On this day, the odds were not in Owen's favor.

Dr. Brady and Ruiz continued to fight for a miracle. He pushed on Owen's chest, his eyes darting to Lacey, who was wailing in grief over her husband, his patient that he tried to do everything to save.

"Push epi! Again!" His voice begged as he gave the directive. In his mind, he knew it was hopeless.

"Frank," said Dr. Forrest, who made eye contact with his colleague. All he had to do was slowly shake his head side to side. It was over.

Dr. Brady stepped back from Owen's bed and angrily ripped his gloves off and slammed them to the floor. "Time of death, 9:34."

The entire medical team looked down at Owen's dead body, tears rolling down their cheeks. One by one, they stopped to offer their condolences to Lacey and Tucker, who held each other as they wailed in agony. Finally, Dr. Brady apologized for not saving Owen and left them alone. For nearly an hour, they sobbed at his bedside. Hugging him. Squeezing his hand. Imploring God to make this nightmare end. Begging Him to bring back a loving husband and father who didn't deserve to die.

PART IV

———————

Day seventeen, Sunday, November 3

CHAPTER TWENTY-SEVEN

Sunday, November 3
Hickory, North Carolina

The next day, Peter woke up to the smell of bacon sizzling in a cast-iron skillet. The warmth from the wood-burning stove heated the Spencers' home while the top burners provided a cooktop to prepare warm meals. Peter said good morning to Anna and Charles before scampering outside to an outhouse that hadn't been used by the family for nearly eighty years. It had been placed back into service when the power went out permanently.

It was colder than the day before, and Peter shivered as he tried to urinate. He was anxious to get into town to learn more about these Uber trips, as Charles called them. He wasn't sure what he could trade, but he would try to gain a seat on one of the trucks heading south.

During their breakfast together, Peter was elated to learn that Charles was going to drive him into town and introduce him to a fellow truck driver he was loosely acquainted with. He thought an introduction would go a long way to gaining a ride.

The two men went alone so Anna could keep an eye on the

house. She and Peter shed a few tears as they said their goodbyes. He was in awe at the woman's fortitude and ability to keep her spirits up. Her husband had serious lung issues that required medical attention that was no longer available. His eventual death would likely be slow and painful.

They entered the Hickory Farmers Market, which was normally held at Union Square on Saturdays. Prior to the attacks, it had been so popular that the organizers had maintained a website complete with a calendar letting attendees know what vegetables they could expect to buy during what period of the year.

The town square was filled with pop-up shops, built in the morning and removed at night. Before the bombs fell, this had been a bustling public market filled with playing children, colorful flags and balloons, and customers who drove up from Charlotte to enjoy the ambience.

The mood was far different that morning. A single entrance forced people to file past the leery eyes of the market's organizers. To enter, you had to show residency or be accompanied by a resident. Peter would've never been granted access without Charles alongside. There were no children present. In the early days after the market began operating again, hungry kids would steal a handful of produce from the farmers. Rather than punish them, the organizers forbade them from being there.

Once inside, Peter began to study the faces of the attendees. They were lifeless. There was no laughter. No chatter. No greetings between old acquaintances. The shoppers wandered past the vendors' booths, gripping their barter item as if it were a bar of gold from Fort Knox. Only it wasn't nearly that valuable. Some held their wedding bands in their nervous, sweaty palms. Others carried a grocery tote bag of canned goods. And then there were those who offered themselves up in trade. Strong young men who offered to work the fields or act as security to the vendors. Women who offered up anything the vendors asked in exchange for food.

It was desperate and depressing. Peter couldn't believe America had been reduced to this. A nation that was once the greatest country on Earth was now something straight out of a dystopian movie. He took a deep breath and tried to put the despair out of his mind. He began to study the vendors as he searched for the truck drivers Charles had mentioned.

In that part of North Carolina, for early November, apples, leafy greens and broccoli were most prevalent. Throughout the year, there were plenty of peanuts and sweet potatoes. Today, the vendors sold more than locally harvested crops. There were tables with guns, ammunition, knives, and even swords. One man was selling gallons of gasoline while another offered a variety of pharmaceuticals.

Barter was the name of the game, and the most sought-after form of currency was precious metals like gold and silver. Many people toted drawstring bags full of pre-1964 U.S.-minted coins because they consisted of ninety percent silver. A few of the larger booths included jewelers with their magnifying equipment and jewelry tools. Some jewelers charged a fee to issue a letter of authenticity for a bracelet or ring. The customer would take the piece with the letter to another booth and make their purchase.

Credit cards were worthless, and most vendors considered U.S. paper currency to be a joke. Peter was fascinated by the dickering back and forth between the buyers and sellers. As he followed Charles through the crowd, he gripped his AR-15 a little tighter as many of the attendees eyed the powerful rifle. He wanted to loiter around the gun traders to determine what it was worth, but Charles, who was toting his oxygen tank on a wheeled cart, was on a mission to find a truck driver he recognized.

"There they are," said Charles as he turned his body slightly to address Peter. Peter was watching a transaction between an ammunition maker and a customer. It reminded him that bullets came at a premium as he heard the prices the ammo seller was demanding.

Peter turned his attention to Charles and followed him as the old man picked up the pace through the crowd. Just ahead was a man in his late sixties standing behind a folding table full of a variety of guns. Hunting rifles, shotguns, and several types of pistols. He unconsciously slid his AR-15 behind his back in a weak attempt to hide it from the prying eyes of the man and his two husky sidekicks, who turned out to be his children. Each of the boys held a shotgun at low ready as they stood guard over the truck-driver-turned-arms-dealer-turned-Uber-driver.

"Mornin'," the man mumbled to Charles as he sized up his customers. He exchanged a glance with one of his sons, who provided him an imperceptible nod. From that point, the young man never took his eyes off Peter's. "What can we do ya fer?" He had a heavy country accent that was all the more difficult to understand because he rolled a protruding toothpick around his mouth.

Charles furrowed his brow. "Aren't you Harvey Lawson's nephew? I used to drive trucks with him."

"I am. Who are you?" The man's response and demeanor were brusque.

"Charles Spencer and this here is Peter Albright. He's looking for a ride to Florida."

The man glanced at his other son and then looked around Charles to get a better look at Peter. He rose from the folding chair where he'd been seated.

"Well, this is your lucky day, Petey," the man began sarcastically. "We're pulling out for the Sunshine State this afternoon." His sons began to laugh at the reference to Florida as the Sunshine State. Apparently, the sun was no longer shining there, either.

"Okay," said Peter hesitantly. "I'd like a ride. Where in Florida are you headed?"

The sons laughed again. "We thought we'd see Mickey freakin' Mouse. Sound good to you, slim?" The bulky belly of one of the young men shook as he laughed.

"What you got to trade? That AR?" the father asked.

Peter sighed. He hadn't used the weapon yet, but it would be a great source of protection in a shoot-out. However, if he had a ride, the prospect of getting into a gun battle with a bunch of bad people was less likely. He began to remove the gun from his shoulder when Charles reached his hand over to stop him.

"Something better," began Charles in response. "How about I fill your tanks with diesel when you return?"

"They's seventy gallons in there." One of the sons spoke up, drawing a scowl from his father.

"Deal," the man responded before Charles could change his mind. The man asked to confirm that Charles actually had it, and it was agreed that the nephew of the former truck driving acquaintance could come over at lunch time to see for himself. After a handshake and a somewhat toothless smile from the truck's owner, Peter was told to return at two o'clock.

CHAPTER TWENTY-EIGHT

Sunday, November 3
Hickory, North Carolina

Peter returned at one, an hour sooner than he'd been instructed to by the man he began to refer to in his mind as Mr. Uber and his sons, Greyhound and Mack. The slighter thinner, taller son was Greyhound, as in the bus line. The shorter, chubbier son was Mack, as in the dump truck. The men had never offered their real names, and Peter didn't really care. He just wanted to get to Florida without a hassle.

Unfortunately, the hassle started before they left Union Square. Peter had wheeled in his bicycle with his tote bags after Charles gained him reentry into the market. The first order of business was to trade his bike for food. The best he could do was a box of twelve Clif bars, a nutritious energy snack used by hikers and runners.

He contemplated trading his duffel full of winter-weight hunting apparel but then thought better of it. It was colder everywhere, including Florida, he'd heard by eavesdropping on conversations in the market. He was pretty sure his dad hadn't been storing away fleece-lined cargo pants or woolen socks.

He was making his way toward Mr. Uber when suddenly a fistfight broke out in the center of the market. Two men were walloping on one another over a transaction, and then a third man jumped in. Soon, there were four or five guys pummeling one another, causing the stress levels of everyone in Union Square to rise. Including Mr. Uber.

When Peter arrived at the truck, the father and his sons were packing up their belongings. Mr. Uber's father was there to load up the table and weapons.

Peter stood at the back of the line of refugees waiting to climb aboard the military-surplus truck. A Hispanic man stood in front of him with his wife and son. He turned to Peter and offered his hand to shake.

"I'm Rafael Sosa."

"Peter Albright. Nice to meet you."

"This is my wife, Maria, and my son, Javier. We hope to get to Miami. How about you?"

"I live in the Keys," Peter responded. He nodded toward the truck. Several people were being assisted into the rear, open-air cargo box. "I thought they might cover it for us."

Rafael shrugged. The "M923A1s came with a cover kit as standard issue. This one is so old, it probably tore away over the years."

Peter furrowed his brow. "M what?"

"M923A1. A five-ton six-by-six. We used to call it Big Foot on account of the wheels and tires being so large compared to the frame. It has twice as much cargo capacity as its cousin the M35 deuce-and-a-half."

"We, as in military?" asked Peter.

"Former Army," Rafael replied. "Stationed at Camp Mackall over towards Fayetteville. My family and I were traveling home from vacation at Dollywood. After the nukes hit DC, we decided to head to her family's place in Miami. We ran out of gas and got stuck here. This is the only option as far as we can tell."

"Come on. Hurry up!" Greyhound barked at Rafael's wife and

son. Rafael snapped his head around and cast a dirty look at Greyhound, who sneered in return.

Peter glanced over his shoulder and saw there were a few stragglers waiting behind him. They didn't appear to be together as they nervously kicked at the ground and studied their surroundings.

"Come on, Petey," Greyhound said condescendingly.

Peter adjusted his load and inched toward the back of the military truck, assessing how he was going to hoist everything in the cargo bed.

Mr. Uber rounded the side of the truck. "Hold up! What the hell is all of this?"

Peter was confused, so he didn't respond.

"Come on, Petey," said the man's son. "Ya gotta an explanation?"

"For what?" Peter responded with a question of his own.

Mr. Uber got in Peter's face. "The old man paid for your transportation, pal. Not your worldly belongings. This stuff has to stay behind 'cause there ain't no room for your wardrobe."

"But I can rest them in my—"

"No exceptions, Petey," Greyhound said forcefully. He pointed his finger in Peter's chest.

Peter's blood boiled when the jerk touched him. He slapped his hand away and said with a snarl, "Peter. My name's Peter." He stepped closer toward the man, but Mr. Uber put his hand between them.

"Hey. Hey, now. We can work this out, right? Money solves everything. Here's the thing, Peter. If you look around, everyone has one bag. They're not greedy and entitled like you. You get one bag and a carry-on just like on a freakin' airplane. Wanna tote a duffel bag and a backpack? Fine. Everything else stays behind."

"You guys never told us that," complained Peter. "If I had known, then—"

Mr. Uber cut him off. He got right in front of Peter, and his son inched closer too. "You see these nice people behind you? They want your seat. They'd love for you to get the hell out of their way. Now, do you wanna ride or not?"

Peter glanced back at the anxious faces. They all had a single bag to carry.

"Yes, I wanna ride," Peter responded with gritted teeth, cracking his neck as he finished his sentence.

"Good," said Mr. Uber, stepping back a pace or two. He raised his right hand and waved his fingers toward him. "Gimme the AR."

"What?" Peter was incensed. "We had a deal!"

"Deal's changed, Petey!" yelled Greyhound.

"New deal," said Mr. Uber. "You can carry all this other shit in your lap, but the price of extra baggage is the rifle. Take it or leave it."

Peter sighed and ran his hand down his face. He'd already given up his bicycle, and there were no guarantees the other truck drivers were traveling south or would be any more reasonable than these assholes. He'd already given away the hunting rifle to Charles as a thank-you for his help.

He reluctantly removed the AR-15 from his shoulder and handed it to Mr. Uber. The man smiled and winked at Peter.

"Pleasure doin' business with ya," he said and then glanced over his shoulder at the three disappointed refugees. "Folks, we'll be back in five days to rustle up another load. We'll see ya then."

It was wishful thinking by Mr. Uber.

CHAPTER TWENTY-NINE

Sunday, November 3
Driftwood Key

Hank and Sonny waited nervously on the front porch of the main house for the first invited guest to Driftwood Key since the collapse. Well, invited was a term that simply differentiated Sonny's ex-sister-in-law, Monroe County Mayor Lindsey Free, from the armed attackers of the day before.

Word had spread quickly throughout Marathon of the nighttime gun battle. By the next morning, it was the topic of conversation at the daily briefing held by the Board of County Commissioners in Key West. Mayor Free, who'd been elected to represent District 2 encompassing Big Pine Key, had been elected mayor as well just over four years ago. Previously, she'd sat on the Marathon City Council and had been elected mayor of Marathon prior to that. Her relationship to the Albrights went back to childhood, as she was only a few years younger than Mike. Mayor Free's ex-husband was also the youngest of Sonny's five siblings.

Hank had been told in advance by Mike to expect something other than a social visit. It was going to be more of a courtesy call than anything. The sheriff, in light of the attack on Driftwood Key, felt compelled to give Mike a heads-up. In an unrelated decision reached by the Board of Commissioners, Mayor Free was prepared to take a tighter grip on her constituents.

"Sonny, you really shouldn't be here for this," said Hank as he finished a protein shake. He set it on the table next to his old friend's partially empty bowl of watered-down Frosted Flakes. They had powdered milk in their storage pantry, but Sonny thought it would be wasted on cereal.

"Let me at least say hello. Otherwise, she might think I'm hiding from her. Lindsey's a viper, Hank. If she smells weakness, you're a goner. Ask my brother."

"I heard. No wonder she's a politician. It suits her."

"So what does she want?" asked Sonny.

"I don't know for sure, but we're about to find out," replied Hank as he stood and pointed toward the driveway. A deputy sheriff driving a marked SUV slowly pulled toward the parking area joined to the bromeliad-lined walkway in front of the main house. The tropical plant bloomed once in its lifetime although the flowers usually lasted for a fairly long period of time. It was one of the features Hank's wife had introduced to greet guests with a lovely first impression when they walked to the front porch. Each day since nuclear winter began to take its toll, the beautiful tropical flowers withered and died.

Sonny walked down the steps to greet his former sister-in-law. "Hi, Lindsey. Well, I mean, Madam Mayor. This is official business, right?"

Hank chuckled to himself. *Nice touch, wingman.*

Lindsey leaned in to accept a peck on the cheek from Sonny before she responded, "Oh, not really. I heard this morning what happened to you folks last night. I've always held the Albrights in high esteem, and I simply worried about them, and you, of course."

Hank managed a smile. She was every bit the snake as she was growing up when she pitted boys against one another for the chance to kiss that picture-perfect smile while gazing into her enchanting hazel eyes. Many a man had been caught off guard by Lindsey's wily ways. He took a deep breath and was inwardly thankful he'd engaged in the gun battle last night. It better prepared him for what was coming.

"Good morning, Mayor," said Hank nonchalantly as he eased his hands into the pockets of his linen slacks. It was a little cool that morning, but he didn't have much else to wear. He'd bloodied his khakis moving dead bodies out of the way so a county flatbed wrecker could get the disabled pickup truck removed.

"Hi, Hank!" she said in a little too friendly manner. *She's up to something*, Hank thought. His level of awareness had just reached its peak.

Sonny excused himself and opened the door for the visiting dignitary and Hank. Her bodyguard deputy took up a position outside on the porch while Sonny made himself scarce. Hank and the mayor made small talk until they were settled into his office with the door closed. Then Hank utilized a communication method that had unnerved his kids on those few occasions they'd gotten out of line.

He said nothing.

After a moment of awkward silence, the mayor, who obviously had an agenda, spoke up.

"Hank, the deeper we get into this crisis, the more difficult it has become for me to both protect and care for our neighbors. None of us asked for this, and we're all trying to find a path forward that is both safe from the criminal element and sustainable by providing basic necessities to those who need it most."

"I bet you never imagined something like this when you were elected mayor," said Hank.

He was making a point that she may or may not have understood. Politicians need to be more than the people who spend tax dollars. They need to be visionaries of progress and collapse. To Hank, it's easy to be a politician when a nation or community is at its best. It's when the society begins to decline, and they all do, as history has proven, that the real leaders step up to shepherd their constituents through it.

"You're right about that," she replied before getting back to her agenda. "In any event, we've made great strides in removing nonresidents and preventing any newcomers from entering the Keys through our implementation of checkpoints. This has also enabled us to keep our law enforcement professionals like Jessica and Mike fully employed."

"They're very grateful for that. I imagine their paycheck will be pretty big when the county is able to actually deliver it."

Hank wished he'd never made the statement. He resented his family having to leave Driftwood Key when armed gunmen were roaming around with nefarious intentions. That said, they'd both impressed upon him the importance of having access to the world beyond Driftwood Key to gather information and acquire necessary supplies.

The mayor bristled at the implication the county's essential employees were working without pay despite the fact it was true. "I'm sure there will be a relief package coming out of Washington or Tallahassee when this is all over that compensates everyone. However, Hank, we have to get to the point where we turn the corner. That's why I'm here."

"How can I help?" he asked and then gulped. *Dammit, Hank. Two unforced errors. Get in the game!*

"Well, I'm glad you asked. I'm calling on everyone, business owners and local residents alike, to pitch in to help their neighbors. I refer to it as *shared sacrifice*. During these unprecedented times, we need those who have a little extra to assist those who are barely scraping by or who are without."

"Okay," said Hank, stretching the word out as he prepared for the big reveal.

"How are you folks making out here on Driftwood Key?" She glanced around Hank's office and through the windows. If one didn't know better, nothing appeared out of the ordinary except for the perpetually soot-filled cloudy skies and the lack of resort guests.

"We're, um, okay. Thanks."

The mayor leaned forward to the edge of the chair to look Hank in the eye. "I wasn't referring to how you were doing, Hank. I'm referring to what you can contribute to help sustain your neighbors and the community which you're a part of."

"What exactly are you asking for, Lindsey?" She was no longer the mayor in Hank's mind but, rather, Sonny's ex-sister-in-law.

"For one, we need more deputies to protect the community, as you well know."

Her tone of voice indicated to Hank that the conversation was now adversarial. He tried not to bare fangs.

"We gave at the office. Mike. Jessica. Remember them?"

The mayor wasn't satisfied with those already in her employ. "You, Phoebe, and Sonny are too old for the tasks we have in mind. Jimmy, however, would be a great addition to our border guards."

"We can't spare him. Jimmy's fishing abilities feed my family."

"I'll assign him a night shift so he can continue to do the fishing chores for you. Besides, did you forget how to fish since all this started?"

Dammit! Hank was cornered. He looked for an out. "I'll have to speak to his mom and dad." He tried to remind Lindsey that Jimmy had loved ones, and he wasn't just a tool he could loan out.

"Do that, and let Mike know so the sheriff can work him into the schedule. Now, let's talk about your hydroponics and greenhouses. How are they producing?"

"Not enough to feed the Florida Keys," replied Hank angrily. She'd already collected one scalp—Jimmy's. Now she wanted Hank to feed the Keys?

The mayor leaned back in her chair and crossed her legs. She studied Hank for a moment. It was time to play hardball.

"Listen, are you aware of the president's declaration of martial law?"

"No. Well, vaguely. Haven't had a chance to mosey down to the post office to read it."

"Well, let me give you the CliffsNotes, okay?" She stretched her hands away from her body with her palms face up to create an imaginary scale. One was much higher than the other.

She continued. "Here's how shared sacrifice works. Up here. In this hand, is Hank with his Driftwood Key Inn. Now, it's producing enough food out back to feed the Albrights, the Frees, and the many guests who normally fill your fancy bungalows.

"In this hand are a dozen or so families, your neighbors, who can't grow their own food or who couldn't afford to empty the store shelves before the wealthy did. Now they're hungry and they're desperate, and some are even dying of starvation. If we don't do something to help them, they're gonna be at your gate again tonight out of desperation.

"You might be able to kill them or turn them away. But tomorrow night, there'll be another group and then another and then another." She paused to catch her breath and allow the scales of shared sacrifice to even out.

"This is where shared sacrifice comes in. Driftwood Key contributes the food it would ordinarily feed to its guests. Otherwise, it might just go to waste, right? Meanwhile, that food goes to all of these families, which keeps them alive and, more importantly, content, so they don't do something rash like attack your precious inn."

She allowed her arms to wave up and down until they eventually balanced out. She adjusted herself in the chair and then gently folded her hands in her lap.

"Are you getting the picture, Hank?" she said with a toothy, disingenuous grin. "And let me make it just a little clearer for you. The president's declaration gives me the absolute authority to make it happen by whatever means necessary."

The conversation was over.

CHAPTER THIRTY

Sunday, November 3
Mount Weather Emergency Operations Center
Northern Virginia

As predicted by some in the Helton administration, China invaded North Korea. Following the near total destruction of Pyongyang and strategic DPRK military bases by U.S. nuclear missile strikes, the Beijing government ordered troops to the North Korean border. With South Korea in disarray as it tried to recover from the North Korean attack on Seoul, China saw an opening.

From a geopolitical perspective, China could never allow the U.S. to hold influence over the North, whether it be through improved relations with Pyongyang or the takeover of the Korean peninsula by Seoul.

The Chinese military incursion into North Korea occurred with remarkable swiftness. There was little left of the North Korean military, so they were unable to mount a defense. After the Chinese tanks crossed the Yalu River and their Chengdu J-20 fighter jets strafed the countryside to eliminate any pockets of resistance, they were welcomed by the North Korean people with open arms.

Chief of Staff Chandler had been a constant fixture by the president's side since those first few hours at Mount Weather. Now he was surrounded by a steady stream of aides who relayed messages to the president from world leaders. The two men cleared the president's office to speak privately.

"They've got to be out of their minds," the president lamented as he read the communiqués from world leaders. They want us to order the Chinese to stand down. I'm forced to beg them for parts to fix the damn power grid! I'm in no position to move on them militarily. And for what purpose? Defend North Korea?"

Chandler dropped the rest of the messages on the president's desk in front of him. The president swiped them to the side and began wringing his hands.

"Carter," began Chandler, who remained on a first-name basis with his friend when out of earshot of others, "in case nobody's noticed, we're screwed on our own. I don't see any of these nations shipping humanitarian aid or relief workers to the U.S. Where's the UN? Nobody is stepping in to bail us out. They always take from us, but now we need them to return the favor, and it's crickets on the other end of the line."

"Yeah, well, you're right, and the world will soon see what I think about fighting everyone else's battles," added the president. "Have you confirmed that the secretary of defense has recalled all of our military personnel except for the bare minimum necessary to defend our assets abroad?"

"They will be returning home within days. Now, are you okay without making a formal announcement? Normally, these things require press releases at a minimum."

"Screw 'em," said the president as he pulled the messages into a pile and dropped them into the trash can next to his desk. "Transparency is overrated. Let's talk about Texas."

Chandler plopped into the chair in front of the president's desk. He loosened his tie and glanced over toward the bar. This conversation required a drink. He glanced at his watch and thought, *It's five o'clock somewhere.* It was a phrase referencing happy hour, although it was used to justify having a cocktail prior to five in the afternoon. He got up from the chair, removed his jacket, and poured them both a scotch whisky, neat.

"Texas?" the president repeated as he stared at his old friend over the rim of his glass.

"Texas has taken the bold step of closing its entire state line, or border, if you will, to Americans traveling south."

"Harrison, yesterday that was rumor. Today, it's fact?"

"I'm afraid it's been confirmed. Their grid survived the cascading failure, and the EMP generated over Colorado barely reached the Panhandle. After Mexico closed its border with the U.S. to prevent an influx of our refugees, Texas stopped the flow of people crossing the state en route to Central America and even South America."

The president took another swig of his drink and winced. He remained calm as he spoke. "They can't do that. Do I need to personally call the governor and straighten her out?"

"Yes, I believe you should try. You know Texans. They're fiercely independent. They've managed to keep their power grid separate from the Eastern and Western Interconnection. As a result, they're positioned to recover from all of this faster than the rest of the nation."

"Maybe so, but that doesn't give them the right to reject American citizens in need. You can bet your ass they'd have their hand out if Dallas took a direct hit. They'd be begging for FEMA to send MREs and build tent cities."

Carter stood and refilled their glasses as he relayed more information to the president. "Apparently, this independent streak is contagious."

"Oh?" said the president in a tone reflective of his curiosity. "Is Hawaii threatening to secede?"

"No," Chandler replied as he got settled into his chair once again. "Monroe County, Florida."

"Where the hell is that?"

"The Florida Keys, mostly. Parts of the county extend on to the mainland, but it's the Keys that have pulled another one of these closed-borders stunts."

"How?"

"They've sent armed personnel to block the two bridges that connect the Keys to South Florida. First, they evicted any nonresidents. Then they established roadblocks to prevent any refugees who couldn't prove residency from entering. As a result, Miami has been inundated with homeless and stranded travelers, and the mayor is having a hissy fit."

"What's the Florida governor say?"

"He's just like his counterpart in Texas, complaining that he has a duty to protect the lives and property of his residents. He's considering similar measures at his state line at Georgia and Alabama."

"Geez," said the president, who shook his head in disbelief. "I'll reach out to him as well. He needs to be reminded the federal government and his fellow Americans are there for Floridians during hurricane season. He needs to be open to accept Americans who are trying to survive. And he'd better straighten out those people in the Keys, or I will."

CHAPTER THIRTY-ONE

Sunday, November 3
Central North Carolina

"Let's do this!" shouted Greyhound as he exchanged high fives with his portly brother. The younger man drove off with his grandfather, leaving Greyhound to drive the military cargo truck and his dad to navigate. The father and son had made this trip once before, attempting to use the interstate to travel. It had been a frustrating drive as they dodged gas-thirsty, stalled cars and people running along trying to climb into the cargo box. This trip, they'd take back roads.

Once they were on their way that afternoon, the paid passengers breathed a collective sigh of relief. The group was packed together on wooden bench seats with slat rails for backs. Their feet were buried under luggage. They huddled within themselves, partly out of apprehension surrounding the treatment by their escorts but mostly because of a chilling wind that began to blow from the north.

Peter sat next to Rafael and his family at the rear of the cargo box. There were a dozen others on board, including a family, several couples, and some single riders. They were a hodgepodge of refugees across the demographic spectrum. After twenty minutes of exchanging names and destinations, they began to tell their stories. Most were seeking warmer climates and rumors of fully functioning electricity. Others, like Peter, were hoping to reunite with family.

Only one person, Peter, had witnessed one of the warheads detonating in Washington. Everyone wanted to hear about it. Yet they didn't. Peter could see it in their eyes and changed demeanor as he continued. An overwhelming sadness seemed to come over the group as the realization of what had happened to America soaked in.

The cargo truck rumbled along through the small community of Hildebran before approaching the underpass at Interstate 40 west of Charlotte. The group was silent as they watched thousands of people walking toward the mountains. Some pushed shopping carts while others pulled luggage on wheels. They were all seeking refuge away from the cities.

The truck chugged along down Henry River Road when it suddenly slowed. The passengers became nervous, and Peter eased his hand into his backpack to get a grip on his pistol. He was relieved that Mr. Uber and his dimwit son hadn't confiscated all of his weapons.

On the left side of the truck, a tall wooden fence appeared along the roadway. Through the heavily wooded forest, a smattering of buildings could be seen. Then a gated entry came into view with several armed guards patrolling behind it. A long gravel driveway led up a hill through a canopy of oak trees.

"What's this place?" asked one of the passengers.

"That's where they filmed the *Hunger Games* movies," replied an older man.

"Really?" asked a child who was sitting next to him.

The old man explained, "This was once Henry River Mills Village, an old ghost town that used to be a yarn factory. This part of Carolina was booming back then, and little communities like this sprang up everywhere. When the big factories moved into Charlotte, the people left the village for the city."

"You said something about the *Hunger Games* movie," interrupted the child's mother.

"Yeah, right. Anyway, the place was abandoned, and the folks who bought it years ago allowed it to be used as a movie set. This was used as the setting for District 12 where the start of the movie took place."

"It doesn't look like a movie set now," mumbled Peter.

"Those guys were ex-military," whispered Rafael as he leaned into Peter. "They were disciplined and carried themselves like they were well-trained operatives."

The older man continued. "Anyway, recently, the place was bought by a couple out of Florida. Supposedly won the lottery. They fenced the entire place like a fortress or some such."

The truck slowly rumbled across a bridge high above the Henry River. Two more armed guards were positioned on the other side behind concrete barriers. They never blinked as their eyes scanned the cargo truck and its passengers. They held their weapons at low ready, just in case.

Peter craned his neck to study the compound from the south side of the river as they continued up a hill. Eventually, the former movie set turned haven, for some, disappeared from sight. He got settled in with the others as the monotonous drone of the diesel engines began to put nearly everyone to sleep.

Their trip took them through the heart of the Old South. Towns like Gaffney, Saluda, and Barnwell in South Carolina were encountered without incident. Once in Georgia, they drove through Statesboro toward Jesup.

They'd been on the road for nearly eight hours, and the passengers were getting antsy. Mr. Uber had only afforded them one pit stop, as he called it, to stretch their legs and relieve their bladders in a looted Huddle House. He and his son swapped driving duties, during which time a passenger overheard them say they planned on stopping near Jesup, Georgia, to refuel and sleep.

During the ride, Peter struck up conversations with every one of his fellow passengers. Some were more open than others about their destination and the price they'd paid for inclusion on the trip. Most had traded guns or silver coins. The elderly couple had given up their wedding bands. One family had turned over the keys to their vacation home outside Asheville, North Carolina.

The two people he was most concerned about were a mother in her late thirties and her daughter, who appeared to be college age. They were closed off about where they were headed and why. Plus, they shut Peter down when he asked what they'd had to barter to get a ride on the truck. The daughter closed her eyes and hung her head low. Her mother shed a tear and looked away as she wiped her face with her sweater sleeve.

Peter had heard rumors of women being forced to trade sex for food, gasoline, and, apparently, a lift to Florida. It angered him that the two men sitting in the heated cab, laughing and swapping a bottle of whiskey, had enticed these two women with a ride by demanding them to humiliate themselves that way.

At one point toward the end of the ride, murderous thoughts crept into his head. He replayed the events in the CVS pharmacy that night. Was that murder or self-defense? Or was his shooting of the four men in rapid succession a preemptive first strike? A kill-or-be-killed scenario that required him to murder others to protect himself.

Then he took his analysis further. Did he have the right to take the lives of Mr. Uber and his ingrate son because they'd asked for, and received, sexual favors in exchange for an uncomfortable seat on this truck? Had America descended into a level of lawlessness where killing could be justified on moral grounds?

Peter grappled with these issues for miles, and as a result, the time flew by as Greyhound slowed the cargo truck at the entrance of the aptly named Motel Jesup. The twenty-two bungalow-style units were arranged in an L-shaped structure connected by covered walkways. The affordable accommodations were the epitome of the quintessential, roadside motor court of days gone by. Before the nation's interstate system provided travelers the opportunity to zip from one point to another at seventy-plus miles an hour, state and federal highways had connected small towns together. Within each small town, there were motor courts.

Many had been built in the late forties as soldiers returned from war and families reconnected by taking long driving trips. The freestanding buildings were quaint and modestly furnished in order to keep the nightly room rate low. Most had a bed and foldout sofa.

The Motel Jesup had plenty of vacancies that night. As in, all of the rooms were empty. Looters had broken into them to take the bedding. They'd stolen the remaining complimentary bottled water and Lance crackers. The toilet paper and towels had been removed, as were the trial-size toiletries. All that remained were the mattresses and perhaps a few pillows.

The cargo truck rumbled to a stop, and Mr. Uber stumbled out of the cab. He reeked of liquor as he waddled to the back gate.

"All right, people, this is where we'll hole up for the night." His words came out slowly and slurred.

His son, Greyhound, was less inebriated and began to order everyone out of the truck. "You heard him. Let's go! It'll be dark soon. And cold, too."

Peter had been the last to be loaded into the cargo compartment, so he was the first to be removed. He tossed his duffel bags out first and began to climb out of the back when Greyhound interfered.

"Hey, let me give you a hand."

Instead of helping Peter, he tugged on his pants leg, causing his foot to slide off the steel bumper. Peter slipped and lost his grip on the back gate. He struck his chin hard on the metal and landed flat on his back with a thud, reinjuring the bruises he'd received days before.

Had he not lost his breath momentarily, matters might have escalated. That, and Rafael's quick actions saved a life—either Peter's or Greyhound's. He jumped out of the truck and helped Peter sit up. He turned and faced Greyhound.

"We've got this," he snarled.

"Good for you, beaner," hissed Greyhound, using a derogatory slur often associated with people of Mexican descent.

Rafael was undeterred. "I'm Cuban," he fired back although he didn't expect the racist to understand why the *beaner* reference was misdirected.

Greyhound sneered at Rafael and said, "No matter. My precious cargo is the last to unload. Move it!"

The rest of the group made their way out of the cargo hold. Peter lagged behind while everyone else chose a cabin. He watched as the mother and daughter hesitantly exited the truck. They knew what was in store for them, as did Peter. The question was what, if anything, would he do about it.

CHAPTER THIRTY-TWO

Sunday, November 3
Jesup, Georgia

The Federal Correctional Institution located just south of Jesup was a medium-security prison that housed male inmates primarily incarcerated for drug and white-collar crimes. During the rolling blackouts that swept the southeast, state and federal prison officials were faced with a significant challenge. They were responsible for tens of thousands of inmates who'd been incarcerated for a wide range of crimes from petty offenses to capital murder. As the grid failed, they found themselves unable to perform the basic functions required to house the inmates. So they turned to the courts for guidance.

Like most governmental agencies, the United States court system was in disarray following the nuclear attacks. All hearings were cancelled. Judges and their staffs remained home as the blackouts began to occur. The Department of Justice offered little in the way of guidance as the entire federal government adopted a wait-and-see approach.

Then the temporary rolling blackouts became permanent. As a result, prison administrators began to make judgment calls. With their correctional staff operating at a bare minimum, they were unable to control, much less feed, their entire populations. Their solution was to review the case files of the inmates and release them from prison based upon their level of offense. Short-termers and nonviolent offenders were sent out in the first wave. The medical inmates with harsher sentences were next. Then on day eight following the nuclear attack on the U.S., the floodgates were opened.

Day after day, these inmates were given street clothes and a kick in the pants as the prison doors were opened. They were reminded that they were not truly free, as they were expected to report back to their designated prison facility once the crisis was over. Most of the inmates were unable to hide the smirks on their faces when given this instruction. In their minds, once they left, they were free.

However, they had no place to go and no way to contact friends and family. At FCI Jesup, two thousand federal prisoners walked through Wayne County, Georgia, aimlessly, most without a plan as to what to do next.

That morning, the final group of eight inmates was released from the medium-security facility. They were the *snitches*, informants who'd cooperated with authorities to help convict others like them. They were eight men who'd committed crimes of murder in various degrees, but because of their cooperation with the DOJ, they were given more relaxed, bucolic accommodations than the concrete and steel environs of the federal penitentiary in Atlanta.

Chris Stengel and his cellmate, Benjie Reyes, had spent eight years at the Jesup prison. They'd both committed gang-related murders in Atlanta before rolling on their brethren. At Jesup, they'd managed to avoid the scrutiny of correctional officers as they ran their hustles ranging from bringing in contraband cell phones to drugs in exchange for commissary and other favors.

That afternoon, they walked out together and immediately contemplated a variety of criminal acts to make their lives better. Booze. Drugs. Stolen vehicle. Women. Their laundry list was not imaginative. They were like wild animals released from captivity.

Both men had family in Savannah, and they'd always daydreamed about living on the ocean. As far as they were concerned, the real estate market was wide open for them. They'd find a nice McMansion on the sea. Kill the owners. And get settled into a beach chair with their toes buried in the sand.

As they walked up the highway, they tried to recall the distance to Savannah. Stengel thought it was about sixty miles or so. The two men had remained fit by walking the track around the outer perimeter of the medium-security facility. Exercising made up the vast majority of their day when they weren't working their jobs in the kitchen at eighteen cents per hour. A five-hour walk at a steady pace would yield fifteen to twenty miles of exercise. With their adrenaline levels, they'd committed to doubling that pace, which meant they could roll into Savannah sometime the next evening.

They walked northbound on U.S. 301 after grabbing some snacks and a couple of bottles of tequila from a liquor store in the process of being looted. Reyes found a tire iron lying outside the motorcycle repair shop nearby, a favorite tool utilized by burglars of commercial buildings.

It came in handy when they approached Babs's insurance. They didn't expect to find anything of value in the small office building, but the place hadn't been looted yet, so the two decided to take a look. Twenty minutes later, they emerged with a backpack full of snacks and bottled water, together with some clothing found in a coat closet. Most importantly, for Stengel anyway, he scored an aluminum softball bat. Before they left, he even got in a few practice swings.

The famed New York Yankees manager, Casey Stengel, would've been impressed by his very distant relative's swing. Former inmate Stengel bashed to smithereens virtually everything in the office that was breakable. There was no particular reason to do so other than the fact he had more than a decade of pent-up violent tendencies to satisfy.

However, the smashing of the insurance agency wasn't enough. He had other urges, too. And as Stengel and Reyes walked up the highway, high on tequila and their newfound freedom, opportunity crossed their path at the Motel Jesup.

CHAPTER THIRTY-THREE

Sunday, November 3
Motel Jesup
Jesup, Georgia

Peter entered the motel room at the far end of the complex from where Mr. Uber and Greyhound took up residency for the night. As he suspected, the mother and daughter must've agreed to trade their bodies for a ride to Florida. Through gritted teeth, Peter watched the two men paw all over the women as they led them to their respective rooms. It was obvious they were being forced into having sex with the men, as the daughter began to cry after Mr. Uber and her mother shut the door behind them.

Peter considered his options as his blood boiled inside him. He paced the floor of his room, trying to put the visual of what was about to happen to the women out of his mind. He retrieved both of his handguns from his sling backpack and confirmed the magazines were full of bullets. He shoved one into the waistband of his pants, and he held the other inside his coat pocket. With firm resolve, he marched back outside and began to walk on the covered sidewalk toward the other side of the motel.

Suddenly, Mr. Uber emerged from his room and began pounding on his son's door. The still-dressed degenerate appeared, angry at the interruption. The two men exchanged words, and after hurling threats at the two women, warning them to stay in their room, they marched off with purpose toward the cargo truck. Seconds later, they were pulling out and heading north on the highway in the direction they'd just come from.

Peter was confused by the activity, but he used their absence to make his move. He hustled along the walkway, narrowly avoiding a collision with several of the refugees, who'd exited their rooms at the sound of the loud diesel truck leaving the motel.

"What's going on?"

"Are they leaving us?"

Peter ignored their questions because he didn't have any answers. He supposed they were stranded or, he thought, they might have a rendezvous nearby to refuel. Mr. Uber seemed to know the area well enough to have the Motel Jesup as his planned stop for the evening. He must have someone nearby providing him diesel fuel for the large-capacity tank.

By the time he reached the two end units near the motel's office, everyone was commiserating in the parking lot except for the mother and daughter. Peter approached the mother's room first. He knocked brusquely on the door.

"Ma'am, this is Peter. They've left for now. Will you please open up?"

He could hear her shuffling around the room. A shadow appeared by the curtains, and then the door slowly opened. Her eyes were swollen from crying, and her nose continued to run. She nervously wiped the mucus onto her sleeve.

"Did they leave?" she said in a loud whisper, her eyes darting around in fear.

"Yes, but I don't know why," replied Peter.

"I do," said a sheepish voice to his right. It was the daughter.

The two women ran into each other's arms and began to cry uncontrollably. After a moment, they broke their embrace, and the mother searched her daughter's eyes for answers to the obvious question.

Peter had watched similar scenes unfold on television programs, but nothing compared to the real-life angst shared by two women who dreaded the inevitable assault they would be forced to endure. In that moment, he knew what had to be done, and he would carry out the task without remorse or compunction.

He averted his eyes to scan the parking lot. With no electricity and, thus far, no other traffic, the rumbling of the Cummings diesel engine would provide him some warning of the men's return. However, he needed to come up with a plan.

"Ladies, um, I'm sorry. Um, you said you know why they left."

"Yes," replied the daughter. "They have a friend who works at the paper mill we passed. He's going to let them fill up their truck."

Peter's suspicions were confirmed. Now for the hard part. He addressed the mother.

"Listen. We don't have much time. Are they going to …?" His voice trailed off. He didn't have the courage to say the word rape out loud. Not that it mattered. The mother knew exactly what he wanted to ask. She simply nodded rapidly and began to cry. The women held each other again, shaking as the tears rolled down their faces. Peter imagined the deal with Mr. Uber and son had been struck with trepidation back at Hickory. However, reality had hit them, and they clearly were unable to go through with it. Nor should they.

Rafael approached them. "What's going on?"

Peter motioned for him to step a few paces away from the women. "Those assholes went back up the highway to refuel. Rafael, we don't have much time. They're gonna rape these two. Plain and simple. And I'm not gonna let it happen."

Rafael studied Peter's eyes and glanced over at the mother and daughter, who continued to cry, before looking toward the highway. Then he said something Peter hadn't asked for, much less expected.

"I'll help you."

"Wait, you can't. Your family might be—"

Rafael cut him off by calling for his wife. "Maria! Please. Come!"

Maria walked briskly across the parking lot, and Rafael met her halfway. After a brief exchange, they approached the two women. Peter joined them.

"This is my wife, Maria," Rafael began as the two women focused their attention toward her. "Please go with her to our room and stay for a while."

"But he said he would—" The daughter tried to relay the threat she'd received before Maria interrupted.

"No, honey. None of that is going to happen. You must hurry. Come with me."

The mother turned to Peter with sullen, but hopeful eyes. "Are you sure? They have guns."

"We're sure. Go."

Rafael gently placed his arm behind their backs and urged them to follow his wife. Then he issued instructions to the rest of the passengers.

"Everyone! Listen to me. Go back to your rooms and barricade the doors. Stay away from the windows and don't come out until we say so. Do you understand?"

"Why?"

"What's happening?"

"Why did they leave us?"

Off in the distance, the roar of the cargo truck's engine could be heard as the driver shifted gears. Peter ran to Rafael's side. He pulled the weapon from his waistband and handed it to Rafael grip first.

"They're coming back."

Rafael shouted at the others, "Hurry. Get in your rooms. Now!"

At the sight of the two men brandishing their weapons, the other passengers became frightened and scampered back to their rooms. Peter and Rafael eased back under the canopy and prepared to fight.

"What are you thinking?" asked Peter.

"We wait in the rooms for them. They're expecting the women to be there. They'll find us instead."

"Take 'em out?" asked Peter, wanting to confirm Rafael was prepared to kill the men, just as he was.

"Without hesitation," came the response.

Peter made a fist and presented it to Rafael, who immediately bumped it in return. They moved quickly to get into position.

Barely a minute later, the truck slowed and eased into the parking lot of the motel. Peter's heart raced as he assumed the role of assassin. He wiped the beads of sweat off his forehead that began to drip toward his eyebrows despite the chilly temperatures. The truck shut off, and the sound of the heavy steel doors slamming indicated the men were heading his way. Using the barrel of his gun, he nudged the musty nylon curtain aside to watch for Mr. Uber's approach. Then his eyes grew wide.

"What the hell?"

CHAPTER THIRTY-FOUR

Sunday, November 3
Driftwood Key

One would think during the apocalypse that people would have all kinds of free time on their hands. No jobs. No television. No extracurricular activities. Wrong. Every moment of every day was dedicated to sustaining themselves through growing food or fishing. Plus, as external threats grew, security became tantamount. If you can't defend it, it isn't yours.

It took a day and a half after the mayor's contentious visit for Hank to meet with Sonny, Phoebe and Jimmy. This was followed by a serious conversation with Mike and Jessica around the bonfire on the beach. For the first time that Hank could remember, the group discussed the fate of Driftwood Key without passing out adult beverages.

"What did you think of the martial law declaration?" Hank asked his brother.

Mike paced through the sand, periodically stopping to mindlessly flatten out a mound only to build it up again with his feet. "It's pretty simple. The only people around here who are *free* happen to have that word as their last name. The president has taken over every aspect of our country while eviscerating the Bill of Rights. Lindsey's threats are real and could be backed up by force if necessary."

Jessica wasn't so sure. "Come on, guys. How far would she go?"

"I don't know, Jess," replied Mike. "But the way that thing reads, what's ours is theirs. Hell, they could strip it all away if they want. Food. Guns. Boats. The damn deed to the property!"

"I just can't believe it would go that far," said Jessica. "People would never stand for it."

"Some might," mumbled Hank.

"Whadya mean?" she asked.

"Think about it. How many residents or businesses have an operation close to what we have here? Very few, if any. Right? So who's gonna stand up to Lindsey and whatever kind of force she employs to take what we have? Us and a handful of others. The majority of the rest might welcome her actions."

Jessica grimaced. She still couldn't believe these types of drastic measures were being contemplated. "But, Hank, the mayor has to know if they took everything we have and kicked us off the Keys, there wouldn't be enough to feed all the mouths who weren't ready for this."

"Jessica, if you saw the look in her eyes yesterday, you'd know that she meant business. We've known Lindsey for a long time. She's conniving, but once she has the power, she doesn't bluff."

Mike finally sat down. "What's the plan?"

Hank took a deep breath and relayed his thoughts. "We give them something. Just a little bit at a time."

"Like what?" asked Jessica.

"For starters, Jimmy has volunteered to be deputized."

"Jesus!" said Mike, who leapt out of his chair and began pacing again. "Do you know what they're doing with these deputies? They're sending them with a rifle to the checkpoints to process people who want in. People demanding entry pull weapons at the border checkpoint all the time."

"Shhh." Jessica admonished her husband to keep his voice down. "Don't tell Phoebe and Sonny. They'll freak out."

Hank asked, "Can you work with the sheriff to keep him off the checkpoints?"

"I can try, but Lindsey has him wrapped around her finger. The whole department is talking about the change he's undergone. Prior to the last several days, there was never any love lost between them. Now they're thick as thieves."

Hank laughed. "Maybe that's it. To the victors go the spoils."

"Whadya mean?" asked Jessica.

"What I mean is this happens all the time when political leaders get too much power. They make sure they get theirs and their families are taken care of. The rest of us have to go along with this shared sacrifice notion, but the same rules don't apply to them."

Mike stopped pacing. "Rules for thee but not for me."

"Pretty much," mumbled Hank.

Jessica asked, "After we send them Jimmy, weakening our own defenses, then what? They want food, too?"

"Yes, but I don't plan on giving it to them," replied Hank. "I've gotta talk with Sonny and Phoebe about cutting back our production to feed just us."

"Patrick, too?" asked Jessica.

"Squirrely scumbag," said Mike, who was in a testy mood. "The more I interact with that guy, the more I'm ready to send him packin'."

"I can't disagree, Mike," said Hank. "I'm still not sure why he wasn't ready to go to the hospital after he was up and moving around. And his story seems to be changing."

"I'm getting the same vibe," said Jessica. "He tells me one thing about his recollection of that night, but it's different than what he's told Sonny or Phoebe."

"He doesn't tell me anything," said Mike.

"Sit down, Mike. Please," said Hank, urging his brother to stop pacing. The detective slid into his Adirondack chair and listened as Hank relayed his thoughts. "He seems capable of speaking freely with everyone but you and me. He won't respond to you at all, feigning amnesia or some such. When he talks to me and the subject comes up, he acts like he's on his last dying breath and needs rest. Yet Jimmy tells me that Patrick turns into some kind of Chatty Cathy when he's around."

"Like I said, squirrely," said Mike.

"What do we do?" asked Jessica.

"Let's work on easing him out," replied Hank. "He's become more mobile, even finding his way onto the porch of his bungalow. I'm gonna get Sonny and Phoebe on board with helping him build up his strength with the ultimate goal of sending him to his own house."

Mike added, "I don't like the thought of him wandering around the inn. Nobody has seen our resources."

Hank added, "Even Lindsey, whose view was obscured by palm trees and plants."

"We'll keep tabs on Patrick," said Jessica.

Hank closed out the Patrick topic. "The other thing that concerns me about him being here is if word gets back to Lindsey. She'll counter my refusal to feed all of Marathon with an alternative."

"Like what?" asked Jessica.

Hank frowned as he made eye contact with the others. "Like moving the displaced and homeless into the inn."

CHAPTER THIRTY-FIVE

Sunday, November 3
Motel Jesup
Jesup, Georgia

Out of nowhere, two men came racing from behind the motel's office, screaming like banshees. One was waving a tire iron over his head while the other pointed toward Greyhound with an aluminum baseball bat. The attack caught Mr. Uber and his son off guard. The two men closed on them in a matter of seconds, and the initial blows sustained were near fatal.

The man with the tire iron did the most damage. He embedded the hooked end into the back of Mr. Uber, who immediately crashed to the asphalt pavement. Greyhound tried to shield his body from the vicious swing taken by the man with the aluminum baseball bat. From inside the motel room, Peter could hear the bones in his forearm shatter over the cries of pain.

The other man slammed a foot on Mr. Uber's back and tried to wrestle the tire iron free. He pushed it forward and back, then side to side until it came loose along with bone, tissue and blood. He released an evil laugh and reached back for another blow. Only one was necessary, but multiple were dealt. Like a deranged lunatic, the man pummeled Mr. Uber's neck and the back of his head until it was unrecognizable. It was a gruesome, gory display of anger and horror.

Inspired by his accomplice's acts, the second man took another swing at Greyhound with the aluminum bat, striking the defenseless man's ribs. The audible crack caused chills to run through Peter's body. Chills that forced him into action.

He'd been frozen in place by the display of murderous brutality. Somehow, the beatdown administered by the two men was barbaric compared to the more humane method of a bullet to the skull that Peter had planned for them. Nonetheless, he had to act as he observed the tire-iron killer retrieve the cargo truck's keys from Mr. Uber's pockets. Now he had to defend his group's greatest asset, the truck.

Peter ran out of the motel room with his gun pointed at the men, who were now rushing toward the cargo truck. "Stop, or I'll shoot!"

It was a phrase that came to mind, and one he immediately regretted saying. It only served to warn the men, who rushed around the back side of the truck for safety. The sound of the driver's side door creaking gave Peter a new sense of urgency.

Rafael emerged from his room, and he ran toward the truck with his weapon drawn. He was forty feet away when shots rang out. Bullets skipped along the pavement, splitting the distance between Peter and Rafael. One of the men had retrieved a weapon from inside the truck and was now firing bullets toward them from underneath.

Rafael peeled off to the left to encircle the back of the truck. Peter didn't know what to do, so he moved to the right and then immediately back to the left to avoid being a stationary target. He fired a couple of rounds under the truck chassis in an attempt to distract the shooter or at least provide Rafael some cover.

Then a barrage of gunfire filled the air. Rafael had reached the back of the cargo truck and was firing at the shooter. Peter added a couple of rounds of his own, which ripped up the asphalt underneath the truck.

Without warning, the passenger-side door flung open, and Peter suddenly found himself exposed. Several shots were fired by the second gunman, which ricocheted off the pavement at Peter's feet. He danced to the left and fired two rounds into the door, which easily repelled them.

Rafael fired again and hit his target. The man groaned in pain, and Peter saw his body hit the ground at the truck's left front fender. A single gunshot rang out as Rafael confirmed the kill.

The truck's engine started, blowing a thick puff of black smoke out of the exhaust.

"Hell no!" shouted Peter as he ran toward the passenger side.

The truck lurched forward as the driver popped the clutch too quickly. Peter closed the gap and was about to grab the door handle when another shot was fired. Blood and brain matter sprayed throughout the cab, coating the passenger window.

Peter was startled by the sudden appearance of the attacker's brain matter on the glass and fell backwards onto the asphalt. He groaned as his tailbone struck the parking lot.

"You okay?" Rafael shouted his question.

Peter sat upright and rested his elbows on his knees as he caught his breath. His handgun lay on the ground in front of him. "Um, yeah! Are they dead?"

"Two KIA," he replied as he shut off the motor.

Seconds later, the second attacker fell to the pavement with a thud, joining his partner's dead body. Peter stared at the two bloodied corpses for a moment before turning his attention to the battered bodies of Mr. Uber and his son. He tried to recall the massacre he'd experienced in Abu Dhabi. He closed his eyes and shook his head in disbelief. It was all so senseless. But then, so was everything that had happened since Tehran nuked Israel. That had triggered a series of events that led him to committing murder. He looked to the sky and then glanced toward the south. He wondered what he'd encounter between there and home.

CHAPTER THIRTY-SIX

Sunday, November 3
La Junta, Colorado

The night before, Lacey had been given a sedative to force her to rest. She was terribly distraught over losing the love of her life. She and Tucker comforted one another, and eventually the medical staff tried to step in to get Lacey to rest. The thought of being apart agitated them both, something Dr. Brady was trying to avoid. After Lacey had been returned to her room, a leather recliner used by many a father-to-be in the birthing suites of the ob-gyn department was brought in for Tucker.

He'd rejected the offer of medications to relieve his anxiety and help him rest. That night he fought sleep out of fear that he'd never awaken. Eventually, his mental exhaustion won the battle, and he slept soundly next to his mother's bed until morning, when the ICU nurses began to make their rounds.

Lacey was the first to wake. She quietly eased out of bed and made her way to the bathroom without the assistance of the wheelchair or the walker the nurses had provided her. As she sat on the toilet, emptying her bladder, she buried her face in her hands as the realization of Owen's death continued to soak into her.

The world had gone to shit. Their life filled with love and happiness and successes had been replaced with a home likely destroyed by a nuclear warhead and a husband who'd been taken away by a fluke weather event. As she finished, she implored herself to hike up her big-girl panties and be the rock her teenage son needed to cope with the loss of his father. However, if she couldn't deal with Owen's death, how could she expect Tucker to do so?

When she came out of the bathroom, she found the lights in her room dimmed and Tucker gone. Her door was cracked slightly, so she presumed he'd slipped out quietly without telling her. She looked around the room and noticed one of her duffel bags sitting on a small table in the corner.

With her strength rapidly coming back to her, she decided it was time to clean up a little bit, hoping the change of appearance and clothing might drag her out of this melancholy state of mind.

She ran her hands down the flannel pajamas given to her by one of the local residents. She assumed they were hers to keep, but just in case, she folded them neatly on a chair after she took them off. She quickly slipped on her favorite hiking pants, a thermal undershirt, and a hooded, camouflage sweatshirt. She looked like she was going hunting, but in reality, she planned on leaving the hospital that day although she presumed the doctors would insist she was putting herself at risk.

Lacey needed to deal with Owen's burial, but moreover, she needed to get away from the place where he died. She didn't fault the medical team at Arkansas Valley in the least. They'd done an admirable job in treating her entire family under the circumstances. But for Lacey, it was part of the healing process to leave the place where her husband had died less than a day before.

She'd just finished dressing and turned her lights up when Tucker reappeared, followed by Sheriff Mobley.

"Mom, there's somebody I'd like you to meet."

Lacey stood next to her bed and casually rested her left hand on the mattress. She didn't want anyone to notice that she was still unsteady on her feet.

"Hi, Mrs. McDowell, I'm Sheriff Shawn Mobley. Please, um, please know that our entire community is grieving with you and Tucker. Our hearts ache for you, and I want you to know that Owen's memory will live on in Otero County for many years."

Lacey smiled and then wiped away a few tears. Throughout the ordeal, she'd appreciated the kindness and love everyone had shown them.

"Thank you, Sheriff. I wish you could've known Owen. He was perfect in so many ways."

Tucker walked toward his mother and provided her a cup of coffee. He'd added just the right amount of cream and sugar. She took a sip and smiled at her son as she mouthed the words *thank you.*

"Some ladies made you a few pastries. You know, if Dr. Brady approves."

The door opened wider, and Dr. Brady suddenly appeared with a clipboard, a Styrofoam cup of coffee, and a disapproving look.

"Lacey, just where do you think you're going?" he asked as he looked her up and down.

"Good morning, Doctor. I'm feeling much better, and there are some things I need to deal with."

"More important than your health?" he asked, confirming he wasn't happy with her actions.

"It's just. Well, I need to breathe. I mean, I need to get out—"

Tucker noticed his mom getting emotional, so he rushed to her side. He hugged her and then helped her sit down.

Dr. Brady set the clipboard on the bed and handed his coffee to Sheriff Mobley, who continued to watch with a concerned look on his face. Dr. Brady approached Lacey and crouched in front of her.

"Lacey, I get it. You wanna run as fast as you can and as far away from here as you can. I don't blame you. But you're not a hundred percent yet. I'm talking about mentally and physically."

Lacey was sobbing. She choked up as she spit out the words. "I feel better. I even dressed myself. I'm fine."

"You're still recovering from a dangerous, traumatic injury. Coupled with your loss, it's premature to be galivanting around. Please consider staying in the hospital one more day."

"Are you not gonna discharge me?" she asked, wiping away the tears.

He chuckled. "We're a little short on formalities nowadays. Of course you're free to go. I'm just concerned for you."

She began to reel off a litany of things she needed to do, from getting their truck fixed to finding gasoline. Sheriff Mobley stepped in to reassure her.

"Mrs. McDowell—" he began before she interrupted him.

"Lacey."

"Okay, Lacey. We have your truck right down the street, and it's repaired. We've filled up your fuel cans. The only thing left to do was a suggestion I made to Tucker."

"What was it?"

"Black & Blue stands out too much for a long trip, Mom. We need to make it look busted up."

"You want to bust up Owen's truck?" she asked, causing a few more tears to flow.

Sheriff Mobley quickly replied, "No. No. Not at all. Just a unique paint job to make it less noticeable, that's all. You can fix it back later."

She furrowed her brow and then thought for a moment. "I have to bury my husband."

Dr. Brady and Sheriff Mobley exchanged glances. "Lacey, the ground is frozen solid now. I took the liberty to speak with Curtis Peacock at the funeral home down the street. He has a crematory at their place. It'll take some creative work with our portable generators, but he said he can help."

The cremation process requires superheating the retort, or the cremation chamber, to a temperature ranging between fourteen and eighteen hundred degrees Fahrenheit. The device needed a combination of electricity and propane gas to operate.

"That would be okay," mumbled Lacey. "May I take his ashes with us? If he has something …" Lacey's voice trailed off as she began to cry again. Tucker welled up in tears in despair over his mother's sadness. He tried to calm her down.

Dr. Brady saw the grief they continued to experience and tried to convince them to stay in the hospital. He offered them a vacant room on the top floor, far away from any activity, where they could be alone.

Lacey recovered and thanked him but declined. She was adamant and finally gained his acquiescence. The doctor made her agree to one more physical examination and to promise to dutifully take the medications he would obtain for her.

She agreed by providing him a simple nod. She suddenly found herself unable to speak again.

PART V

———————

Day eighteen, Monday, November 4

CHAPTER THIRTY-SEVEN

Monday, November 4
North Florida

That night, Peter and Rafael dragged the bodies behind the motel and covered them with a tarp they found. The two men piled cinder blocks on top to provide them some protection from wild critters that roamed the woods behind the buildings. The two men didn't think the four deserved a proper burial. They were the worst kind of criminal opportunists, who preyed on the innocents, and therefore, they got what they deserved.

The rest of the group helped clean up the truck and later thanked the guys for their bravery. None of them questioned their motives, especially after they learned of Mr. Uber and Greyhound's plans for the two women. After a cold night in which Peter and Rafael took turns standing watch, they piled into the military-surplus cargo truck and began their ride south along U.S. 301 that would take them through the heart of Old Florida toward the Tampa Bay area.

It was agreed that Rafael and his family would keep the truck.

They promised to deliver everyone to their destinations if their fuel supply allowed.

Early that morning, with everyone else, including Peter, bundled up in the cargo bed, they made their way through Jesup and then into rural southern Georgia. They crossed the Florida state line, expecting warmer temperatures to greet them. They were disappointed, but not surprised. Even the palm trees had a dusting of white snow mixed with grayish soot.

Along the way, they encountered more refugees on foot. Stalled cars had been abandoned. Some had been broken into while others had their doors left open, hoping to come back to them intact someday. The carcasses of vehicles blocked the roads at times, causing Rafael to use his knowledge of the military truck to drive off road.

They encountered dead bodies more frequently. People were dying of thirst. Many people had stretched their bodies to their limits by not drinking seemingly polluted water for three days. Then, out of desperation, they'd thirstily slurp up any water source they came across. The brackish ponds and streams filling the St. Mary's River looked drinkable, but the combination of fallout and bacteria caused many refugees to contract dysentery.

This exacerbated their dehydrated condition. The bacteria swirled through their bodies, causing bloody diarrhea, abdominal pain, and fever. Unknowing travelers tried to combat the aches, pains, and fever by drinking more fluids. They died within days. Corpses were lying in ditches or leaned up against trees, lifeless eyes staring into space.

Soon, the passengers heading south stopped looking. The dead were no longer a spectacle to be gawked at. They were another part of the landscape they traversed in their effort to get home or to a place of safety.

Rafael was careful to avoid slowing down near large packs of pedestrian travelers. On several occasions, they were surrounded by people who wanted to climb in the back of the truck, further cramping the paid travelers. It was difficult to pass up the hopeless and anguished. However, it was a decision Peter forced them to make before they left the Motel Jesup. The time to make an emotional, heart-wrenching decision was not when the sad eyes were looking into yours, he'd told everyone. The agreement not to take on any new passengers had been unanimous at the time although with each encounter, it was increasingly difficult to say no.

The first couple was dropped off about fifteen miles west of Jacksonville. They lived in a beachside community, but Rafael explained it was too dangerous for him to take the truck that close to the city.

The same was true for the mother and daughter, who asked to be dropped off in Gainesville. Her ex-husband still lived there, and the daughter was a sophomore at the University of Florida. They were dropped off along U.S. 301 in Waldo, just to the east of the college town.

The goodbyes exchanged with the two women were the most difficult for Peter. Their tears flowed as they expressed their appreciation for what he'd done to protect them. There were offers for him to come stay at the ex-husband's horse farm near the Gainesville airport. The mom even offered up one of the man's farm pickups for Peter to drive to the Keys.

He declined and said he planned on riding with Rafael as far as the fuel tank would carry them. He gave them one of Mr. Uber's handguns along with a quick tutorial on how to use it. The mother and daughter had been opposed to guns prior to the night before. Now they understood how they could be used to defend themselves.

It turned out two of the older couples lived in The Villages north of Orlando. They shared stories and learned they had several mutual acquaintances. Then they both gloated how their golf carts were solar operated. The battery banks were powered by solar panels on the roofs of the golf carts, a primary method of transportation around the large retirement community. They were in high spirits when Rafael eased into the Wawa parking lot, a convenience store chain that operated up and down the Atlantic

Seaboard. They also heaped thanks on the two men and promised to pray for them as they continued their trip.

Peter wasn't ordinarily religious, but in the throes of a post-apocalyptic world, he found himself looking to God for guidance. He also found himself begging for forgiveness. At one point, he swore he wouldn't fire his weapon at anyone again. He promised not to take another man's life.

Eventually, that would change.

CHAPTER THIRTY-EIGHT

Monday, November 4
Driftwood Key

Patrick had become attuned to his surroundings and the people who surrounded him. Like many serial killers who oftentimes functioned on a highly intellectual level that allowed them to evade capture, Patrick was the consummate con man. He knew what button to push on some people and what conversations to avoid with others. It was all designed to achieve a goal—remain at Driftwood Key for as long as possible, if not forever.

Patrick sensed they were ready for him to leave. There was a level of wariness from Jimmy. Hank seemed to be more questioning about what had happened to him as each day passed. Sonny and Phoebe were no match for his wits although they both seemed to be more withdrawn around him.

And then there were the cops: Nurse Jessie, as he thought of Jessica, and Detective Mikey, the guy who was so full of himself that he didn't realize Patrick was practically under the same roof. Detective Mikey was lucky Patrick hadn't totally regained his strength. If he had, he'd declare himself to be King Kraken of the Key by murdering the whole lot of them.

He lay in bed, trying to put his finger on what had happened to raise their suspicions. He recalled every conversation he'd had with them. Did his story change? What about his demeanor? He acknowledged he hadn't been a hundred percent lucid those first few days as he recovered from the beatdown. Maybe he'd let something slip?

Then his mind raced to the worst-case scenarios. Had Detective Mikey extracted his DNA and come up with a match to the murder victims? Had somebody identified Patricia and given a sketch artist all the details? Patrick had become adept at applying makeup after years of practice, but were they somehow able to study him against the composite sketch while he was sleeping?

All of this troubled him that day. And when they started taking him for limited walks and constantly badgered him about regaining his strength, warning lights flashed in his mind. *They're getting ready to vote me off the island just like they did everyone else in the Keys who didn't belong as far as they were concerned.*

Patrick weighed his options. He thought about who was the most vulnerable and open to manipulation. At first, he'd thought it would be Jimmy, but Patrick began to realize he was sending the young guy signals that he shouldn't have. He'd changed his approach to Jimmy in the last day, but it might have been too late.

Then he thought about Phoebe. She was compassionate. Motherly. In a mother hen sort of way. He could tug on her heartstrings if necessary.

So, equipped with a plan, Patrick decided to give them what they wanted. A more mobile, rapidly recovering patient who should be ready to leave in a week at the most. Only, his leaving was gonna be on his timetable.

As in—never.

CHAPTER THIRTY-NINE

Monday, November 4
Central Florida

After their final passenger drop-off, Peter relieved Rafael behind the wheel. He and the family of three squeezed onto the bench seat, with Javier sitting in his dad's lap against the passenger door. It was the young man who first caught a glimpse of the traffic on Interstate 75 near Thonotosassa, where they'd dropped off the last of their passengers.

"Look at all those Army trucks, Dad!" the young man exclaimed, his eyes wide with excitement.

Peter had pulled into a funeral home's circle drive and was making a wide turn through their memory gardens when the interstate came into view. One transport truck and troop carrier after another ambled along the highway toward Brandon, a bedroom community to the east of Tampa.

"That's a heckuva convoy," commented Peter as he slowed to view the Desert Storm–era, khaki-colored trucks. In addition to the transport trucks like the one they were driving, several Humvees were interspersed throughout the slow-moving vehicles.

"They're mobilizing for something," Rafael opined. "My first thought would've been MacDill Air Force Base just south of the city. But these guys are heading southbound."

"The only other military base I can think of anywhere near the Gulf is at Homestead," added Peter.

"The air reserve base?" asked Rafael. "Doesn't make sense. These are guard units. Maybe …?" His voice trailed off.

"What, honey?" asked his wife.

Rafael tapped his knuckle on the passenger window and pointed toward Tampa and the lower end of St. Petersburg. Black smoke was rising into the sky from several locations on the horizon.

"Unrest?" said Peter inquisitively.

Rafael grimaced and nodded. "Yeah. Probably in Miami, too."

"What's that mean, Dad?" asked young Javier.

Rafael adjusted his son in his lap so he could rub his hand through the boy's long locks. "It means some people got out of line, and the National Guard needs to straighten them out."

"Do you still think it's safe to go to your parents'?" asked Maria.

"Where do they live?" asked Peter.

"West of Kendall. The south part of Miami-Dade. This road will take us through a handful of small towns and eventually run into South Trail."

"Tamiami Trail?" asked Peter. U.S. Highway 41 ran along Florida's Gulf Coast through Sarasota, Fort Myers, and Naples before turning east toward Miami. Kendall was a residential area in the vicinity of where U.S. 41 ended.

"That's right. I thought it would be easy to take this route to get you into the Keys."

Rafael leaned closer to his wife to study the truck's gauges. Peter picked up on his intentions and immediately looked to the fuel gauge. He noticed the look of concern on Rafael's face and spoke first.

"You'll never make it all the way to Driftwood Key and back to Miami. You're gonna have to drop me off."

Rafael and Maria exchanged looks. "We made a promise," she said.

Peter smiled. He focused on the road but glanced in their direction as he spoke. "Guys, when the blast wave threw me off into the ditch, all I could hope for in that moment was staying alive. Then I reconciled myself to walking twelve hundred miles. After that, a man was kind enough to give me a bicycle. You know the rest of the story."

"But ..." Javier began to protest, but he knew Peter was right. They'd never make the round trip from Kendall to Marathon and back. Peter waved his hand to prevent him from picking up on his thought.

"Listen, we're talking about fifty or sixty miles to the Upper Keys. From there, I can find a ride down U.S. 1. My uncle's a cop. I'm sure I can hitch a ride with one of the deputies."

Maria spontaneously leaned over to plant a kiss on Peter's cheek. He blushed and looked down shyly. He'd bonded with the family through the ordeal and vowed to look them up when it was over. For a brief moment, he considered encouraging them to come to Driftwood Key. Maria and Javier would fit in well with his family and the Frees. Not to mention that Rafael would be nice to have around because of his military training. In the end, he decided not to bring it up, as their own family needed them more than Driftwood Key did.

As darkness approached that afternoon, Peter pulled over to the side of the road across the street from the Miccosukee Resort. The normally full hotel and casino complex stood vacant at the intersection. They nervously shuffled around the cargo box while Peter gathered his things.

He divided up the potassium iodide to provide the family enough dosage for another ten days. He wanted to do more, but he had to consider his own family's needs. He allowed Rafael to keep the handgun and extra magazines. He was confident he could make this final stretch of his journey with the guns he'd taken from Mr. Uber and son.

The group exchanged hugs and tearful goodbyes. Peter stood and waved to the family as they continued on toward Miami. He strained his eyes as he tried to focus on the Miami skyline. However, the hazy, darkening skies made it difficult. What he expected to observe, but didn't, were the plumes of black smoke dotting the landscape like in Tampa. In fact, there was no indication of structure fires whatsoever.

This puzzled Peter. If the National Guard was traveling this way, he figured the unrest must've been worse than Tampa-St. Pete. It didn't make sense.

He shook off the thought and began the final trek toward the Keys, full of anticipation.

CHAPTER FORTY

Monday, November 4
Homestead, Florida

It was pitch dark as Peter approached Homestead. He elected to take a residential side street to avoid walking through the heart of town. It was well known that Homestead had its issues with drugs and homelessness, problems certainly exacerbated by the power outage. The detour added about thirty minutes to his walk toward the Keys, but it was uneventful, something he needed at this point in the long journey south.

He was about thirty miles from the Blackwater Siren, a well-known bar and grill at the entrance to the Upper Keys. He'd stopped there many times to pick up fish tacos to munch on in the car when he traveled between his home and college.

Despite the late hour, he could see the proverbial light at the end of the tunnel. The long day coupled with little sleep had taken its toll. However, his adrenaline-fueled body began to visualize sleeping in his old bedroom at the main house.

As he walked the deserted streets to come closer to U.S. 1, he began to hear the low rumble of trucks approaching from the north.

His mind immediately recalled the large convoy of vehicles headed down the interstate near Tampa. He and Rafael had speculated whether they were headed to Homestead Air Reserve Base or Miami. As it turned out, they were both wrong.

Peter walked along the center median of Palm Drive when he noticed a glowing light in the distance. The dark surroundings made it stand out even more. That, coupled with the low ceiling of clouds and haze, caused the reflection to emanate for miles away from its source.

He reached U.S. 1 and stopped in the middle of the road amidst a trio of crashed cars. Two teenage boys were sitting on the tailgate of a pickup truck, passing a cigarette back and forth. With his hand on the grip of his pistol, he cautiously approached them.

"How's it goin'?" Peter asked casually.

"Not bad. You?" The young man was equally nonchalant.

Peter reached the side of the truck and stopped just short of exposing himself completely to the boys. He was able to see over the truck bed and felt satisfied that they were unarmed.

"I've been on the road trying to get home. I haven't seen much in the way of lights anywhere. Are they racing tonight?" Peter knew Palm Drive ran past the Homestead-Miami Speedway, where NASCAR races were held.

The guys laughed, which served to relax both parties. Peter let go of his weapon and eased around the side of the truck.

"We were gonna check it out, but the military has a roadblock set up about a mile from here. They've got all the roads blocked, actually."

"To the racetrack?" asked Peter.

So far, only one of the boys had engaged in conversation with Peter. "Yeah. There have been military trucks passing through town all afternoon. They've been coming from Miami, mostly."

"Why here?" asked Peter.

The other boy laughed. "Ain't you heard? On account of the Keys."

Peter stood a little taller as fear overcame him. He couldn't imagine why another country would want to drop a nuclear warhead on the Florida Keys. His first thought was a wayward missile fell off course or maybe was shot down, resulting in radioactive fallout.

"Did they get hit with a nuke?"

"Nah, man," said the first boy. "They've lost their dang minds."

Peter sighed. He was tired of talking in riddles.

"What exactly happened, and why would the government send the National Guard down here?"

The talkative teen took one last drag off the cigarette and flicked the butt end over end until it rolled under one of the other wrecked vehicles. He slid off the tailgate and rolled his neck around his shoulders.

"After the bombs hit, they started kicking people out. You know. Tourists. Bums. Anybody who didn't actually live down there."

"Yeah, and the poor bastards all came here," said the other teen.

"Okay," said Peter, drawing out the word, as he was still unsure what that had to do with the National Guard presence. If anything, in his mind, it would be prudent to move anyone out who didn't belong there. His father had done the same thing at the inn for the guests' own good.

The boy continued. "Well, I guess that was only half of what they did. When it started getting colder everywhere, people started looking to head south. They figured the Keys was their best bet."

"Or Mexico," said the other boy before adding, "But we heard they locked down their borders, too."

"What do you mean by *too*?" asked Peter.

"That's what Monroe County did," said the talkative teen. "They threw as many people out as they could, and then they blocked access to the Keys. They piled about a hundred of them concrete barriers like these ones in the middle of the toll bridge." He pointed at the concrete road construction barriers that lined the median on the east side of the intersection.

"They even have armed deputies manning the bridge," said the other teen.

"They ain't real, though. Hell, down there, if you own a gun, you can be a deputy."

Peter scowled and slowly walked toward the barriers and then stared down the boulevard toward the speedway. There must be more to the story.

"What about U.S. 1? Is it barricaded, too?"

"They blocked it off with dump trucks just this side of Jewfish Creek. Anybody approaching by car is turned around unless you're a resident. Same if you're on foot. You have to show proof of residency to get in."

"Are you guys serious?"

"As a heart attack. You live down there?"

"Yeah, sort of. I live, um, lived near DC now. My family lives near Marathon."

"You got photo ID?"

"Yeah, but it's ..." Peter's voice trailed off before he added the word Virginia. He realized the problem he was facing. His Virginia driver's license wasn't going to gain him access into the Keys. He'd have to use his father's name and address. But the two boys indicated they'd deputized all kinds of Keys' residents. Unless he got lucky and his uncle Mike or aunt Jess were present, he might not be able to get through.

"Are you gonna go for it?" the talkative young man asked.

Peter looked at him and then over toward the speedway again. He pointed as he spoke. "And you think they're here because of these roadblocks?"

"I know they are. They told everyone in town to stay away from the Overseas Highway and Card Sound Road. I think they're gonna invade."

Peter laughed at the thought, and when he noticed the boys weren't laughing, he became suddenly serious. He took a deep breath, thanked them, and began jogging down the highway toward Key Largo.

CHAPTER FORTY-ONE

Monday, November 4
Otero County Sheriff's Department
La Junta, Colorado

By the time arrangements could be made for Owen's body and the truck could be readied for their lengthy road trip to Driftwood Key, it was near dark. Lacey and Tucker decided it was safer to stay in La Junta that night and to get a fresh start in the morning. Plus, Lacey admitted to herself, she could use one more night to regain her strength.

They said their goodbyes to Dr. Brady, Dr. Forrest and virtually everyone who worked in the hospital. Dr. Brady provided them both plenty of medications to fight infection and to relieve pain. He also provided them the proper dosage of potassium iodide in case they encountered a site with nuclear fallout. Communications between cities was minimal other than ham radio chatter. The locations of where the warheads had actually been detonated were still uncertain.

Deputy Ochoa picked them up at the hospital and drove them to the sheriff's department, where Deputy Hostetler had just arrived with their Bronco. Lacey gasped and covered her mouth when she soaked in the transformation.

"That's badass!" said Tucker. "Very Mad Max."

Lacey sighed at her teenage son's excitement over the defiling of Owen's prized toy. It was hard to approve the paint job. However, she trusted Sheriff Mobley's judgment, and the man had proven his ability to prepare for a catastrophic event like this one.

They were escorted inside after their belongings were secured in the back of the Bronco. Everything was neatly arranged, and Tucker was the first to notice several additions to their gear. A green and brown leather rifle case was lying on the floorboard of the back seat. Stuffed behind each of the Bronco's bucket seats were several green ammo cans. Finally, a few picnic baskets full of baked goods and Mason jars full of canned foods gave them more than a week's worth of food.

Lacey greeted Sheriff Mobley as they walked in. He extended his hand to shake, but she wrapped her arms around him instead. The hug was well deserved.

"We can't thank you enough for saving our lives," she began. She made eye contact with all of the deputies, who were gathered around the front entrance to the sheriff's department. "Had it not been for you, Owen would've never had a chance, and we ..." Her voice trailed off as she reached out to squeeze Tucker's hand.

"This is what we do, ma'am," said Sheriff Mobley as he smiled and nodded at his team. "I regret that we couldn't do more for your husband."

Tucker stuck his hand out, and the sheriff shook it. "We'll never forget you guys. Thanks."

"You're welcome," said Sheriff Mobley. He took a deep breath. "Okay. You've decided to leave, and I understand you're anxious. I'll offer our hospitality one more time, just in case."

Lacey smiled but shook her head side to side. "No, thanks. We're ready."

"I figured as much. We've added a few things to your supplies. All of your fuel tanks are topped off. My mechanic performed some calculations based upon fuel mileage for this model Bronco. With your extra gas cans, you should be able to make it twelve hundred miles before you run out completely."

"I studied the map last night," interjected Tucker. "That's more than halfway. We can make it to Mississippi or possibly Alabama."

"About that, let me show you something," said Sheriff Mobley. He led the McDowells into the department's communications room, where they were introduced to the 9-1-1 operator who now monitored the ham radio base set. He had a large map of the United States hung on the wall next to a map of Otero County. There were strips of Post-it notes taped at various points along a route toward Florida. Once he had their attention, he explained.

"We have reliable information to the effect that Texas has closed their borders to all outsiders," he said.

"What? Can they do that?" asked Lacey.

"It's hard to tell what's truth and what's fiction right now. Accurate information is a precious commodity. Speculation and conjecture are plentiful. I do know this, though. The Texas electrical grid, operated by ERCOT, their utility, is separate from the rest of America's. Here in Colorado, we're part of the Western Interconnection, and those utilities east of the Mississippi River are part of the Eastern Interconnection.

"The nukes caused blackouts around the country. Eventually, the entire grid failed as the system got overloaded. Texas wasn't affected because their grid isn't connected to the Western and Eastern."

"So they have power, and nobody else does?" asked Tucker.

"Well, that's the rumor via our ham radio network. There are parts of the Texas Panhandle, you know, near Amarillo and Lubbock, that were affected by the same EMP that hit us. Otherwise, the state's power wasn't shut down."

"Who closed their border? The president?"

Sheriff Mobley sighed as he hitched up his utility belt. "Supposedly, the Texas governor did it. They convened an emergency session of the legislature and declared a statewide crisis to be in effect. They're not letting any nonresidents in."

"Wow, that's so trash," said Tucker as he traced his fingers along the thirty-eight hundred miles making up Texas's perimeter. "But think about it. Everybody would want to move to Texas if they didn't close their borders. Right?"

None of the adults in the room could argue with the teen's logic.

"You can see the tabs I've placed on the map," continued the sheriff as he directed their attention back to the wall map. "There really isn't a need to try to cross into Texas although their wide-open country roads would make for a safer trip. If you follow U.S. 50 over to Dodge City in Kansas—"

Lacey interrupted him. "That was part of our original plan. Then we were gonna make our way toward the Florida Panhandle, avoiding any populated cities if we could."

"Very smart," said the sheriff. He reached onto the table and retrieved a foldable paper map from AAA. He opened it up to show them. "I'm not telling you what to do, but this is the route I would take." He pointed out an erratic line drawn by a black marker on the map. The route went through Oklahoma, Arkansas, Louisiana, and across the Mississippi River.

Lacey took a look for a moment and then folded it up. "Thank you for this. And, um, Tucker noticed a few extra things in the back seat, like picnic baskets and, um ..." She hesitated to continue since there were others in the room.

Sheriff Mobley smiled. "From time to time, in the course of our duties, we have to confiscate weapons and ammunition from criminals. We have a few that are on the destroy list, but we've been a little busy to do it. I thought you might be able to take them with you and discard them when you arrive in the Keys."

Lacey smiled. "Glad to help out, Sheriff."

"Lastly, take this with you." He gave her a small, cloth zippered pouch. She opened it and viewed the contents.

"A two-way?"

"It's a portable ham radio with a cigarette lighter charger and instructions. It also has our call signs and frequently monitored channels preprogrammed. You'll have a way to communicate with others and listen for information on the emergency channels, too."

Lacey teared up again at the sheriff's generosity. She gave him another hug and thanked him. After a few more words of sage advice, Lacey and Tucker left the building and stood behind their truck.

"It's so different," said Lacey. "They did a good job of ruining it, if you know what I mean."

"Badass," muttered Tucker. He stepped past his mom. Ignoring her disapproving look, he headed for the passenger door.

"Wait. Where are you going?" she asked.

"I thought we were leaving?"

"We are. But you get the first shift." She tossed the keys into the air until they struck Tucker in the chest. He fumbled to catch them before they hit the ground.

"Really?"

She nodded and smiled at her young man, who'd grown up so fast since they left Hayward.

"Yeet!" he shouted as he opened the passenger door for his mom like a gentleman. "Here you are, madam. Don't forget to buckle up."

"Trust me. I wish there were two buckles."

CHAPTER FORTY-TWO

Monday, November 4
Key Largo Checkpoint
Florida Keys

"Okay, people. Listen up!" Sergeant Franklin of the Monroe County Sheriff's Department was used to bellowing at his charges. He'd supervised many watch shifts during his career although he'd never had to deal with an undisciplined bunch of newly deputized civilians with no training. It was midmorning, and he gathered up the new deputies while his experienced crew stopped processing refugees trying to travel down Overseas Highway. The sergeant waited for everyone to calm down and give him their complete attention. Satisfied, he began.

"I'm looking for experienced divers. Anybody here fit that bill?"

Reflexively, Jimmy almost raised his hand and then caught himself. He'd been warned by everyone, especially Mike, not to engage in conversation with the deputies unless forced to. They were not his friends, Mike had warned him. They were only going to use him for things they didn't want to do themselves.

Several of the young guys eagerly raised their arms under the assumption they'd be pulled off the ungrateful checkpoint duties, where they were verbally abused and threatened all day. As it turned out, they were right, but what they'd volunteered for was wholly unexpected.

Sergeant Franklin pulled them out of the crowd and turned them over to Jessica's boss on the Water Emergency Team. They piled into several sheriff's department vans that appeared to be full of SCUBA gear before traveling back toward Jewfish Creek, using the ramp leading to the water's edge.

Jimmy regretted his decision to remain silent. He was not an adversarial person by nature and truly hated conflict of any kind. The loss of manpower at the checkpoint meant he'd have to shoulder a greater part of the load and possibly work a much longer shift that day.

In addition to the hostilities he encountered while working the checkpoint, his heart was broken by the desperation exhibited by those who were being removed from the Keys and those who were trying every ploy to get in.

On the one hand, the Keys offered the new arrivals hope of living in a more hospitable climate with the opportunities to survive through fishing or growing crops. There were many people who tried to sell themselves to the gatekeepers with offers of heirloom seeds and farming expertise.

Then there were the evictees. Travelers who came to Key West, mostly, to let their hair down and enjoy the mirage that was Margaritaville. The power grid collapsed. The hotels threw them out. Their cars ran out of gas. And now, with the entirety of their earthly belongings consisting of swimsuits, shorts, tee shirts, and flip-flops, they shivered as they were escorted out of the Keys to become someone else's problem.

It was a display of humanity that he only thought he'd see in the movies. It disgusted him and broke his heart at the same time. However, it also reminded him how lucky he was to be a part of Driftwood Key. At first, he didn't want anything to do with becoming a quasi-deputy. It was his father who convinced him it would be a short-term sacrifice to protect his family and their home until Hank could come up with a solution to his aunt's demands.

He watched another group of the poor and downtrodden who were being removed from the Keys. He shook his head in disappointment at the decision made by his aunt Lindsey, the mayor of the Conch Republic, as many of his newly deputized associates called her.

Jimmy, who wasn't much for deep reflection or an analysis of the world around him, did realize his ex-aunt would be judged by her actions one day. Perhaps harshly. For him, family came first, at all costs. Not just his parents, but the Albrights, too.

CHAPTER FORTY-THREE

Monday, November 4
Near Cushing, Oklahoma

They'd made great time on the road. Sticking to the route suggested by Sheriff Mobley, they rode through Kansas without incident, stopping once to swap drivers and top off the gas tanks with fuel. He'd suggested to them that they keep the truck's fuel tank as close to full as possible in the event someone stole their gas cans. At least their truck could travel on.

It was approaching five o'clock when they stopped next to Cushing Lake, just west of the small town located equidistant between Tulsa and Oklahoma City. They'd come upon an Oklahoma Department of Transportation facility, where salt and sand trucks were ready to clear the roads as winter set in. However, the place was locked up and lacking any activity. Even the United States and Oklahoma state flags had been lowered and stored away.

Tucker took a chance and used the bolt cutters he'd found to open the chain that padlocked the fenced entry. Lacey drove into the maintenance yard and found a place at the back to park their truck. They topped up the fuel tank, had a snack, and relieved their bladders. Then they set about looking for more gasoline.

Lacey was the first to spy the two zero-turn riding lawn mowers tucked away in the back of the open maintenance shed. She shouted for Tucker, who came running. He easily broke open the small padlocks with the heavy-duty bolt cutters and found four five-gallon cans. Three were full, and one was half full.

Then he found a water hose and cut it into a six-foot length using the bolt cutters. Although he'd never done it before, he figured out how to siphon the gasoline out of the mowers until the fourth can was full. Then he took the time to transfer the newly found gas into their own empty camouflage containers.

"Mom, this was a great score. We might be able to make it home on what we have now."

Lacey wandered away from him and into the darkness that had overtaken Oklahoma. She turned her head sideways and squinted her eyes to focus.

"Do you hear that?"

Tucker, who was breathing heavily after hoisting the fuel cans back on top of the Bronco, joined her side. He tried to control his breathing so he could hear better.

"What? I can't—"

The roar of an engine grew louder as it approached.

Lacey was on the move. "Something's coming. We've got to get ready."

"Crap!" he said as he fished the truck's keys out of his pocket and rushed toward the driver's door. Lacey followed him and swung open the passenger door. Before climbing in, she pulled the seat up and retrieved one of the handguns they'd been carrying.

The vehicle, which had appeared to be traveling at a high rate of speed as it came upon the maintenance facility, suddenly slowed at the gate. It skidded to a stop in the gravel.

Tucker had parked the Bronco behind the single-story metal building near a wood privacy fence surrounding a dumpster. They were unable to see the gated entry, but in the quiet, powerless world, any sound was amplified.

Both he and Lacey rolled down their windows to listen. Suddenly, the vehicle revved its engines and spun out, throwing gravel against the undercarriage. The headlights told the story as it washed the trees to their right and then the side of the building they were hiding behind.

They could hear voices as the vehicle raced through the gates. People were laughing, and the sound of a bottle crashing against the No Trespassing sign affixed to the fence could be heard.

Tucker leaned forward in his seat and nervously fiddled with the keys in the ignition. He glanced over his left shoulder to see if the headlights gave away the newcomers' intentions. As best he could tell, they were stationary, shining on the front of the corrugated steel building he and Lacey were hiding behind.

"Maybe they'll leave," Lacey whispered to her son. She hadn't blinked since the vehicle pulled through the gate.

A car door slammed. Followed by another. They were exiting the vehicle and talking loudly.

Tucker kept his fingers on the keys, ready to fire the ignition as soon as he felt he had a chance.

The sound of breaking glass startled them both. The new arrivals broke into the DOT offices and were clearing out the excess shards so they could climb through.

Tucker's mind raced. He turned to his mom. "Gimme the gun."

"Why?" she questioned.

"Because their truck is on my side. Trust me."

Lacey hesitated but then handed it over to him. Tucker flipped off the safety and gripped it in his left hand. He turned to his mom in the darkness.

"Hold on tight, Mom."

Lacey nodded and braced herself using the dashboard. Her eyes darted between her son and the chain-link fence a few hundred feet in front of them.

Tucker started the Bronco. The noisy motor immediately

grabbed the attention of the newcomers, as their excited shouts from inside the building indicated. Tucker wasted no time in moving from behind the building. He whipped the wheel to the left, causing the top-heavy truck to sway to the side. He and Lacey were both thrown toward the passenger side before he corrected and drove around a Caterpillar backhoe.

He held the handgun in his left hand, allowing his arm to dangle out the window. He slowed slightly as he reached the corner of the building, where he came across their late-model, charcoal gray Mustang. It was pointed toward the front of the maintenance building.

Tucker took a deep breath, took aim at the left rear tire of the Mustang, and pulled the trigger. The first shot embedded in the car's fender. However, the next shot found its mark, causing the tire to explode.

Tucker took off toward the gate, spinning gravel and kicking dust into the air. The newcomers ran through the parking lot toward them, but within seconds, Tucker had put plenty of distance between them. After handing the gun back to his mom, he swerved to the left, placing them back on the county road heading east.

His adrenaline was racing, and Lacey had gripped anything she could find to hold onto until her knuckles turned white. Tucker drove at a high rate of speed until Lacey finally convinced him to slow down.

"Whew!" an exhilarated Tucker shouted as he turned onto another county road headed south.

"What was that all about?" asked Lacey.

"I didn't want them to follow us."

"So you shot out their tire?"

"Good idea, right?"

Lacey wasn't sure she agreed. "What if they had a gun and shot back? What if you missed and they did chase us down?"

"They didn't," Tucker argued.

Lacey rested her chin on her hand and looked out the passenger window. A farmhouse sat off the road a couple of hundred yards. Its downstairs windows were lit up with flickering candlelight. She decided not to get into an argument with her son, although she thought the risky maneuver should be addressed before something like that happened again.

She sighed and then unfolded the map. With a penlight provided by Dr. Brady, she studied their location. She wanted to make it into Arkansas before they stopped for the night. It meant traveling another five hours or so. Then something struck her as odd.

"Tucker, what kind of car was that?"

"One of those new Must—" he began before cutting himself off. "Mom, it was a new car. That means Sheriff Mobley was right. There are gonna be other cars now."

Lacey sighed. Things were about to change, and she wasn't certain they would be for the better.

CHAPTER FORTY-FOUR

Monday, November 4
Mount Weather Emergency Operations Center
Northern Virginia

In the U.S., a law called the Posse Comitatus Act prohibited the domestic use of military for law enforcement purposes without specific congressional authorization. There was another law, the Insurrection Act, which provided the president authorization to use the military under certain circumstances. Throughout American history, the Insurrection Act of 1807 had been invoked on numerous occasions but generally to quell unrest in large urban environments. It's considered an action of last resort to be used in the event state authorities were unable to give their citizens the protection of law enforcement.

Pursuant to the declaration of martial law, the president was able to invoke the provisions of the Insurrection Act without the input of the states' governors. Both the governors of Florida and Texas refused to take action as he'd requested. Texas doubled down and ordered the Texas Army National Guard to assist law enforcement to create roadblocks at any road entering the state.

214

Those roads they couldn't patrol were blocked with concrete barriers and razor wire.

In Florida, the governor set up roadblocks at the state line to ask for proof of residency. He didn't use the Florida National Guard, as it was occupied tamping down unrest in Miami, Orlando, and the Tampa Bay area. Likewise, the governor of Florida refused to intervene in the actions of the Monroe County government.

The Florida Keys represented a very small part of the state's population, and their actions didn't threaten any lives, although the evicted nonresidents argued to the contrary. Nonetheless, he refused to take action, and this angered the president every bit as much as the Texas border issue.

In response to the perceived insolence on the part of the two governors, the president elected to use a show of force to make them capitulate. He sent available troops from regional military bases toward Texas. They were instructed to amass at major highways entering the state as if they planned to invade. Whether that actually came to pass was yet to be determined. He hoped the Texas governor would back down from her quasi-secession attempt.

In Florida, he needed to make an example of the Florida Keys. Across the country, communities and towns were learning of these quasi-secessionist movements so were also following Texas's lead. Federal highways that passed through towns were being blocked, and travelers, few that they were, had been denied entry. Pockets of rural communities across the southeastern states had armed citizens engaging in hostilities with refugees seeking help. If they weren't residents, they were told to leave. If they didn't leave of their own accord, they were forced to at gunpoint.

The president saw this type of activity as lawless, and it ran contrary to the spirit of cooperation he thought the nation needed to help one another through the crisis.

During the daily briefing that morning, Secretary of Agriculture Erin Bergmann was called upon by Chief of Staff Chandler to provide the president some insight into the mindset of these rural communities. She very succinctly equated it to the Helton administration's position on assisting Israel and India during the outbreak of nuclear war. The president's duty, similar to that of governors, county executives, and mayors, is to protect the citizens within his charge. Rural communities don't get the kind of attention large cities do in times of unrest. They had to fend for themselves, she explained.

This honest assessment was the proverbial nail in Erin's coffin. The president was interested in surrounding himself with *yes-men*, those who agreed with every one of his proposals. He wasn't interested in contrarian points of view at the moment. Although Erin responded with her opinion when called upon, following the meeting, the president instructed Chandler to begin looking for her replacement. He hoped, by her forced resignation and expulsion from Mount Weather, other cabinet members who chose to challenge his approach to the governing of the U.S. would fall in line.

He instructed the chairman of the Joint Chiefs to assemble regional strike forces to move into the rural areas of America, where communities tried to isolate themselves from the rest of the nation. They were instructed to open highways, by force, if necessary. If a community failed to cooperate, a larger contingent would be ordered in to sweep the homes for weapons and hoarded food.

As for the Keys, he saw the importance of the southernmost point in the U.S. to the rebuilding effort. Their location in the southernmost latitudes of the country provided an opportunity to grow food and raise livestock. Of course, it would require a colossal effort to remove buildings and hard surfaces to make way for truckloads of topsoil. The Keys would be converted from a tourist mecca to America's new breadbasket until the clouds of soot and smoke lifted. After that, it could become a national park for all he cared.

The president pulled Chandler into his office and gave the orders. He wanted U.S. military troops from outside of Florida to deal with the problems in the Keys. He'd already dealt with military leaders at Fort Hood and Fort Bliss, who refused to follow orders because their loyalties had shifted to their home state. He ordered the troop contingent to halt the insurrection in the Keys to be deployed from Fort Benning on the Alabama-Georgia border just outside Columbus.

Within hours, the eighty-eight-vehicle convoy of Humvees, troop carriers and logistics support vehicles were traveling down Interstate 75 toward the rally point at Homestead Motor Speedway.

PART VI

Day nineteen, Tuesday, November 5

CHAPTER FORTY-FIVE

Tuesday, November 5
Overseas Highway at Cross Key
Florida Keys

It was the middle of the night when Peter entered the stretch of Overseas Highway that connected the Mainland to the Upper Keys. The tiny islands upon which the two-lane divided highway was built were mostly uninhabitable except for the Manatee Bay Club approximately five miles from the point where the boys said the roadblock was set up.

Peter knew the location well. An access road had been built on both sides of U.S. 1 leading to Gilbert's Resort, a small hotel and tiki bar known for being home to a number of racing catamarans. The access road looped under the highway, so any cars denied access could be directed back toward Homestead.

At this hour, he assumed the road would be desolate. He was wrong. In addition to abandoned vehicles, there were pedestrians walking in both directions. Occasionally, a vehicle would force its way through the throngs of people.

Conversations were had across the concrete divider as those

who wanted access to the Keys quizzed those leaving about the requirements to get in. Many tried to develop stories to con their way past the many armed guards who stood vigil at the entrance.

Friend of a friend. Long-lost family member. Dual residency. Been off to college. Lost my license. Identity theft.

The list of excuses for not being able to show photo identification was long. Peter wasn't sure how he was going to overcome the deficiency. He simply hoped a familiar face would be present. Or, at the very least, someone who knew the Albright family well enough to confirm his story.

He joined a pack of refugees shuffling past the aqueduct's pump station. Fresh water was pumped to the Florida Keys through a series of aqueducts connected to a one-hundred-thirty-mile-long water main. It was the only source of fresh water and was used by the Albright family to fill its own water tower on Driftwood Key. Now, with the power grid down, the pump station wasn't working, causing survival in the Keys to be even more improbable for most people.

He walked another thousand feet until Barnes Sound was on his left. Because of the darkness, he couldn't see across the fairly large body of water toward the toll bridge. As the people in front of him began to bunch together, waiting their turn to enter the Keys, he realized he was more than a mile away. He shook his head in disbelief and prepared himself to wait hours for the opportunity to enter.

As he shuffled along with the others, he continued to eavesdrop on conversations. He was amazed at the quest for information. For many, it appeared to be more important than food and water. Misinformation seemed to run rampant as well.

Rumors of more nuclear missile strikes on U.S. soil were common. Confirmation of Mexico shutting out American refugees was confirmed by a number of people. Texas had closed off their borders to outsiders. It was believed they were still operating their power grid without a single blackout episode.

None of them seemed to be aware of the National Guard

presence at the speedway. He didn't dare ask, as he preferred not to draw attention to himself. However, when nobody made reference to it, he began to question the veracity of the teenage boys he'd spoken with.

Having witnessed the number of stalled cars on the Overseas Highway coupled with the throngs of people making their way in both directions in the middle of the night made him wonder how they'd cross the sound to begin with. And if the barricades were in place as the teens said, that bridge would be impassable without a significant amount of work by some heavy-duty Caterpillar front-end loaders.

The wave of refugees came to an abrupt halt, and they began to bunch together. Some eased down the embankment and fought along the mangrove trees to cut ahead of the others. This drew the ire of some, and hostile words were exchanged.

Peter noticed the number of refugees heading off the Keys was less, so he sat on the concrete barrier and swung a leg over to the other side, followed by the other. To avoid walking against the flow of pedestrian traffic, he opted to shuffle along the silt fence separating the soft, sandy shoulder and the riprap that prevented it from washing into the water. He was moving much faster than the other side of the road, and soon others joined him.

Pushing and shoving broke out as those who felt people like Peter were cutting in line tried to stop them. Shouts filled the air, and a couple of fistfights resulted in a near brawl next to a stranded DHL delivery van.

As daylight came, Peter pressed forward despite being shoved ever closer toward the water's edge. He gripped his pistol and contemplated pulling it so he could defend himself. The melee, however, was on the other side of the barrier as people began to push forward, crushing those ahead of them into those standing in line.

Raised voices broke the relative silence he'd enjoyed until this point. People were scared and agitated. The shouting and fighting rose to a crescendo until a single sound quietened everyone, stifling their voices.

An explosion rocked the waters of Barnes Sound. A massive blast sent a fireball high into the air from the direction of the Monroe County Toll Bridge. The sound of concrete crumbling and the extremely heavy concrete barriers falling into the water roared across the glass-like water.

Then the hundreds of people surrounding Peter reacted. As if on cue, in unison, they screamed at the top of their lungs. Voices shouted out warnings.

"They're bombing us!"

"It's the Air Force!"

"There's gonna be a tidal wave!"

"Run!"

A panicked stampede was headed Peter's way. Some people from the right side of the road jumped the barrier and began to flee the Keys. Those who were already shuffling their way to the mainland ran for their lives.

He was at risk of being trampled, so he stepped over the silt fencing and found a gap in a guardrail that marked the last thousand feet before the access road entrance came into view.

Peter didn't know what had happened, and he doubted anybody's air force had bombed the bridge or the pedestrians on it. He did see an opportunity to use the chaos as a way of getting to the front of the line. He considered it to be his best opportunity to get onto Key Largo.

Or die trying.

CHAPTER FORTY-SIX

Tuesday, November 5
Mount Weather Emergency Operations Center
Northern Virginia

It was during the predawn hours of November 5 when the president assembled his military leaders. His day was filled with meetings and included his first encounter with the outside world since the nuclear attacks. Marine One, the presidential helicopter, was going to take him on a tour of Washington, DC, followed by a flyover of Philadelphia. He wanted to end his day on a positive note.

The president's first meeting was with Chandler and his military leaders about the progress they were making toward his goal of establishing a new center of government in Pennsylvania. In order to secure the necessary facilities to house Congress and other government agencies, residents and businesses in downtown Philadelphia had to be displaced. This resulted in pushback in the form of violent protests that distracted the military from fulfilling the president's directives. Many lives had been lost on both sides during the unrest, creating a boondoggle for President Helton.

During their briefing, the subject matter turned to the Florida

Keys. The governor of Florida was no longer responding to the Helton administration's attempts to intervene. Even direct communication attempts with Monroe County leaders failed.

"They're calling themselves the Conch Republic, Mr. President," said the chief of staff of the Army.

"You can't be serious," said the president sarcastically. "Are they actually claiming to secede from the Union?"

The general rolled his eyes and smiled. "Sir, they claim they already did many decades ago. Now they're simply formalizing their declaration. Their words, not mine, sir."

"Well, our nation, and this administration, will not be insulted by their insolent declarations of independence, or whatever's on their minds. It's insurrection against our government, and I want it quashed by whatever means necessary. I can't allow this concept of a Conch Republic, or banana republic, to take hold. Texas is a difficult enough situation to deal with. Counties or geographic areas trying to assert their separation from our nation need to be dealt with harshly."

The general continued. "Sir, as we speak, our troops are pulling out of the rally point in Homestead, halfway between Miami-Dade and the two bridges being held by the locals. We will use Army logistics bulldozers to force the concrete barriers off the bridges. Our troops, led by armored personnel carriers, will enter Key Largo. We suspect the locals will lay down their arms or run screaming into the night."

The general had just finished his sentence and laughed along with the other military personnel in the briefing. Suddenly, one of his aides entered the conference room and interrupted their playful banter at the expense of the Florida Keys. He read the note and then nodded to his aide, who scurried out of the conference room.

"Mr. President, I'm afraid you'll have to excuse me," the general said as he rose from the table. "We have reports that the locals have detonated explosives under the supports of one of the bridges. A two-hundred-foot span has collapsed into the water."

"Explosives? Collapsed? Were any of our people hurt?"

"Unknown at this time, sir." He turned his body toward the door.

"Wait. Did you say there was a second bridge?"

The general nodded.

"Protect it, dammit! Use air support. The Coast Guard. Whatever it takes. Do not allow them to cut themselves off!"

CHAPTER FORTY-SEVEN

Tuesday, November 5
Overseas Highway at Cross Key
Florida Keys

Eventually the lane leading off the Keys contained only a handful of elderly people and families who walked away from the checkpoint. Around the bend, floodlights washed the highway as more concrete barriers blocked both sides of the road in a staggered fashion. This was apparently designed to let vehicles through one car at a time. On the other side of the highway, the grassy shoulder was littered with stalled cars that had been pushed off the pavement to make way for others.

Voices were raised as he approached the checkpoint, where armed guards threatened to shoot the refugees despite the fact some of those who were trying to gain access claimed to have proof of residency. A scrum of several dozen people was occurring around the folding tables where men and women in plain clothes processed the refugees.

Peter had to take a second look when he saw the blue flags of the Conch Republic flying in the breeze behind the intake tables. At first, he rolled his eyes at the lunacy. *You can't secede from the United States.* Then he thought, *Or could you?*

Regardless, he needed to get through the checkpoint because the only other option was to hop over the barrier and wade through the mangroves. That was a surefire way to get snakebit or lose a limb to an alligator.

One of the gatekeepers shouted to his personnel, "We've got to move it along, people! I've got orders to shut it down."

The crowd of refugees immediately responded.

"Shut what down? You can't!"

"Let us in first!"

"Please, we came all this way!"

"We're so close. You gotta let us in."

Peter sensed what was about to happen. Whoever had dreamed up this secession thing must be aware of the troops amassing in Homestead. Out of fear, they planned to isolate themselves from the rest of the country. Blowing up the toll bridge was just the first step. They might destroy the short span over Jewfish Creek at Anchorage Resort or the longer stretch that crossed Lake Surprise. Either way, his access to home would be taken away.

He furrowed his brow and set his jaw. Being polite wasn't gonna get him anywhere. He shoved his way past several people, who became agitated. Peter didn't care. He needed to get someone's attention before they pulled the entire operation to the other side of those two bridges.

He elbowed his way past several men, who grabbed at his backpack in an attempt to sling him to the ground. Peter angrily swung around and pulled his pistol on them.

"Gun!"

"He's got a gun!"

"It's the man in camo!"

The supervisor of the intake process had had enough. "That's it, people. We're outta here."

"You heard the man, soldiers! Weapons hot!"

Peter stopped in his tracks. He knew enough about military

parlance to realize there were soldiers of some nature standing on the other side of those barriers with what could be automatic weapons. They'd cut him and everyone around him to ribbons if he forced the issue.

"Please! Let us in, mister!"

"Yeah, we have a condo in Islamorada. I have our deed with me!"

Peter was unsure of what to do. He had no identification that showed residency. He didn't have a deed to a condo. He didn't have a library card. All he had was his name.

He used the same ploy that had worked when he walked out of the conference center in Abu Dhabi. It had worked when he approached the old couple in North Carolina, who'd proven so helpful. He holstered his weapon and raised his hands as he pushed his way to the front.

"Hey! I'm Peter Albright. Does anybody know me?"

CHAPTER FORTY-EIGHT

Tuesday, November 5
Nashville, Arkansas

That night, after hours upon hours of traversing the back roads of four states, they found a secluded place to sleep in the back of a cemetery just west of Nashville, Arkansas. While they both found it creepy sleeping among the dead, they also felt they were less likely to encounter other people in the offbeat location.

The farther they drove south and east, the more traffic they encountered. Gas stations were closed and mostly looted. The types of vehicles varied, but they were few and far between. Lacey surmised gasoline would be even more difficult to find now. In the several-hundred-mile radius surrounding the Denver metropolitan area where the electromagnetic pulse had the greatest impact, new vehicles were disabled. Owners of vintage trucks like the McDowells' and the Otero County Sheriff's Department were the few who truly needed gasoline for transportation purposes.

They decided to renew their search for sources to replenish their spent gas cans during the daytime. As Tucker recognized, at night, the farms or businesses they approached would hear and see them coming before they began their search. It would make them ripe for an ambush.

During their travels, they talked about Owen. They cried. They laughed. They reminisced. They patted each other on the back for their determination to get home to Driftwood Key.

They also recalled the conversations they'd had with Owen before their debacle east of Pueblo. They'd dreamed up as many scenarios as their creative minds could imagine that would result in trouble along the way. Every one of their concerns revolved around conflict with their fellow man.

After a decent night's rest, during which Lacey stretched out in the back seat and Tucker curled up in the front, they awoke before dawn and hit the road. A light dusting of snow had coated their truck, and the roads were somewhat slick as they made their way toward Interstate 20, an east-west route that would take them across the Mississippi River near Vicksburg.

They were about to turn up the on-ramp in Cheniere, Arkansas, when Tucker slapped the dashboard and pointed ahead.

"Mom, the entrance is blocked by those military Humvees. Keep going straight."

"But we need to cross the river at Vicksburg," she argued and kept going. She drove up to the National Guardsmen, who approached their vehicle with their weapons at low ready. They were studying Lacey and Tucker through the windshield as they approached.

Lacey rolled her window down and spoke to them before they arrived. "We need to get to Vicksburg."

"Not this way, ma'am," the man gruffly replied. "All lanes are closed to civilian traffic."

Lacey looked ahead and then to her left to observe the highway. "I don't see any traffic at all."

"It's coming, ma'am. Now, back down the ramp and move along."

"Well, when can we cross the bridge?"

The soldier shook his head and glanced over at his partner. He was wearing a shemagh around his mouth and nose, so Lacey could only see his eyes.

"Move back, lady!" the other soldier shouted, growing impatient with Lacey's questioning. "We have the authority to confiscate this vehicle and everything within it per the president's martial law declaration. We've got better things to do, but if you insist ..." He purposefully let his last few words dangle in the air as he raised his automatic weapon in Tucker's direction.

"Mom, we should go."

Lacey didn't bother to roll up her window. She glanced in her side mirrors to ensure nobody was parked behind her before slowly easing down the ramp. Tucker never took his eyes off the soldiers. He was still gripping the pistol he'd retrieved from the glove box as the men first approached the truck.

Lacey continued south through the country roads that ran parallel to the Mississippi River. The next available crossing was U.S. Highway 425 at Natchez, Mississippi. This was not a route they'd mapped out that morning, and the first comment Tucker made related to the waste of gasoline.

Lacey drove slower than she had prior to this point in an effort to conserve fuel and to watch for opportunities to obtain more. While they thought they might have enough to get into Central Florida, if not farther, they were constantly on the lookout. This unexpected detour gave them a greater sense of urgency to fill up.

U.S. Highway 84 turned into Route 425, where it began to run along the banks of the Mississippi. It also took them through a series of small communities as they approached Vidalia, Louisiana. There was more traffic and quite a few people milling about on the side of the road. Lacey was beginning to feel uneasy, as those without transportation had the distinct look of envy on their faces as they scowled at the moving vehicles.

They entered the small town of Vidalia, perched on the west side of the Mississippi. The closer they got to the bridge, the more traffic built up in front of them.

Tucker rolled down his window and tried to see ahead. The hazy conditions restricted visibility to less than a mile. All he could see was a single lane of taillights.

Tucker was surprised at what he saw. "A traffic jam? Seriously?"

"Nobody is coming off the bridge in our direction. Are they all headed east?" Lacey asked.

Tucker looked around, and then he suddenly opened his door. "I'll be right back."

Before Lacey could ask where he was going, he'd exited the vehicle and bounded across the parking lot to the overhang of the Craws, Claws & Tails patio restaurant. He spoke with a group of teenagers and a couple of older men sitting in rocking chairs underneath the sloped roof overhang. He looked back at their truck several times to see if Lacey had advanced any. She had not. Tucker bumped fists with the young men, and he ran back to the truck.

After he was back in the truck, he pointed to his right at a small residential street that ran next to the restaurant. "Mom, take a right here. We can't cross the bridge."

"Why not?"

"They're confiscating gasoline and weapons on the other side. The Mississippi governor, acting on the president's orders, is searching every vehicle that enters. The martial law declaration allows them to take our guns, ammo, and stored gasoline, leaving us only what's in the tanks."

"That's ridiculous!" shouted Lacey in disbelief. She wheeled the Bronco across the parking lot, where Tucker waved to the group, who gave him a thumbs-up.

"Take a left up ahead and then an immediate right. These county roads drive along the river and will take us to a small town called New Roads. Supposedly the highway is open to cross there since both sides of the river are in Louisiana."

"It still leads us into Mississippi, right?" asked Lacey although she knew the answer to her question. "We're just gonna run into the same problem."

"Eventually, yes. According to those guys, the bridge is open. The next crossings are in Baton Rouge and New Orleans, which are unsafe. They said New Orleans is on fire."

"Whadya mean?"

Tucker raised his eyebrows and nodded slowly. "I mean they said the city is on fire. People are killing each other in the streets. One of the old men said the cops and National Guard won't even go in there."

Lacey shook her head. This meant they had one shot to get across the Mississippi without giving up everything they needed to get to the Keys. She was growing weary of the constant threats and uncertainty. She took a deep breath. Then she got a firm grip on the wheel as well as herself.

CHAPTER FORTY-NINE

Tuesday, November 5
Driftwood Key

Dress for success were the words Patrick Hollister's father had ingrained in him growing up. When he entered the banking world, he was always impeccably dressed in custom-tailored suits and Italian shoes. While most of the professional world in the Florida Keys adopted a laid-back appearance, Patrick's pride in himself prevented him from lowering the standards his father had taught him.

He studied himself in the mirror, and the person who stared back was hardly recognizable. He hadn't shaved in more than a week, resulting in a shaggy beard that certainly hadn't adorned his face since the day he was born. Likewise, his hair was long and unkept.

The clothing had been given to him by Hank out of his musty closet. Hank was the type of man to keep those unworn size thirty-six jeans he'd bought online many years ago for when he lost a few pounds. Of course, that never happened, and the size forty waistline meant the jeans remained new-with-tag, as they say on eBay.

The long-sleeve sweatshirt with the Driftwood Key Inn logo was ironic. Patrick had every intention of becoming a part of the operation here. In fact, the title of *sole proprietor* seemed to suit him just fine.

So, with a final adjustment of his sweatshirt and a half-hearted attempt to straighten his hair, Patrick emerged from bungalow three to take a little tour of the grounds.

He was somewhat familiar with the twenty-nine acres that made up Driftwood Key from his prior visits to Hank years ago. When he'd first solicited the Albrights' business, he did his homework. He studied the property assessor's records online and then viewed images posted on Google by guests or the hotel staff. As a banker, when he set his sights on a prospective business client, he made the extra effort to learn all he could about their operation in order to impress them in some small way.

He didn't earn Hank Albright's business on that day, but it certainly benefitted him on the day he planned on taking it away from him.

Patrick stepped onto the sugary white sand of Driftwood Key. It was cold. Until now, he'd played up his recovery by remaining inside the bungalow or on the porch. He moaned and groaned when he moved in their presence. He'd winced so many times he wondered if he'd need Botox after this was over. If Botox was still a thing someday.

However, Patrick saw the handwriting on the wall. They were ready for him to leave. He'd worn out his welcome to the point they were getting suspicious. Truth be told, he was ready to live again. He was tired of the bedridden days and nights filled with an insatiable hunger to kill.

It was time.

Throughout his time in the bungalow, he tried to watch everyone's movements through the windows. He had a clear view of the drive connecting the front gate and the main house. He eavesdropped on their conversations when he sat on the front porch. He engaged in casual conversation with Jessica and Phoebe, especially, when they came to tend to his wounds or feed him.

For the last several days in particular, they all used a sneaky ploy that didn't work with the man who'd mastered deception. Small talk was generally followed by pointed questions as to how Patrick had suffered his injuries. Patrick was interested in small talk, so he did everything he could to extend the casual discussions. He was gathering information while his adversaries were setting him up to extract theirs. It was a game of mental chess that he was winning easily.

Their routine had changed in the last day or so. He'd overheard that Jimmy, his favorite, had been pulled away to work for the sheriff's department. The poor boy must be exhausted, Patrick had thought to himself the night before as he fell asleep. Eight hours away. Eight hours doing chores and fishing. More hours on patrol with a few hours of sleep a day.

Then there was Jessica. She was pulling double duty outside Driftwood Key. She was gone most of the afternoon and didn't return until close to midnight. On more than one occasion, her truck pulled in as Detective Mikey's pulled out.

Sonny spent his days in his precious greenhouses, doting over their vegetables after a long night of patrolling the grounds and manning the gate. He'd disappear to sleep, presumably from late afternoon through the early evening until around eleven. Phoebe was tethered to the kitchen. When she wasn't planning and preparing meals for everyone, she was constantly checking their supply inventory. The woman was borderline obsessive-compulsive about all of that stuff. However, Patrick thought, she'd be his first hire if he were staffing the inn. Unfortunately, on this day, she'd be the first fire.

Patrick turned his attention toward the soon-to-be-former-sole-proprietor of Driftwood Key, *Mr. Hank*. Even in Patrick's mind, he managed to say the words sarcastically. He found it so annoying that the Frees referred to him as Mr. Hank. C'mon, people! It's

Hank. Or Mr. Albright. Or boss. Or sir. Or something other than some plantation-speak like Mr. Hank.

Regardless, good old Hank had to go; otherwise a new sole proprietor couldn't be anointed.

So Patrick began to wander the grounds of Driftwood Key. He came across one or two of them throughout the day, and they were cordial while keeping their distance. He knew what they wanted—a healthy enough patient capable of hitting the road and going home. He was going to raise their hopes while laying the groundwork to have one helluva party that night.

For hours, with only an occasional stop to take a rest, Patrick took mental inventory of the main buildings and their locations. He began to lay out a time frame to make his move.

Phoebe fed him like clockwork around six every evening. She tended to stick to the house after dark, she'd told him. Sonny ate early and went to bed to get some sleep before the graveyard shift. Then she fed Patrick.

His dinners were delivered on a bamboo tray complete with plastic utensils, of course, befitting any inmate. You must feed your prisoners, but you certainly don't give them a knife and fork, right? Patrick laughed when he analyzed this part of his daily routine. Clearly, someone at Driftwood Key had watched *Silence of the Lambs*.

After the meals were served, Hank, Jessica, and Mike would gather by a bonfire next to the water's edge. Sometimes they'd drink, and their conversations varied. In the dead calm of the post-apocalyptic world, *oceanfront edition*, their voices carried, and Patrick made a point to settle in on the bungalow's porch to listen. Jessica didn't always join the guys because she was still working. With a little luck, she'd be off saving lives while Patrick was drumming up some business for her back at home.

Jimmy hadn't been home at the evening hour for days, so he wasn't likely to get in the way. With a little luck in terms of timing, Patrick could dispose of the others and Jessica, upon her return, leaving Jimmy all alone.

. . .

239

As Patrick wandered, so did his mind. He thought of all the ways he'd killed in the past. He considered himself a versatile and imaginative serial killer. Guns would be easy. He laughed at this as he saw Hank walking along the water's edge with a rifle slung over his shoulder. Everyone wanted to do away with guns. *Gimme a knife and I'll show you how to kill. Better yet, I wonder if Sonny has a cordless Sawzall he'd be willing to loan me for a few hours.*

He tried to enter the toolshed and found that the paranoid Sonny had double padlocked it. Patrick grabbed the chain and gave it an angry shake before moving on to the greenhouses. He walked through, stopping periodically to examine a hand trowel or a three-pronged weeder. He took the weeder and raised it over his head, slamming it downward into the two-by-four surround of a planting bed.

"Dull," he muttered as he tossed it into the tomato plants. "Don't you people have a hatchet? How do you split open your coconuts?"

Frustrated, Patrick continued to roam the grounds in search of a weapon. Anything that was capable of piercing skin or crushing a skull would do. After a few hours, he became concerned he was drawing suspicion, so he made his way back to his bungalow without a killing tool. He'd have to come up with a plan B. Or, better yet, fall back on his instincts that had served him well those many nights sitting on a bar stool, waiting for his next victim.

CHAPTER FIFTY

Tuesday, November 5
New Roads, Louisiana

Lacey and Tucker rode mostly in silence as they mindlessly traveled south along the side of the Mississippi River lowlands. They'd begun to lose their focus and were tiring of the trip although they still had over nine hundred miles to travel. Tucker had tried to cheerily look on the bright side that they were more than halfway to Driftwood Key, but both of them recognized the challenges were becoming more frequent.

They passed through the small riverfront town of New Roads, Louisiana, without incident. The old Bronco chugged up the John James Audubon Bridge, a two-mile-long crossing that rose to five hundred feet above the Mississippi River.

As they drove up the fairly steep slope, more of their surroundings came into view. To their left sat the Big Cajun 2 Power Plant, a fifteen-hundred-megawatt gas and coal-fired power plant along the Mississippi. Louisiana's first coal-fired station, it now appeared to be nothing more than skeletal remains as it sat dormant below them. The power station relied upon power to generate more electricity for the region. In order to function, computers were required to monitor and control the process. When the cascading failure of the Eastern and Western Interconnection occurred, it took Big Cajun 2 down with it. It would sit empty and useless for nearly a decade as it waited for replacement parts necessary for its operation.

At the top of the bridge span, Lacey slowed their progress to take in the view. They were shocked as they realized they were barely able to see the river. At five hundred feet above ground, they were immersed in the gray, ashen clouds of soot that hung over the earth. It prevented them from seeing into the distance, which meant they'd be driving blind into the lowlands on the other side of the river. If there were roadblocks ahead, they wouldn't know until they were on top of them.

"We're committed now," said Lacey as she caught Tucker's look of apprehension. He obviously shared her concerns by the way he gripped the rifle he'd pulled out of the back seat before entering New Roads.

"I know, Mom. We're stuck on this road for a few miles, and then we pick up Highway 61. We'll be changing roads a lot until we get to Florida unless you wanna chance getting on I-10."

"Too much traffic. We've only got a few hours of daylight left, so let's keep rolling."

"I can drive," Tucker offered.

"Let's wait until dark. Your eyesight is better than mine right now. My vision has been getting blurry at the end of the day since I woke up."

Tucker understood. His mom had been injured more by the flash freeze than he was. He was amazed that she hadn't experienced more issues during the two long days of traveling.

Their drive through the back country of Eastern Louisiana was relaxing. They both began to feel better about their prospects of getting to the Keys by the next evening. Tucker vowed to drive late into the night. By his calculations, they could make it to beyond

Tallahassee by midnight, maybe even to Lake City in north-central Florida.

They were able to enter Mississippi at Bogalusa before turning south. They ran into a large group of refugees walking in the middle of the road toward the coast. Tucker was driving now, but he still laid a handgun in his lap as he approached the group. His mother did the same. The two of them had discussed the use of firearms after Lacey broached the subject of Tucker shooting at the vehicle in Arkansas. They'd agreed he'd exercise restraint and only use his gun in self-defense.

Initially, the group of people politely stepped to the shoulders on both side of the two-lane road as Tucker drove past them. Their faces were haggard, and their eyes were sunken into their sockets. Each of them appeared exhausted, hungry and defeated.

Lacey was curious about where they were headed because they didn't seem to be part of a cohesive group. Rather, they seemed to have banded together for protection, not unlike animals who stick together in herds or flocks.

"Where are you going?" she asked after rolling down her window.

"We're headed to a FEMA camp in Slidell. It's been there for years following the hurricanes."

"We're headed to the marina at Bay St. Louis," said another woman, who was holding the hands of two young children who barely kept up. "We heard boats are leaving for South Florida, where it's still warm."

"Hey, that's what I like to hear," whispered Tucker.

Another woman joined in with her opinion. "Supposedly the weather's decent and doesn't have all these clouds. Something about the way the wind blows."

A man caught up to the group and said, "Those boats aren't cruise ships or anything. They're just fishing charters trying to make a buck. And they're really expensive."

Lacey became genuinely curious. "Like what?" she asked as Tucker continued to roll along slowly, matching the pace of the refugees. As his mom asked questions, he watched his mirrors and all sides of the truck in case somebody decided to move on them.

"Like, trade your truck for two seats. Crazy expensive."

"Say, lady," said one of the men, "let me ride by standing on your bumper. I can hold on to the roof rack if you won't go too fast."

The suggestion urged others around the Bronco to make similar offers. They began to draw closer to the truck, making Tucker nervous.

"I'll do that if you'll let my little girls ride in the back seat," said one of the women. "They don't take up much room."

"No! Me! I can pay, too!"

"Tucker?" questioned Lacey apprehensively.

"I know, Mom. I know."

Tucker pressed on the gas pedal and tried to move the refugees out of the way who'd tried to surround the truck. They were becoming belligerent. Several tried to slam on the hood in an attempt to get him to stop. One attempted to open Lacey's passenger door.

"Dammit, they asked for this," said Tucker. He furrowed his brow, set his jaw, and began to push through them without regard to whether they might get hurt. In his mind, they were on a street made for vehicles, not pedestrians. It was a risk they chose to take.

He blared on the horn, which only served to make the mob angrier. He slammed on the brakes as one man tried to jump on the hood. He slid all the way across and landed hard on the pavement. Tucker slammed his foot down on the gas, causing the Bronco to surge forward into a slight gap in the crowd. It was all the opening he needed, and he never looked back. Several people tried to chase them, and one managed to get a foot on the nerf bar before being knocked sideways and spinning to the ground. He sped off, hitting sixty-five miles an hour, the loaded-down Bronco's top speed, before finally responding to his mother's pleas to let off the gas.

"Tucker, this is getting old."

"I agree, Mom. But what choice do we have? I mean, we're almost to Florida."

"Yeah, think about that for a minute. If the word is spreading around that Florida is still the Sunshine State, we're gonna run into more and more groups like this one. Only, the next bunch might have guns pointed at us."

Tucker took a deep breath and thought for a moment. They had the ham radio, and they could try to use it to monitor things like traffic and mobs of people walking down the road. However, he doubted they could trust something like that. This group they'd just encountered had come out of nowhere.

"What about the boats?" he asked.

"Bay St. Louis?" Lacey had given it some thought as well.

"Obviously, we may not be able to trust what those people said, but it was more than one who seemed to know about it."

Lacey stared out the window and then up at the sky. "We have to drive past there anyway, right?"

"Well," began Tucker in response, stretching the word out as he spoke, "sort of. If we take I-10, absolutely. If we cut across Mississippi and Alabama just above the interstate like we planned, it would be about twenty miles out of our way."

"Is it worth looking into?" she asked. "We could avoid another thousand miles of this type of stuff. No more hunting for gasoline or sleeping in cemeteries."

"Mom, you heard that guy. We'd have to give up Dad's truck."

Lacey nodded and fought back tears. She'd be letting yet another part of Owen get away from her. Then she glanced over at her son. He was a part of both Owen and her. The most important part. Trucks can be replaced. Kids can't. She made a decision.

"Let's check it out. If it doesn't pan out, we'll keep going the best we can."

CHAPTER FIFTY-ONE

Tuesday, November 5
Driftwood Key

Phoebe settled in for the evening. The generator was turned off after dinnertime, so she was following her early evening kitchen routine by candlelight. Having a structured day had helped her cope with this sudden change in their way of life. She once thrived on working full days that began at dawn and lasted well into the evening, seven days a week. She didn't complain. She had a work ethic instilled in her by her parents and the genetics of their parents before them.

Hank had commended her repeatedly throughout the collapse. She was indispensable and she knew it. But she didn't look at her value to the inn through the prism of an employee seeking higher compensation. They were family. Sonny, Jimmy and all the Albrights were all blood relatives in her mind.

She lit the last candle next to the small work desk nearest the entrance to the kitchen. As had been her practice, she retrieved the handgun from the desk drawer and set it on top of the journal she used to record their daily usage of supplies. She flipped through the pages to the menu she had planned for the next day, and since Sonny had gone to bed more than thirty minutes ago, Phoebe thought she'd do a little advance meal prep.

She set up her workstation next to the kitchen sink. A well-worn cutting board was pulled down from a shelf attached to a wall cabinet, and she pulled a serrated butcher knife out of the teak block on the counter. Finally, a peeler was retrieved from the drawer.

Phoebe chuckled as she surveyed all the tools it took to peel and slice up a carrot bunch.

She was a smart cook, not a gourmet chef. Sure, she was capable of producing a plate worthy of some Food Network program, but that was not her passion. Practical cooking was, and that certainly suited the times they lived in.

For example, many cooks don't bother cleaning up a carrot bunch. They buy prepackaged sliced, shredded, or cut carrots at the grocery store and prepare a dish. Not Phoebe. She used the entire bunch, including the tops, the leafy green part of the carrot that grew above ground. She set some aside to regrow and cooked a few as well. While bitter, they could be prepared with olive oil, garlic and other greens to provide bulk to a meal. *Not to mention,* she thought as she began cutting the tops off, *they help you poop.*

Phoebe was mindlessly chopping away when suddenly the back door opened, causing her to nick the end of her finger. Blood spurted out onto part of the carrots, drawing a few choice curse words in her mind. Phoebe dropped the knife and spun around to see who had rudely interrupted her.

"You startled me!" exclaimed Phoebe as she angrily turned on the water tap and ran cold water over her finger. "Patrick?"

"I'm sorry, Phoebe. That wasn't my intention. I thought I was doing a good thing by returning my tray to save you a trip in the morning."

Phoebe took a deep breath and exhaled, almost blowing out the candle next to her cutting board. Admittedly, she'd been a little jumpy, so the self-inflicted cut was as much her fault as it was Patrick's.

"No problem, Patrick. That's very kind of you. Would you mind setting it in the sink over here while I rinse this out?" She turned back to the sink and continued to run water over the gash on top of her knuckle. It was in one of those locations that would take forever to heal because the finger was constantly bending.

Patrick walked slowly toward her, his eyes darting around the room to assess his options. Everything was perfect to start his big night. As predicted, Jimmy and Jessica were off Driftwood Key, performing their duties for the sheriff's department. He'd hidden among the palm trees as Sonny turned off the generator. He'd followed him through the trails as he went to the caretaker's house located behind the greenhouses to catch several hours of sleep before he relieved Hank at the gate. Patrick sighed as he thought of how easy it would've been to kill Sonny along the path. If only he'd had a knife.

Hank, along with Mike, was manning the entrance to Driftwood Key. With both Jimmy and Jessica off-island, they weren't able to have their usual fireside chat on the beach.

As he got closer to the sink and the countertop where she was cutting the carrots, his eyes adjusted to the candlelit room. He saw the butcher block with the cutting utensils protruding out, handle first. Scissors. Steak knives. Several butcher knives. Even a sharpener. It was a serial killer's dream.

Patrick's heart raced as Phoebe droned on about something or another. She spewed meaningless words like anyone who was nervous in a tense situation. His adrenaline had reached a level he hadn't experienced since he'd fought off his attackers that night. Unfortunately, he had been outnumbered by three drug-fueled maniacs who got the better of him.

He gently set the tray on the kitchen island behind Phoebe and eased up behind her. She turned off the water faucet and reached for a kitchen towel to her right. Patrick made his move.

He rushed forward and reached for the butcher knife. It slipped out of his hands, so he lunged again, pressing his body against Phoebe's.

She was pinned against the kitchen counter.

"What are you doin'?" she shouted as she tried to twist away.

Her eyes caught a glimpse of Patrick reaching for the knife that had slid off the cutting board. She writhed and squirmed to get away, but couldn't.

Patrick grasped the knife and made a clumsy attempt to pull the knife toward Phoebe's chest. The blade tore through her shirt and sliced open her right shoulder blade.

"Arrggh! Help!" she shouted as loud as her surprised mind would allow.

Phoebe dropped to her knees and grasped her shoulder to stem the flow of blood pouring through her fingers. No longer pinned down, she tried to scramble away from Patrick.

He, too, dropped to his knees and grabbed one of her ankles. He tugged at her but only managed to pull off her sock and sneaker.

"Help! Anyone! Help me!" Primal fear had overtaken Phoebe as she begged for someone to help her. She continued to pull herself along the floor with one arm, but Patrick grabbed her other ankle, arresting her advance.

He raised the knife high over his head and thrust it downward to stab her again. He nicked her calf but just barely.

The tip of the bloodied knife embedded in the wood floor, and Phoebe jerked her leg from the sharp, serrated edge. Shocked by the pain soaring through her body, she began crawling again until she reached the work desk where her journal was laid open. She reached up with her left hand and felt around the tabletop until she found what she was looking for.

Phoebe swung around and fired blindly in Patrick's direction. Bullets flew around the kitchen, obliterating glassware and penetrating the cabinets.

Patrick was still coming.

Phoebe's hand shook as she tried to steady her aim. He growled, emitting a guttural snarl that frightened her into shooting again. She found her target.

The bullet struck Patrick in the side, striking just below the rib cage near the liver. Having missed anything solid other than layers of fat and connective tissue, it went through him before plugging the front of the refrigerator.

Patrick's body spun around, and he fell backwards from the force of the impact. Phoebe fired again, striking his left hand, shattering the bones and severing the ulnar artery.

"Dammit!" shouted Patrick in pain and frustration. He crawled behind the kitchen island and managed to stand to rush out the door. This was going horribly wrong, and now he had to find a way to escape.

CHAPTER FIFTY-TWO

Tuesday, November 5
Driftwood Key

Still clutching the knife in his right hand while his fractured left hand tried to stem the bleeding from his side, Patrick stumbled out of the main house into the darkness. The confidence and mental acuity he'd possessed when he began his attack on Phoebe was lost. Now he was wounded, frightened, and on the run, in search of a way off Driftwood Key.

He'd lost track of where he was. The loss of blood and excruciating pain resulted in a sort of brain fog that clouded his thinking. His mind raced as he tried to recall all his options. A debate raged within him.

Do I run across the bridge, retracing the steps I took that night to get here? Wait, Mike and Hank might be there. No, they always drink down by the water after dinner. Not tonight, Patrick. They're manning the front gate. You can't go that way. Steal a boat. They'll never find you in the dark. What if I run down the dock and the keys aren't there? I'll be trapped.

His mind finally screamed at him as the voices of Mike, Hank and Sonny shouting filled the air. *Just hide!*

He raced behind the main house to the densely vegetated part of the key. He stumbled along a path, lowering his head to avoid the palms that seemed to defy gravity by growing sideways. He was sweating profusely and made the mistake of wiping his brow with the sleeve of his sweatshirt. Patrick wasn't sure if the blood was his or Phoebe's. Regardless, it smeared across his face and into his eyes, causing them to burn.

Then he ran head-on into Sonny. The two men collided and knocked one another backwards. Patrick dropped the knife and reached around the ground in search of it.

"Arrrgghhh!" shouted Sonny as he pounced on top of Patrick's legs.

Sonny threw a punch that hit his already bruised kidneys, causing Patrick to yell in pain. As Patrick struggled to get out from under Sonny's weight, he found the knife's handle. He swung his arm around with a slicing motion in an attempt to cut into Sonny's arm. He was holding the knife backwards, so the sharp edge missed its target.

Phoebe shouted, "Sonny! Help me!"

Sonny became distracted, giving Patrick an opening. He thrust his hips upward and threw Sonny off to the side. Patrick rolled away, found his footing, and continued running down the path. He could hear Phoebe call her husband's name again, and Sonny responded. His heavy footsteps pounded the crushed shell mixed with sand as he rushed to the kitchen's back door.

Patrick's heart was pounding in his chest, and the sweat continued to pour out of him despite the cold temperatures. He ran into a thick cluster of palm trees and leaned his back against one of them as he tried to regroup.

"Think. Think, dammit. Where are you?"

He turned slightly to get oriented. A slight breeze washed over him off the Gulf. He turned his back to it and pointed toward Marathon with his knife.

"That way."

He started moving deliberately and quietly through the trails that led past the Frees' home and toward the brackish water separating the two keys. From there, he'd be able to walk through the mix of mangroves and tropical plants until he found the gate. It was his only hope.

Hank and Mike arrived at the main house just as Sonny emerged from the trail. All three men rushed into the kitchen and found Phoebe leaning against the kitchen island, favoring her wounded leg. She was shaking, pointing the gun at the door as the men entered, her hand wavering with her nervous finger on the trigger.

"Stop, or I'll shoot!"

Sonny responded quickly to reassure her. "Phoebe, it's okay. It's just us."

Phoebe began to sob. Until that moment, she'd mustered all the strength and courage within her to survive. The knife wounds were sending searing pain through her body, but it was her nerves that caused her to break down in tears.

Sonny gently held her as Mike peppered her with questions.

"Who did this?"

"Patrick," she and Sonny responded in unison.

"Son of a—" started Hank, but Mike interrupted him.

He looked to Sonny in the dim, candlelit space. "How did you know?"

"I ran into him on the path leading to our place. He tried to stab me, but I got lucky."

"I shot him," interjected Phoebe. "Twice. Once in the side and once in the hand. Left, I think. It all happened so fast."

Mike looked at Hank. "The gate."

Hank didn't hesitate. He cradled the AR-15 in his right arm and bolted through the open kitchen door.

Mike turned to Sonny. "Did you see him?"

"Yeah, on the trail to our house."

"Take care of her and lock the door."

Sonny nodded, and then Mike took off down the trail in search of Patrick.

While Hank took the more direct route toward the driveway gate, Mike followed the trail, using his flashlight to follow the trail of blood left by Patrick. He illuminated the path, and then he realized Patrick only had one option. With his gun drawn in his right hand and crossed over his left wrist, Mike picked up the pace, running toward the water and the narrow path that snaked its way through the mangrove hammocks clustered along the water's edge.

"Give it up, Patrick," he shouted as he spotted another glimpse of blood. "You'll never get off the key alive if you don't stop now. I will kill you!"

Mike meant it. There were no investigations associated with officer-involved shootings. Deadly force didn't have to be justified. He wouldn't be restricted to desk duty for weeks while internal affairs found a way to crucify him. In his mind, it was open season on would-be killers. The only thing that confused him was why did Patrick find it necessary to attack Phoebe? He could've left anytime he wanted with everyone's blessing and a picnic basket full of food as a parting gift.

Mike ducked below the fronds of a low-slung palm tree and then twisted his body sideways to slip between the trunks of two more. That was when the six-inch carbon-steel butcher knife was thrust into his chest.

CHAPTER FIFTY-THREE

Tuesday, November 5
Bay St. Louis, Mississippi

Lacey had grown up on the water, and during her childhood, she'd spent a lot of her time around marinas. After parking their truck near the restrooms of the Bay St. Louis Harbor and Pier, they stepped into a moribund version of the vibrant and active marinas of the Florida Keys.

Her eyes surveilled their surroundings. There were no gulls wheeling and diving for bait fish that would normally be seen splashing around the docked boats, scooting away from predators above and below them. There weren't would-be sailors toting their dock carts from ship to shore and vice versa. Only the bell-like clanging of steel cables on aluminum masts reminded her of home.

A misty haze hung over the warm water. Earth's atmosphere and its environs struggled with a form of bipolar disorder. Parts of the planet, at the surface and below, behaved normally. The Gulf waters still managed to remain seasonally warm. However, the air temperatures shattered records around the globe. As the cloud cover increased, and temperatures continued to steadily fall, it was a matter of time before the great oceans of the world would lose the battle and become colder.

A gust of wind caused the sailboats to wobble in their slips, and their rigging became agitated as a result. The clanking sound rose to a crescendo, and then, in a blink of an eye, the wind stopped blowing, allowing the vacant boats to rest.

"C'mon, Tucker. Let's see if the rumors are true."

Lacey led the way toward the marina office near the start of Rutherford Pier. At the end of the eleven-hundred-foot fishing pier, several anglers were trying their luck. Lacey thought about her dad and Jimmy. One of their daily duties on Driftwood Key was to feed the inn's guests, as well as themselves. She imagined fishing took on a whole new level of importance, as it probably did for these people on the pier.

"Hey, Mom. Look over there. It's the, um, third pier out. There's a man talking with a group of people."

They picked up the pace and rushed along the waterfront until soon they were jogging toward Pier 4. The chain-link gate to the last pier of the marina had been held open by a bait bucket with several dead fish inside. The smell forced Tucker to cover his nose. Lacey, however, found it somewhat familiar and comforting.

They turned down the pier, where they were met by an older man walking briskly toward them. Lacey tried to appear cordial, making her best effort to hide her apprehensiveness.

"Excuse me," she began. "We were told there might be charters heading toward Florida. Is that true?" She looked past the crusty old fisherman as she spoke.

"Depends," said the old man.

"On what?" asked Tucker, slightly annoyed that the man was playing games with them. He was concerned about leaving the truck unattended and continuously glanced in the direction of the parking lot as they spoke.

"My boy and me are running some folks to Florida. There's room for two more. The last two seats are pricey."

"We don't have any—" Tucker began before Lacey interrupted him.

"How pricey? We have things to trade."

The man took a deep breath and sighed. "Lady, tell me what you've got, and I'll let you know when it's enough."

"We have gasoline."

"Good start. How much?"

"Maybe thirty gallons, give or take. Plus what's in the truck."

"Can't siphon from these new vehicles," he muttered. He began to walk away from the negotiations.

"It's an older truck. Ford Bronco."

The boat captain's interest was suddenly piqued. "What year?"

"Mom, let's go," said Tucker, reaching for Lacey's hand. He could tell where the conversation was headed.

"Sixty-seven. Pristine condition. Drove it here from California."

"Deal. Truck and fuel for two seats."

"No way! Mom, we can't do this. That's Dad's truck."

The captain laughed. "I'm sure he'll understand. You wanna get—"

"Shut up, asshole!" Tucker was incensed. He walked up to the captain with his fists balled up, ready to fight. "He just died!"

Lacey forcefully grabbed her son by the arm and pulled him back toward her. "Tucker, stop it. He didn't know."

"Hey, listen. I'm sorry. I just have to get a fair deal and—"

"How is taking our truck for a couple of seats on a fishing boat a fair deal?" Tucker demanded.

"It is what it is, kid. Do you two wanna go to Florida or not?"

"Mom, let's go. Okay?" Tucker was morose and sincerely wanted to take his chances on the road rather than give up his dad's truck.

Lacey touched her son's face and smiled. "It's okay, son. Dad would want us to be safe." She turned to the captain.

"Truck and fuel for two seats. And you have to take us to the Keys."

"No way! That requires an extra fuel stop."

Lacey held her hands up, urging him to reconsider. "Before you answer, see what we've got to trade. The other thing, our gear comes with us. It's all we own."

"Show me," he said with a gruff.

The man whistled for his son to join them, and ten minutes later, the deal was struck. Tucker and Lacey carried their belongings toward the end of the pier with the assistance of the boat captain. As they got closer, music could be heard wafting from the old trawler as if they were preparing for a booze cruise.

Half a dozen people milled about on the dock, sizing up Lacey and Tucker as they approached. Between the duffel bags, ammo cans, and their weapons, they made quite an impression on the group. Most of them stood at the edge of the dock as far away from Lacey and Tucker as they could get.

Their fellow passengers came from all walks of life, refugees returning home or seeking a warmer climate. After the passengers realized mother and son weren't a threat, they exchanged pleasantries to break the ice. The newcomers were assisted on board by a man and his wife who had taken up seats on the stern's bench seating alongside their young daughter.

The forty-five-foot fiberglass fishing boat had been used by the captain and his son for years along the coastal waters. Their commercial fishing operation targeted cobia and amberjack for sale to fisheries that package seafood for grocery stores.

The captain instructed them on where to stow their gear, and he showed them the sleeping quarters with bunks for eight people. As they shoved their duffels, weapons, and ammo cans under two of the bunks, Lacey mentally performed a quick head count. There would be ten adults, three children, and the two boat owners on board, requiring them to sleep in shifts. Not that it mattered. Traveling by water would relieve the stresses and danger of the final leg of their journey. Giving up Owen's truck in exchange for their safety was sad, but necessary.

Without warning, the captain started the 855 Cummins diesel engine. The Big Cam, as it was known, produced six hundred horsepower, allowing the vessel to cruise at fourteen knots, or about sixteen miles per hour.

"Looks like we're about to get under way," said Lacey with a hint of excitement. So many memories flooded through her mind of growing up. As a child, she'd loved going fishing with Hank and her uncle Mike. She had been thrilled when he told her, at age twelve, it was time she learned to drive his Hatteras. Lacey had absorbed every detail of traveling on the ocean from her dad. It had been years since she'd taken a boat out on the water. Although this vessel stank of fish and diesel, it was comfortingly familiar.

Tucker, however, was still dejected over the decision to give up Black & Blue. "It sounds like it." His voice trailed off.

Lacey noticed her son was unable to make eye contact with her. "Honey, all of this sucks. All of it. Let's get to Driftwood Key and regroup. Okay?"

Tucker reluctantly nodded. Lacey felt horrible for her son, who was forced to become a man. She didn't want to give up one of the last tangible memories of Owen that they possessed. However, she felt in her gut it was the right thing to do.

And then, as if to reinforce her decision, shouts were heard over the steady rumble of the diesel engine. Tucker scrambled out of the sleeping quarters first, followed close behind by Lacey. They emerged onto the aft deck, where they froze.

The family of three was huddled at the back of the boat, looking toward the pier. A large man led a trio walking briskly toward the boat. His deep voice bellowed, clearly and succinctly heard over the low rumble of Big Cam.

"Get off the boat! Now!"

CHAPTER FIFTY-FOUR

Tuesday, November 5
Driftwood Key

The knife plunged into Mike's chest. It pierced the skin just below his left nipple and sank to a point where it almost pierced his diaphragm near his lungs. The force of impact immediately knocked the air out of him as he spun to the ground. With the knife sticking out of Mike's chest, Patrick pounced at the opportunity to finish him off.

"You're done, Detective Mikey!" he shouted as he tried to grasp the handle of the knife and twist it.

Only, Mike wasn't done. He'd held onto his sidearm despite falling hard to the ground. He raised his knee to block Patrick's attack and then fired a shot into the murderer's already wounded shoulder.

Patrick screamed in agony as the hollow-point round exploded inside his body, tearing tendons away from bones and shattering everything in its path as it tumbled around. Now Mike had the upper hand.

He sat up and groaned. He grasped the knife handle and slowly pulled it away from his body. His adrenaline-amped ears picked up the tearing sound as the serrated edge further damaged his chest cavity. He knew immediately that he might have cut his lung.

He was having difficulty breathing that was made even more difficult as Patrick rose and punched him in the side of his rib cage. The blow caused Mike to lose control of his gun, which flew into a twisted mess of mangrove roots.

Now neither man had a weapon except their fists.

Mike regained his breathing and ignored the incredible pain burning in his chest. He climbed on top of Patrick and began to mercilessly pummel the man in the face, upper body and shoulder where his wounds were the worst.

"Let it all out, Detective Mikey!" Patrick emitted a wicked cackle that caused blood to fly out of his mouth.

Patrick swung back with his right arm, slamming his fist into Mike's rib cage. Mike temporarily lost his balance before rearing back and slamming his fist into Patrick's jaw.

"Why, asshole? Why did you do this?"

"I shouldn't tell you!" Patrick shouted back before having a coughing fit.

Mike stopped slugging him and jammed his fist into the gaping wound where Patrick's left shoulder used to be.

"Arrrgggh!" Patrick screamed again. Then, inexplicably, he began laughing. It was menacing. Evil. Insane.

Mike grabbed him by the neck and started to choke him, causing Patrick to spit blood all over his face.

"Talk!" Mike demanded, releasing the death grip he had on Patrick's larynx.

Patrick began to cough up more blood. He'd lost a lot of blood, and his organs were beginning to shut down. He was on the verge of going into hypovolemic shock. Somehow, he managed enough strength to allow his demented mind to taunt his pursuer.

"You would've never caught me." The words came out in a gurgle.

Mike winced and grimaced as pain shot through his body. Blood was pouring out of his chest, soaking through his sweatshirt. He slugged Patrick again.

"Tell me, dammit!"

"Too easy," Patrick hissed through his blood-covered teeth.

He started to choke and cough violently. Mike tried to maneuver his head to clear his airway. He didn't care if the guy died. He just needed to know why he'd attacked Phoebe, first.

Then, with one last effort coupled with a hideous laugh, Patrick spoke again. "I'm Patricia." He smiled, and blood poured out of both sides of his mouth until he died with his eyes staring into Mike's.

Mike shook Patrick by the arms in an attempt to revive him. He pounded the man's chest to restart his heart.

"What do you mean?" he shouted his question, and then his body convulsed. He suddenly felt like someone had wrapped a belt around his neck and pulled it tight, cutting off his ability to breathe. His eyes grew wide, he gasped for air, and then everything went black.

CHAPTER FIFTY-FIVE

Tuesday, November 5
Bay St. Louis, Mississippi

The men slowed their pace and walked steadily toward the frightened passengers waiting on the dock to board. A few of them had just stepped onto the boat. At the man's instructions, they panicked and scrambled off the fishing vessel, falling hard onto the wood dock before crawling away.

Lacey glanced at the wheelhouse to gauge the captain's reaction. He'd disappeared. She turned her attention back to the men and saw that they all had their guns drawn, pointing them wildly at the trembling passengers on the dock as well as in the direction of the boat.

Unexpectedly, three shots were fired a hundred feet away from down the pier. The son had returned and immediately opened fire on the men. He struck one of the assailants in the back of the head, throwing blood and flesh onto the dockside passengers. They screamed and then jumped into the harbor in fear for their lives.

The remaining men turned on the captain's son and began firing. Each shot several times in the young man's direction, but they all missed. In a gun battle, especially between shooters who are untrained, it's not unusual for over ninety percent of the rounds to miss their marks. However, it just took one to kill.

Lacey jumped at first and then dropped to her knees when the thunderous boom of a shotgun blast occurred from just over her shoulder, immediately followed by another. The captain had emerged with his marine shotgun and wasted no time firing upon the attackers.

They spun around to shoot back, catching Lacey and Tucker in the crossfire. They fell to the deck and scrambled for cover, although the fiberglass sides wouldn't necessarily protect them.

Bullets and shotgun pellets were flying in all directions. Lacey had managed to crawl up the slight slope toward the bow and out of the line of fire. She eased her head over the railing to watch.

There were two dead bodies lying on the dock, surrounded by blood. Both of them had been shot in the head. One of the shooters had dropped to a knee. Bleeding from his chest, he continued to fire at the captain's son until he finally found his target. The young man was struck in the shoulder, spun around, and then fell off the dock but not before striking his head on the transom of a boat as he hit the water.

His father, the boat captain, saw this and unloaded a barrage of shotgun fire. He'd squeeze the trigger, rack another round, and then fire again. He stood strong against the last man standing on the dock, the leader who had demanded everyone get off the boat. Brutally wounded himself, he finished the battle with a kill shot, nailing the captain in the heart, who instantly fell to the deck.

Exhausted, the killer dropped to his knees and began waving his gun around. He tried to shout, but blood gurgled from his throat and into his mouth. His eyes were wild as he became increasingly incoherent.

"Off … my … boat!" he tried to yell, but it was barely audible as he began to lose his breath.

"Mom!" shouted Tucker as he tried to gain his footing only to slip and fall in the captain's blood.

"I'm okay."

"Off!" the man yelled as he spit out more blood. He raised his weapon and tried to shoot in their direction. All that resulted was several clicks barely heard over the still-running diesel engine.

Tucker regained his footing and held onto the rail to greet his mother as she made her way past the wheelhouse. She was incredibly calm under the circumstances.

"Quick, untie the dock lines."

"What?"

"We're leaving," she said as she pushed past him. She pointed toward the bow and carefully made her way past the dead captain. When she reached the entrance to the wheelhouse, she pointed at the man who'd wrapped his arms around his wife and daughter.

"You. Untie that line."

"But ..." He was uncertain if he should follow Lacey's instructions.

"Now! We've gotta go."

The man jumped at her stern tone and nervously began to untie the line. Lacey entered the wheelhouse. The enclosed space included an eating area, a small galley, and a traditional wooden six-spoke ship's wheel.

"We're clear, Mom!"

Lacey turned the wheel and nervously grasped the throttle. This boat was much older than her Dad's, but the basics were all there, including console-mounted electronics. At first, she gave it too much throttle, and the boat rushed forward. Tucker and the family were thrown to the deck.

"Sorry about that!" Lacey shouted.

Tucker responded with a question. "Whadya want me to do with the body?"

Lacey didn't have to think about her answer. "Throw it overboard."

She glanced over her shoulder through the windows above the galley. Tucker and the father slowly hoisted the man onto the side of the boat and dropped him into the harbor. Seconds later, Tucker was by his mom's side, wiping off his bloody hands on a dish towel.

"Are you okay?" she asked, glancing at him while navigating between the jetty and the Rutherford Pier.

"Yeah. You?"

Lacey nodded and then pointed through the front windows. "The sunset looks different than what I remember."

"Weird." Tucker seemed to be recovering from the hectic moments when six men had lost their lives during the gun battle. The two were remarkably calm.

Tucker took a deep breath and reached into his pocket. He dangled a set of keys for his mother to see.

"Are those ...?"

"Yep. The keys to Black & Blue. It's the extra set we have. I was supposed to give them to the captain. Um, I kinda got distracted and forgot."

Lacey smiled and reached her arm around her son to pull him close to her.

"Are you up for an adventure?"

Tucker sighed and smiled. "Grandpa once told me that a rough day at sea is better than any day at work."

Lacey laughed. *One can only hope.*

THANK YOU FOR READING NUCLEAR WINTER: WHITEOUT!

If you enjoyed it, I'd be grateful if you'd take a moment to write a short review (just a few words are needed) and post it on Amazon. Amazon uses complicated algorithms to determine what books are recommended to readers. Sales are, of course, a factor, but so are the quantities of reviews my books get. By taking a few seconds to leave a review, you help me out and also help new readers learn about my work.

Sign up to my email list to learn about upcoming titles, deals, contests, appearances, and more!

Sign up to my email list to learn about upcoming titles, deals, contests, appearances, and more!

Sign up at BobbyAkart.com

VISIT my feature page at Amazon.com/BobbyAkart for more information on my other action-packed thrillers, which includes over forty Amazon #1 bestsellers in forty-plus fiction and nonfiction genres.

**NUCLEAR WINTER: DEVIL STORM, the next installment in
this epic thriller. Available on Amazon.**

"Masterful and suspenseful!" -Reader Review

From the initial firestorm and the spread of smoke to the
destruction of the Earth's ecosystem.
Nuclear winter took no prisoners.

AVAILABLE ON AMAZON

OTHER WORKS BY AMAZON CHARTS TOP 25 AUTHOR BOBBY AKART

Nuclear Winter
First Strike
Armageddon
Whiteout
Devil Storm
Desolation

New Madrid (a standalone, disaster thriller)

Odessa (a Gunner Fox trilogy)
Odessa Reborn
Odessa Rising
Odessa Strikes

The Virus Hunters
Virus Hunters I
Virus Hunters II
Virus Hunters III

The Geostorm Series

The Shift
The Pulse
The Collapse
The Flood
The Tempest
The Pioneers

The Asteroid Series (A Gunner Fox trilogy)

Discovery
Diversion
Destruction

The Doomsday Series

Apocalypse
Haven
Anarchy
Minutemen
Civil War

The Yellowstone Series

Hellfire
Inferno
Fallout
Survival

The Lone Star Series

Axis of Evil
Beyond Borders
Lines in the Sand
Texas Strong
Fifth Column
Suicide Six

The Pandemic Series

Beginnings

The Innocents
Level 6
Quietus

The Blackout Series
36 Hours
Zero Hour
Turning Point
Shiloh Ranch
Hornet's Nest
Devil's Homecoming

The Boston Brahmin Series
The Loyal Nine
Cyber Attack
Martial Law
False Flag
The Mechanics
Choose Freedom
Patriot's Farewell (standalone novel)
Black Friday (standalone novel)
Seeds of Liberty (Companion Guide)

The Prepping for Tomorrow Series
Cyber Warfare
EMP: Electromagnetic Pulse
Economic Collapse

CPSIA information can be obtained
at www.ICGtesting.com
Printed in the USA
LVHW092215050521
686547LV00034B/1988/J